Philip G)66, and lived and worked throughout Europe before settling in Scotland in the 1990s. He first came to Italy in 1994, when he spent some time working for the European Space Agency in Frascati. Philip now works as a teacher, writer and translator, and lives in Venice.

The Venetian Game

PHILIP GWYNNE JONES

Constable • London

CONSTABLE

First published in Great Britain in 2017 by Constable

Giuseppe Tomasi di Lampedusa's *The Leopard*, in the translation by Archibald
Colquhoun, quoted with permission from Penguin Random House.

A CIP catalogue record for this book
is available from the British Library.

ISBN 978-1-47212-397-8 (paperback)

Typeset in Adobe Garamond by Hewer Text UK Ltd, Edinburgh
Printed and bound in Great Britain by Clay Ltd, St Ives plc

Papers used by Constable are from well-managed forests
and other responsible sources

MIX
Paper from
responsible sources
FSC   FSC® C104740
www.fsc.org

Constable
is an imprint of
Little, Brown Book Group
Carmelite House
50 Victoria Embankment
London EC4Y 0DZ

An Hachette UK Company
www.hachette.co.uk

www.littlebrown.co.uk

In memory of Helen Susan Noble, 1968–2014
I miss you

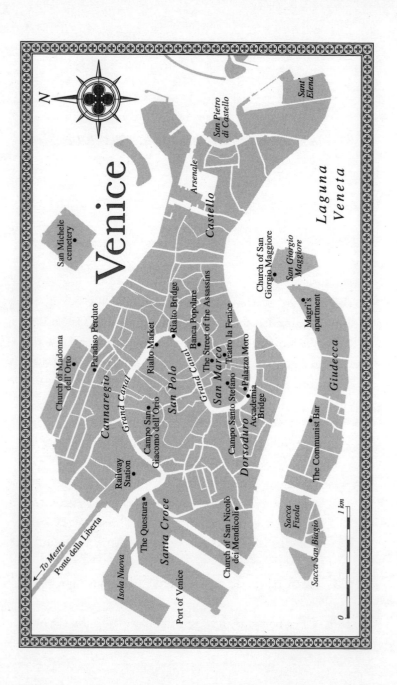

Chapter 1

Her Majesty gazed down serenely from her position on the wall, as the family Mills gazed back at me with rather less equanimity.

The question was coming. Any minute now. But in the meantime I shuffled the papers on my desk, and smiled back at them. She looked tired and red-eyed, he, angry and one step away from a good old shout and swear, the boy, visibly bored.

'That's one hell of a painting,' said Dad, jabbing a finger at *sua Maestà*.

'It is, isn't it? I inherited it from the previous consul. He had a rather larger office than I do. He thought it would create the right atmosphere. A bit less foreign, more reassuring.' I gave her a jaunty salute. 'God bless her, eh?'

A short but awkward silence followed as I swore to myself that I would never, ever again attempt to use humour at work.

Dad looked at the tiny, bedraggled flag dangling from the miniature flagpole on my desk.

'That's seen better days. You think they'd have got you a new one.'

'Erm, it is a new one. It's just difficult to stop the cat playing with it.' I tried to move the conversation on to safer ground. 'There are just a few questions I need to run through with you. Then I'll make some phone calls and you can get back to your holiday. Okay?' I gave them my best disarming smile. 'You've been to the police, of course?'

He nodded.

'You have the reference number?'

He rummaged in his wallet and extracted a crumpled photocopied sheet. I scribbled the details down.

'Right, please bear with me for a few minutes. I just need to phone Milan and make an appointment for you.'

I picked up the phone and started to dial, but he raised his hand. 'I'm sorry, but why do you have to call Milan?'

I replaced the receiver. I smiled, again. 'I need to make an appointment for you at the consulate there; hopefully for tomorrow. That's where you need to go to collect your Emergency Travel Documents. Think of them as temporary passports, just to get you home.'

'Can't we just get them here?'

Bingo. The question. Guaranteed to be raised every time, and twelve months down the line I still hadn't come up with a convincing answer.

'I'm afraid not. I only have an honorary position, I'm not an official consul or ambassador. For passports and travel documents you need to go to the official Consulate General in Milan. Now it's just two hours away on the train. It's a very pleasant city, lots to see. You should only be in the consulate for thirty minutes or so; less if we can get all this documentation sorted out today. My advice is to treat it as another day of your holiday. Don't let all this spoil things for you.'

His wife brightened slightly. 'Milan sounds nice. I've always quite wanted to go there.'

He was having none of it. 'I suppose this isn't going to be free?'

I suppressed a sigh. This, too, was a regular one. 'The ETDs will be one hundred and twenty euros each. And, of course, there'll be the rail fare; but if we get that sorted out straight away we might be able to keep that down to, oh, perhaps a hundred or so euros in total.'

'How much?'

'Well, you're looking at not far south of five hundred euros to get you home. And remember, when you get back, you will need to get those passports replaced as well.'

'I thought you people were supposed to be able to help us?'

This time, the sigh couldn't be suppressed. 'I am helping you Mr . . .' Here I made the briefest of pauses as my eyes flicked over the sheet in front of me. 'Mr Mills. I really am doing everything that's possible.'

'So why can't you just give us these . . . emergency passport things?'

'As I said, I am just an honorary consul. I'm not authorised to do so.'

He shook his head, and forced out a laugh. 'So this is where the taxpayers' money goes, then?'

A full house. When they reached this point I generally didn't feel the need to be polite any more. 'I don't get paid, Mr Mills.'

'And I suppose you're doing this out of the goodness of your heart?' He smiled at his wife. *See, nobody gets the better of me.*

'Exactly that. Now then, I can phone my colleague in Milan and make an appointment for you. Then we can look at the

Trenitalia site – which, I should warn you, is incomprehensible to the novice in both Italian and English – and book your rail tickets. I can even sketch out a pleasant day's itinerary for you and recommend a nice restaurant. Or if you'd prefer, I'm quite happy to let you spend the rest of your holiday sorting all this out yourself. Entirely up to you'.

I started to file the papers away, at which point he threw up his hands. 'No, really. It's okay. I'm sorry, it's just the last day's been a bit difficult. You know.'

I nodded, and picked up the phone again. I smiled at the small boy. 'You'll like Milan, Simon, is it? Simon. Chance to see the San Siro. Who's your favourite then, AC or Inter?'

He gave me a blank look. 'He prefers rugby,' said his mother.

We stared at each other in silence for a few seconds, until Gramsci padded in. The child reached down to stroke him and then snatched his fingers away as if burnt. His mother reached for a paper handkerchief to staunch the blood.

'I'm so sorry. I'm afraid he's not very friendly.'

Gramsci lunged for the flag, but I swatted him away in time. He plopped himself on to the windowsill, the better to gaze down upon the outside world with bad intent. There was another awkward silence. Then, mercifully, the receiver crackled. 'British Consulate, Milan.'

'Helen. It's Nathan here. The usual thing, if you could. Three ETDs needed. Adult male, adult female, male child. I'll fax you the details directly. Can you fit them in tomorrow?'

'Hello, Nathan. Hope things are lovely in Venice? Just checking now. Yes, they're in luck, I can fit them in at one p.m.'

I looked across my desk at *la famiglia Mills*. They stared back with a mixture of confusion and antipathy. Not their fault, I suppose. Some little sod on a water bus had swiped her handbag. Next thing they knew their entire holiday was revolving around police stations and consulates, and any thought of having a good time had become secondary to the sheer bloody hassle of getting home again. Even in a tourist-friendly city like Venice, it must have been annoying and frightening in equal measure. Perhaps I'd been too harsh. I was about to confirm the appointment when he whispered the words 'taxpayers' money' again.

'I'm sorry, Helen, I don't think that's going to be possible for them.'

A brief pause, then, 'In that case they'll have to be here at nine a.m. sharp. Not a minute later. They'll have to leave Venice by six thirty at the latest.'

'That will be fine, Helen. Thanks again. Talk soon!' I replaced the receiver. Childish, perhaps. But you had to take these little victories when you had the chance.

I smiled across the desk. 'I'm so sorry, but it looks as if you're going to have a rather early start . . .'

The family Mills went morosely upon their way. I rested my head on the desk and closed my eyes. Just twenty minutes more and I could close up for the day, and the chances were that nobody would be turning up now.

There was a gentle cough. I gave a start and straightened myself up.

'Sorry. The door was open.'

The speaker was a man in, perhaps, his early sixties. Smartly dressed, perhaps overdressed for the time of year, in a dark three-piece suit that was just ever so slightly too tight. With a thinning widow's peak and clear blue eyes, he might once have been a handsome man. Gramsci, incredibly, was sitting in his arms, purring.

'No, it was my fault. I'm sorry. Please come in.'

He placed Gramsci upon the floor with a surprisingly delicate motion, before sitting himself down.

'Mr Sutherland I presume?'

'That's me. You're honoured, incidentally. He doesn't usually like strangers. Or people in general.'

He took a handkerchief from his top pocket and wiped his hands – perhaps a little theatrically – to be sure of clearing away any stray hairs.

'So, how can I help you Mr . . .?'

'Montgomery. Simple matter, really, and it won't take too much of your time.' He reached into his jacket pocket and withdrew a padded envelope. 'I'd like you to look after this. In the wall safe. Just for a few days.'

He made as if to push the envelope across the table to me, but I held up my hand.

'I'm sorry, could you just say that again? What do you want me to do?'

'This package. Just take care of it for a few days.' He pushed it towards me, ever so gently.

'I really do apologise, but before we go any further you have to understand that I can't possibly do this.'

He inclined his head. 'Yes, I know. You're not a left-luggage facility or anything. But it really will only be for a couple of days.'

I shook my head. 'Really, I can't. I don't even know what's in there.'

He smiled. 'Well now, what do you think it might be?' And he pushed it across the table, more firmly this time.

I turned it over in my hands. 'As far as I know it's a photo of your mother. Or drugs. Or stolen jewellery. Explosives. A computer hard drive with all sorts of beastliness on it.'

He should have been offended, but seemed to find it gently amusing. 'Really?'

'Mr Montgomery, you seem to be a very nice man. More than that, you are perhaps the only person to enter this office that my cat has not attempted to savage. But I can't take a package containing the Lord knows what and stick it in the safe. Can't you use a locker at the station? Or at your hotel?'

'I'd be happier if it was here. I mean, you're British, aren't you?'

'Well, yes. But I'm sorry. I can't help you.'

'Let's just say that it's a photograph of my mother. And that I'm prepared to give you ten thousand euros to look after it for me.'

Every muscle in my body attempted to move two inches upwards, but I managed to restrict myself to a solemn nod of the head. 'Ten thousand euros?'

'Exactly.'

'You must have loved her very much. The answer is still no.'

He nodded. There was silence for a moment, as we stared at each other.

I broke first. 'So. Is there anything else I can do?'

He said nothing, but just continued to stare.

This was becoming annoying. I opened a drawer, withdrew a business card from the stack inside, and passed it over to him. 'Here's my number, just in case you need it. But time is getting on, and if there's nothing else I can do for you . . .'

He reached across the table, but made no move to pick it up. Instead, he reached for the miniature flagpole. He turned it over in his hands, then placed it directly in front of him, and gently bounced his index finger off the point. He pursed his lips in a silent expression of pain. 'That's quite sharp. You want to be careful.'

I kept my eyes on his, as I stretched my hand across, and pulled it back to my side of the table. 'I will be. Now time, I'm afraid, really is getting on . . .'

'That's the second time you've said that.'

'I know, but I should be closing up for the day.'

'You've got ten minutes yet. What are you going to do with them?'

He hadn't raised his voice at all, but I didn't like the turn the conversation was taking. 'Mr Montgomery, I think you should go now.'

He continued to stare, then shook his head as if to clear it and tugged at his collar. An expensive shirt, but just a little too tight. Then he splayed his fingers and drummed them on the table. 'You know, I never had this trouble with your predecessor.'

'My what?' This time I really couldn't suppress a little start.

'Your predecessor. The previous consul.' He lingered over the words as if explaining something to the simple-minded. 'I never had this trouble with him.' He leaned forward, ever so slightly.

I forced myself to remain still. 'There must be some mistake.'

He grinned. 'Oh I don't think so.'

I held his gaze. 'Mr Montgomery, I'd like you to leave now.'

He nodded. He reached down to give the treacherous Gramsci a tickle under the chin, and got to his feet. I decided to give it one last go, for my own curiosity if nothing else.

'I don't suppose you could tell me what's really in there?'

He smiled again, but there was no warmth in it. 'I could. But I don't think I'm going to. Be seeing you.'

Chapter 2

Paradiso Perduto was rammed. The band were not *that* good but the material – covers of Deep Purple, Black Sabbath and, enterprisingly, Jethro Tull – seemed to have attracted every Venetian male of a certain age through the door. It was loud, sweaty and smelled of fish and fried food. In a good way. I thought I was having a good time.

'Does it have to be so loud?'

'You're getting old, Nathan. Of course it has to be loud. I bet you never go to La Fenice and say, this Verdi guy, he has some great tunes but he's too loud eh?'

'I can't afford La Fenice, Dario. And yes, I am too old for all this. This is making my ears bleed.'

There was a sudden moment of silence and I became aware that I was shouting as heads turned to stare at me. Then a burst of synthesiser and a driving, insistent guitar riff. Dario grabbed my shoulder and shook me.

'Pink Floyd! "Astronomy Domine"! Syd Barrett years, from—'

'Dario, how do you know all this shit?'

He looked genuinely affronted. 'Nathan, this is your heritage.'

'Well maybe. I just mean, how do you know so much about all this stuff? I never go on about Gaber or Celentano.'

'But nobody listens to that. Well, they do, but not really. This is proper British music. No other country in the world made music like this. You should be proud!'

'Well, I suppose I am. I just feel . . . I dunno . . . just a bit too old for all this.'

'Look around, Nathan. Everyone's here. Old guys, kids, even grumpy bastards like you.'

It was true. The audience was a mix of students, longhairs and middle-aged guys like us. The bar was serving up portions of fried fish, meatballs, *baccalà*, grilled cuttlefish; whilst Spritzes *al bitter* or *al* Aperol were dispensed and slid across the counter with machine-like efficiency. I took a swig of a disappointing Italian lager. They were always disappointing. On a hot day, they seemed like the best thing in the world for the ten seconds they took to become warm and flabby. I wished I could have a proper beer. A cigarette seemed like a pleasant idea but Dario, I knew, would shout at me.

I drained my glass. 'Same again?' he asked.

'Yeah, why not? It'll dull the pain. And get us a wee octopus, eh?'

Whilst he was gone the band struck up an old Hawkwind song, 'Master of the Universe'. It got an excited 'yay' out of me. By the time Dario returned I was singing along. Gentle air guitar might possibly have been involved.

He smiled, the corners of his eyes crinkling. I'd always wondered about the deep-set lines around his eyes. When we first met, I thought he'd had too much sun. Later, I realised it was that he just smiled a lot. He grabbed my shoulders and shook me again. And when Dario shook you, you stayed shaken.

'You see! I said you'd enjoy it!'

'Yeah well, it's Hawkwind isn't it? Never heard a covers band playing this before.'

'Hawkwind, shit. Let me tell you my Pink Floyd story.'

I set down my beer and fixed him with a cold stare. 'Okay. I'll hear the Pink Floyd story. But if I hear you speak about Hawkwind like that again our friendship is at an end.'

He grinned, and for a moment I feared more backslapping would be involved. 'I'm joking, Nathan. "In Search of Space" is quite good. But the Pink Floyd story . . .'

I munched upon the wee octopus. Little octopus. On a stick. Genius. 'Okay, let's hear it.'

'It's 1994, right? Roger Waters has left, years ago. Nobody thinks the rest of them can do anything without him. And then they make *The Division Bell*. Their last album, and it's a *great* album. And they're going to play in Venice. In *Venice*!

'Now, I've got my ticket of course. But one afternoon, I'm in the office and I get a phone call. It's Maria – she was my wife at the time – and she's on the Zattere. And she's seen them, all three of them, they're sitting outside Nico's having a Spritz.

'I've got to get there, but how? Twenty minutes on the bus from Mestre, and then get a *vaporetto*? No, they'll be gone. I tell my boss I've got to go, I've had an important call, I'll be back in an hour.

'I jump on the bike, it's my old Moto Guzzi Le Mans 850. I'm away down Corso del Popolo, turn in to the Via della Libertà, on to the bridge and then I'm hammering along to

Venice. It's a beautiful day. It's cool, but the sun is shining on the lagoon. The sky is clear. I'm ripping along the outside lane and the old city is getting closer and closer and all I can think of is Pink Floyd are having a drink at Nico's and I've got to get there before they leave.

'I get to the end of the bridge and I turn off towards San Basilio. And then there's a checkpoint, where the old *stazione marittima* used to be. There's a cop there but – and you have to believe this – he's an old friend. We did National Service together. I shout out that I've got to get to Nico's because Pink Floyd are there and he waves me on!

'So I'm at San Basilio and I know I've got to be careful now because there's people everywhere. Everybody is shouting and waving at me, they think I'm a crazy tourist, or a drunk or maybe someone's making a film. I head up the first bridge, and then I'm on the Zattere heading along the side of the canal. There's another bridge, I'm airborne for a moment and then I'm down.

'There they are. Nick Mason. Richard Wright. David Gilmour. I screech to a halt, kick the stand down, take my helmet off. And now I'm shaking. I walk up to them, and say to Gilmour "I just have to say, you are fantastic."

'And Gilmour just looks at the bike and shakes his head. And then he smiles.'

He stopped, and grinned. 'That's what happened. That's my Pink Floyd story.'

I drained my beer.

'You're telling me you rode a motorcycle along the Zattere, just to tell Dave Gilmour how much you loved him?'

'*Sì!*'

I shook my head. If it was almost anybody else I would cry bullshit. But things like this did seem to happen to Dario. I punched his arm and immediately wished I hadn't. It was like punching a brick wall.

'You mad bastard. So what happened?'

'They signed their tablecloth for me!'

'No, what happened about riding a motorcycle through Venice?'

'Oh, I lost my licence for twelve months. Because I lost my licence, I lost my job. Because I lost my job, Maria left me. I couldn't get a job so I ended up rejoining the army. But it was worth it. I still have the tablecloth. I'll show it you the next time you come over.'

The band had laboured through 'Freebird' and were packing up for the night. I checked my watch. Only just past eleven, we still had an hour.

'Are we having another?'

'Better not. I told Valentina I wouldn't be too late.'

'Ah, go on. Just a swift one.'

He stared at his glass, considering the idea. 'No, I need to go. Always better to do what the wife says, eh?'

There was a fleeting, but awkward, silence.

'Sorry.'

I shrugged.

'You okay?'

I shrugged again. 'Yeah. More or less. Most of the time.' I changed the subject. 'You know, I had someone come into the office today who made me an offer I couldn't refuse.'

'What did you do?'

'I refused it.'

'So what was it?'

'He asked me to look after a package for him. Just for a few days, he said.'

'Drugs?'

'Almost certainly. Anyway, I sent him on his way. You sure you won't have another?'

He shook his head. I feared a bone-crushing hug, but he spared me and we went our separate ways. He, back to the railway station for the next train to Mestre; me, back to San Marco. I wondered if I should wander over to Fondamente Nove to take a boat. The *vaporetti* would be less crowded now, and the wait, looking out across the dark waters of the lagoon to the cemetery island of San Michele, would be suitably meditative.

I decided to walk. It was a warm night, just right for wandering the streets. I made my way down through Cannaregio and over the Scalzi Bridge. Then along the Rio Marin Canal, silent now, turning off past the Scuola Grande di San Giovanni Evangelista. Years ago, I'd got lost in Naples in the small hours of the morning and spent an increasingly panicky two hours trying to find my hotel, imagining every footstep behind me belonged to someone with evil on their mind. Venice was not like that. When you needed to get home late at night, you waited for a boat or you walked through its labyrinthine streets. And you never thought twice about it. I liked the feeling of solitude and had taken to walking for hours late at night, when I would hardly see another soul. I rarely got lost these days, which made me feel a little sad.

I emerged into the Campo dei Frari, and smiled, as I always did, at the graffiti sprayed on the side of the convent: 'Silvio, can you dance like Mussolini?' The city was busier here, a few bars and restaurants still open. Then I passed the church of San Pantalon with its brick façade and picked my way through the late-night drinkers sitting on the bridge that led into Campo Santa Margherita. From the way locals spoke of it, you might be forgiven for thinking that the *campo* was twinned with Gomorrah. Truth be told, it wasn't that bad. Music blasted out from every bar as late-night drinkers spilled into the square. In the morning, there would be a sea of bottles, pizza boxes and kebab wrappers to clear away. It must have been hell to live above, but – in comparison to Leith on a Friday night – it just seemed like a slightly shoutier version of Morningside.

A party of Brits were arguing with the doormen refusing to let them into Piccolo Mondo, the only nightclub in the historic centre; but otherwise the streets were becoming quiet again and I had the Accademia Bridge to myself as I crossed over the Grand Canal and into the *sestiere* of San Marco. Nearly home now. Through Campo Santo Stefano, across Campo Sant'Angelo and then into the Calle dei Assassini, where three shadows waited for me. The first time I'd seen them they'd given me a start. Three shadows, cast by the corbelling of the arch that spanned the street, looked for all the world like three figures lying in wait. A suitable image for the Street of the Assassins.

I walked past an antique bookshop that I had never visited, and a small gallery. If the Magical Brazilian Café had been open, I might have been tempted to stop for another drink, but they, like everywhere else at this hour, had closed. Just as well. The urge for a post-midnight Negroni was a clear signal that it was time to go to bed.

I went up to the flat. Gramsci was waiting for me, and mewled insistently until I gave him some more food. I took a bottle of Billa grappa from the fridge, poured myself a glass and sat down on the sofa. It was nearly one o'clock now. Midnight back in the UK. Late, but perhaps not too late. I picked up the telephone and dialled the code for the UK. Then for Edinburgh.

I paused. How many beers had I had? Four, five? If I called now, questions would be asked. We would have to have A Conversation.

Do it now. Call now. Say what you have to say.

Don't be stupid. It's late. You've had a drink.

You haven't spoken in weeks.

She'll think you're an idiot.

And then the killer: *What if someone else answers?*

I dropped the handset back on to the cradle, finished the grappa and poured another. Then I hauled Gramsci on to my lap and gave him a mournful cuddle. He leapt from my arms and on to the table, from where he gazed at me with contempt.

Chapter 3

There was no milk in the fridge, as there hadn't been for days. It gave me an excuse for a coffee and a brioche from the Brazilians downstairs. I leafed through the rack of newspapers.

'No *Unità* this morning?'

Eduardo broke off from polishing glasses. 'Not this morning, maybe never again.'

'What do you mean?'

'They've gone bust, Nathan. Don't you read the papers?'

'I do read the papers. I just read them backwards. Sometimes I don't get to the front bit.'

I pulled a *Manifesto* from the rack, but had barely opened it when my mobile rang.

'*Signor* Sutherland?'

'*Sì.*'

'This is the Accademia Gallery. You left some things in the locker yesterday when you came to visit.'

'I'm sorry, I think there must be some mistake. I wasn't at the gallery yesterday.'

This didn't throw him off. 'When you were here you left your things in the locker. You must collect them today please.'

He hung up.

Strange. I hadn't been there for nearly six months, when Federica had wangled me a ticket for the unveiling of a restored Titian. I couldn't remember having left anything there, but perhaps they'd just made a mistake with the dates. Or perhaps nobody had checked the locker since then. Hell, it was only a ten-minute walk away, and I had no surgery that morning. I did, however, have a large piece of translation work on a lawnmower manual that I'd been putting off. I'd put in a couple of hours' work on that before heading out. I'd stop at the gallery, pick up whatever it was that had been left and then think about lunch.

Charlie Chaplin was standing outside the church of San Vidal, as he had been every day since I arrived in Venice. He twirled his cane, gave his knees a gentle bounce and we exchanged nods. We'd never spoken to each other, and probably never would, but after five years we had at least moved on to acknowledging each other's existence.

Sometimes, typically late at night, it was a genuine pleasure to cross the Accademia Bridge. On a clear autumn evening, free of the daytime crowds, I would stand there and look out towards the church of the Salute lit up against the background of the *bacino* of San Marco. If I was lucky, my friend the lutenist would be playing some baroque music and I would think how I was the luckiest man in the world to be living in this city. And then, at other times, it resembled the Odessa steps sequence from *Battleship Potemkin*. Today was one of the latter occasions.

Gheorghe was waiting at the foot of the bridge, as he always was. I stopped to say hello.

'What's this?' I indicated a piece of cardboard on which two symbols had been scrawled. The first showed a silhouette of a woman staggering under the weight of a large dog as she carried it across the bridge. A large red cross had been felt-tipped though it. The other showed the same woman skipping across as someone else carried the dog for her. This picture was marked with a green tick.

'It's my new scheme,' said Gheorghe in his thick Romanian accent. 'I was thinking, you know how everybody hates us?'

I nodded, cautiously. He was right. If a league table were to be constructed of the popularity of incomers, Romanians – together with Bulgarians, Albanians and anyone from Rome southwards – would be occupying the relegation positions of Serie C.

'Everyone thinks we're all beggars and thieves, right? So I thought, we need to get known for something else. The Africans sell handbags, the Asian guys are all selling darts or lovelocks. The British guys are dressing up as Charlie Chaplin . . .'

'Wait a moment, he's *British*?'

Gheorghe looked surprised. 'Of course he is. You think any Italian would do that? Anyway, I thought we Romanians, we need to have our gimmick too. So what can we do? And I thought of this.'

'So how does it work?'

'Easy. This is a city full of small dogs and bridges. You ever seen a sausage dog struggling over a bridge? And also it's full of old ladies. Old ladies with dogs and shopping trolleys. You see them every day, she's got her trolley in one hand, and pulling the dog in the other and you think she's never going to make it to the other side. But, for just a euro, I pick the dog up and carry it over for her, and she only has to worry about the trolley. Easy money!'

'But wouldn't it make more sense to carry the trolley and let her walk the dog?' I said.

He looked confused, as if I were missing something blindingly obvious. 'But anybody could do that. This way we have a novelty. You need to think outside the box, Nathan.'

I didn't want to scoff. Gheorghe hadn't had the best of times since arriving from Romania. He had at least avoided getting sucked into organised begging and street crime, but life had been difficult. His shoulders dropped, 'You think I'm crazy?'

'Crazy? It's insane. It's an insane idea. But yesterday my best friend told me he once rode a motorcycle through town in order to meet Pink Floyd. Maybe crazy is the way to go.'

This seemed to please him. As we talked, he noticed an elderly lady approaching, visibly labouring with an enormous shopping trolley and a small dog.

'Sorry, Nathan, have to go. Time is money, right?'

He walked towards her, a broad smile on his face. I braced myself for an instant rebuff, and possibly some low-level racism. To my amazement, she nodded and handed over a euro and the dog's lead. Gheorghe scooped the miniature hound into his arms, and strode out across the bridge, as she struggled to keep up with him.

I shook my head. Crazy was indeed the way to go.

The Accademia was cool and smelled of art by dead people. The man at the *guardaroba* gave me a hard time about leaving things in lockers. He hoped I realised how fortunate I was, that these things were normally just thrown out after a couple of days. They were a national museum, not a left luggage facility. If I wanted to leave things in a safe place, why didn't I use the lockers at the station or the hotel safe? I tried explaining that I was not a tourist and whatever it was they'd found it was almost certainly nothing to do with me. He just shook his head, and handed me the package.

It was a jiffy bag, similar to the one Montgomery had tried to pass on to me less than a day previously. The only difference being that a label reading 'Property of Nathan Sutherland, British Consulate, Calle dei Assassini', in elegant copperplate script, had been affixed.

He saw the recognition in my eyes, and smiled in triumph. So it was mine then? Good, obviously he was very happy that I was here to collect it but I had to realise that he'd been to a great deal of trouble. There hadn't even been a contact telephone number. He'd had to check on the Internet. I was fortunate that he'd been on duty that morning, some of the other staff wouldn't have bothered. Next time, please, better to leave valuables in my hotel.

'I don't have a hotel.'

'*Scusa?*' He was being cheeky now, using the familiar form.

'I said I don't have a hotel. I live here. And what's more, this isn't mine.'

He narrowed his eyes. 'Are you sure?'

'Yes, I'm sure. It isn't mine.'

He made to grab it back. 'In that case we'll put it in lost property.'

I snatched the other side of the packet. We glared at each other as we tugged it back and forth across the desk.

'It isn't mine. It belongs to a, well, to a client of mine.'

'A *client*?' He rolled the word around his tongue.

'Yes. The gentleman in question asked me to look after it for him.'

'Why?'

'I don't know.'

'What's in it?'

'I don't know.'

'Why didn't you take it?'

I ran my hand through my hair. Why was it that, sooner or later, everybody in this country turned into a bureaucrat? 'Because I don't know what's in it.'

'Why would someone give you a package to look after?'

I drew myself up to my full height. 'I am Her Majesty's honorary consul in Venice, and that means that, on occasion, her subjects will ask me . . . will ask me to do . . . things.' That last bit, I thought, seemed to lack the necessary gravitas.

'You are the ambassador?'

'No, the consul. The honorary consul, to be precise.'

He nodded, and reached into his desk for a sheaf of papers. 'Okay, I'll need to see some documentation.'

'Why? Five minutes ago you just wanted me to take the bloody thing away!'

'Yes, but that was when I thought the parcel was yours. If it isn't, we must complete a form.'

I looked at the papers in front of him. Three sides, perhaps five signatures required. In a country that required one to sign twenty times in order to open the most basic of bank accounts, this was getting away lightly.

'Passport.'

I took out my identity card. He looked puzzled. 'No passport?'

'I never carry it about. Just my ID card.'

'So you live here?'

'Of course I live here. I'm the British honorary consul. How could I do that if I were just on holiday?'

He nodded. He looked at the card. 'It says here that you are a translator?'

'I am. That's my job.'

'So you are not the consul?'

'I am the consul, but it's not really a job. I don't get paid for doing it. Translation is my real job.'

'You don't get paid?' He whistled. '*Mamma mia.*' For the first time he looked at me with a degree of sympathy. I was one of them, after all.

I took out my business card from the consulate. He gave it a cursory glance and scribbled down something indecipherable. Then he turned the papers towards me. 'Just sign here please . . . and here . . . and here. And here.'

Four signatures for collecting lost property. Not bad really. I slipped the package into my jacket, and we made our farewells. As I left the building, I saw – for an instant only – a stocky gentleman in late middle-age making his way to the upstairs gallery. Montgomery, surely. I followed him up, only to find my way blocked by an attendant who insisted, not unreasonably, that I show her a ticket. I tried to scan the great vault of the first room over her shoulder but if he had ever been there, he was gone by now.

I could, I suppose, have bought a ticket and sprinted through the galleries looking for him. But for what? To tell him to stop sending me parcels? And chances are I was mistaken anyway. More importantly – I checked my watch – it was nearly time for lunch.

I made my way back home. There was, probably, the need to go shopping. The only food in the flat belonged to Gramsci, and I felt I really should have an attempt at seeing if the oven still worked. Yes, I'd walk down to Punto and maybe buy some stuffed pasta. Nothing that required too much effort.

And then, when I walked through Campo Sant'Angelo, I saw him again. No mistake this time. Sitting on the steps at the foot of the unintentionally scatological statue of Nicolò Tommaseo, reading a newspaper. I stopped. The first time was almost certainly a coincidence. This, less so. Should I walk up and confront him? Or just ignore him?

I decided to outwait him. I'd go for lunch at the Bacaro Da Fiore, which would have the advantageous side effect of removing the need to cook anything. And, if I was having lunch, I could outwait anyone.

Paolo, beardy and cheerful, was there as usual. '*Ciao*, Nathan, *come stai?*'

'*Mica male*, Paolo. Any soft-shell crabs on today?'

'Only a few, so you're in luck. They're a bit expensive though.'

'*Beh*, just give me two then. And a couple of meatballs with a half-litre of red. I may be here some time.'

I emerged one hour later, fuller of tummy and lighter of both head and pocket. Montgomery was gone. When I got home, I unlocked the office and plonked the package on the desk.

What to do?

I could either put it in the safe and forget about it, or I could open it up. Was I really going to do that?

Yes. Yes, I was.

I didn't know if Montgomery was coming back. In the event of it containing something illegal I would have to inform the police. Moreover, if it was illegal, I didn't want it on the premises for any longer than necessary.

Gramsci sprang on to the desk, and scratched at the envelope. We stared at each other. I nodded. He was usually right about these things. I took out a letter opener, and went through to the kitchen. Should I open it in the sink, just in case it was explosive? Or did that only work in films? I didn't know much about this sort of thing but I was pretty sure that explosive devices couldn't be deactivated merely by running them under cold water for a few seconds.

I hesitated for a moment, until a miaow of admonishment came from behind me and I slit it open. It contained an envelope on which the words 'Please wear these' had been written in the same copperplate hand, and a larger object in bubble wrap. I picked away at the letter with a degree of trepidation. and took out a pair of thin white cotton gloves.

There seemed no reason not to put them on. Then I gently removed the bubble wrap. The object inside was covered in a layer of tissue paper.

It was a book. Small, perhaps only four inches in length and three across, with a simple black leather cover.

The gloves were fine, nevertheless my fingers felt clumsy and constrained as I turned the pages. The frontispiece bore the simple title *La Vita della Vergine Maria. The Life of the Virgin*. The following page showed the Madonna enthroned in the company of saints. It was beautiful. A tiny jewel of blues and golds and reds, just a few inches across. Then pages of Latin script, indecipherable to my eyes, interspersed with other images. I tried to drag the stories back into my mind. The Immaculate Conception. The Birth of Mary. The Presentation. The Betrothal of Joseph and Mary. The Annunciation. The Flight into Egypt. All of them illustrated so perfectly, so precisely, with colours that shone. All those stories from Sunday School where the terrifying Mrs Walton had convinced me that, at the age of seven, I was a sinner and condemned to hell.

I leafed through it again. It seemed disrespectful, blasphemous almost, not to spend a proper amount of time looking at each one; as if I were a tourist scurrying through the Uffizi to take a selfie with *The Birth of Venus* and then be on my way. I turned it over in my hand, felt its weight. I lifted it to my face and sniffed it. The smell of old libraries mixed with clean leather.

I placed it down upon the desk, almost reverently. Gramsci had an experimental prod but, for once, I managed to stare him down and he slunk away. What to think? An object of veneration, presumably commissioned by someone of considerable wealth and power. How must they have felt to be able to hold this book, this most lovely book, in their hands? To leaf through it and see each and every beautiful image. To think, ' "I made this. For the love of Our Lady, I had this most precious thing made." ' Or perhaps they looked at it and felt nothing but fear? A permanent reminder that they had tried to buy their way into heaven; to atone for their sins by paying for the creation of something so pure and so perfect. They wouldn't have been the last to think that there was no problem that couldn't be resolved by throwing money at it.

Why had Montgomery made sure this had come into my possession? I'd never met him before and yet he could read me so well he knew I wouldn't be able to resist the temptation to open it up. Was it nothing more than he simply wanted it to be looked after for a couple of days, and trusted me enough to treat it with respect? It wasn't a great explanation, but I couldn't think of a better one.

Besides, there was another question and this one seemed more important. The face of the Virgin. Beautiful, of course. Serene, yet capable of expressing all the sorrows in the world. A young woman, yet just a little plump, and slightly rounded of face.

I'd seen her before. But where?

Chapter 4

Venice was drowning under a tsunami of tourists, and Something Had To Be Done. Of that, *Il Gazzettino* was certain. It didn't know what, but it had no doubt that Something, ideally sooner rather than later, Had To Be Done.

I folded the newspaper and threw it on to the growing pile of half-read ones. Gramsci gave a little howl of approval and leapt atop the perilously leaning stack, in order to settle down for a much-needed little sleep.

I often wondered why I bothered with *Il Gazzettino*. Over the years, I'd tried to figure out its political stance and had ultimately concluded that it was centre-miserablist. It was never short of things to complain about. *Grandi Navi*, the grotesque cruise ships, were disfiguring the city. Visitor numbers were making the famous parts of the city no-go areas for *Veneziani*. Crumbling *palazzi* were in need of restoration. Restored *palazzi* hadn't been restored correctly.

The weight of traffic on the Grand Canal, it was generally agreed, was too great. The morning hours saw the area around the Rialto Bridge swarming with *vaporetti*, water taxis, commercial boats making deliveries, refuse collection barges, the Alilaguna service to the airport and gondolas. Sooner or later someone was going to be killed. And so it transpired. Following the death of a tourist, struck by a *vaporetto* that backed into a gondola, everyone agreed that Something Had To Be Done. The response was to reduce the number of *vaporetto* services, leading to angry commuters railing at unfortunate *marinai* when they refused to let them on to already overcrowded boats. This, the newspaper declared, had been decidedly The Wrong Thing To Do.

There was also a fair amount of raging against corruption, but at least that particular form of miserabilism was shared with every other newspaper in Italy. Everyone was in agreement that Something Had To Be Done. Similarly, there was a general accord that It Probably Wouldn't.

The one thing there was little to complain about, in Venice at least, was crime. Oh yes, there was regular thievery, graffiti, crap merchants selling a mixture of the illegal and the useless on every bridge and occasional bad behaviour from tourists; but for proper crime – dirty, violent, big city crime – you had to leave the charmed environment of the lagoon and head over the bridge to Mestre.

Dario had once told me that the best time to have lived in Venice was twenty-five years ago. Or, more precisely, that the best time to have lived in Venice was always twenty-five years ago. He was probably right. Yet whenever we found something new to complain about, I felt that we should head over the bridge to *terra firma*, to spend a few hours in a normal, unlovely town; to remind ourselves of how lucky we were.

Gramsci scrabbled around sleepily, causing the pile to shift alarmingly. He gave a long stretch, and yawned, as if wondering if there was something going on in the world that he needed to be outraged about. He decided there wasn't, and settled back down to sleep, atop his own personal tower of grumpiness.

The telephone rang. I didn't recognise the number.

'*Pronto.*'

'*Ciao,* Nathan. It's Vanni.'

I paused, struggling to remember the name.

'Vanni, from the *Questura.*'

'Vanni? How are things?'

'Not so bad. Listen, can you come in? We brought a couple of kids in last night. For possession.'

'Do you need me? I mean, really? Don't you normally just shout at them? Give them a scare and send them on their way?'

'Not this time. Too much stuff. Looks like they were dealing. A *barista* in Santa Margherita tipped us off.'

'*Beh.* Yeah, okay. I'll be right along.'

I remembered the first time I took a call from the *Questura.* It seemed ever so slightly thrilling, glamorous even. I'd imagined defending my fellow citizens, fighting miscarriages of justice, tearful farewells and hugs outside the police station. That sort of thing.

In reality, it typically meant little more than spending hours in the company of scared kids, there for a bit of drunken silliness or for smoking something they shouldn't have. There is precious little you can do to help. You do not storm in swearing to fight injustice wherever it may be found. Still, if you've done something wrong when you're abroad, it doesn't matter how well the police speak English. You just want someone with a British accent to come along and tell you everything's going to be all right.

Most cases never came to very much anyway. A night in the cells, and free in the morning with a slap on the wrist. Nobody wanted the hassle of prosecuting kids for a misdemeanour. But possession with the intention of dealing was different. They could have been looking at a prison sentence. If that seemed likely the case would be booted upstairs to Milan, but, for the time being, it was my responsibility.

The police headquarters had been over in Castello, opposite the church of San Lorenzo, a pleasant stroll from the flat. We used to like going down there to feed the stray cats that sheltered outside the church, and to get ice cream from Mela Verde. But the *Questura* had moved long before I'd ever had need to go there. The new building was just off the bus terminus at Piazzale Roma, near the end of the Ponte della Libertà that linked Venice with the mainland. It seemed colder, less reassuring; although I had to concede that looking reassuring was probably not high on the list of design requirements for a police station. Going there always made me feel slightly uneasy, in the same way as a visit to the dentist's.

Vanni's English was reasonable, but one of the kids was insisting on having a native English speaker there. One of them was long haired and unshaven, with a T-shirt bearing the name of a popular beat combo vaguely familiar to me. The other was shorter and neater, with glasses and a centre parting. They both looked as if they should still be at school.

We shook hands and ran through the formalities. Yes, they knew why they were there. There'd been a terrible misunderstanding and all they wanted was for it to be sorted out so they could go home, no hard feelings. I ran through what I could do for them. If you need a lawyer, I can get you one. If you need to contact people in the UK, I can contact them. A priest? I can get you one, any denomination you like.

Silence. I took a closer look at Long Hair's T-shirt. Beneath the name of the popular beat combo was an inverted, flaming crucifix. Okay, maybe not a priest. An interpreter?

Glasses, looking increasingly bored, stuck a cigarette in his mouth and reached for a lighter. 'Can I smoke?'

I shook my head and pointed at the *Vietato Fumare* sign.

'Why not?' I was unsure if he really needed one or if it was just for face. 'I saw one of them' – he gestured towards the *poliziotto* who was standing at the door – 'having one earlier.' The guard stiffened.

'First of all,' I said, 'he's a policeman and can do what he likes. Secondly, some of *them*' – I lingered over the word, and mirrored his gesture – 'speak English. So it's as well to be polite.'

He stared at me in silence for a moment, before replacing the cigarette in the packet. He toyed with the lighter, flicking it occasionally in challenge. 'Can't you just have a word?' He made quotation marks in the air with his fingers.

'I can't. I'm sorry, but I can't do that.'

'What would you say if *he* wasn't here?' He gestured towards the *poliziotto* again.

I threw the cop a glance, and made a brief apology in Italian. Then I turned back to Glasses. 'I would say exactly the same. There are things I can do to help, but they are limited.'

He tapped the lighter gently but repeatedly on the table. This was starting to become irritating. 'Not much, is it?'

'Well, it's up to you. Are you sure you don't want me to call anyone? Mum and Dad, for example?'

Silence. 'As I said before, I can put you in touch with a lawyer. Would you like me to do that?'

Silence. I shrugged, and started to gather my notes together. 'In that case, there's very little I can do. If you do change your mind, let the police know and they'll contact me.' I packed my notes into my bag, and stood up. 'There is one thing you need to know. In the event of your being charged, and given its seriousness, I will have to inform the authorities back in the UK.'

Long Hair was staring ever more fixedly at the table. I looked at Glasses, but he refused to meet my gaze. The cockiness had gone, as if he'd finally realised that I wasn't going to be able to wave a magic wand. I nodded at the *poliziotto*, 'Okay, I think we're finished.'

I walked to the door and then decided I'd give them one last chance. 'By the way. Have you heard of a man called Giorgio Napolitano?'

'Plays for Juventus, doesn't he?' It was, inevitably, Glasses who spoke. A last touch of braggadocio.

'He used to be the President of the Republic. He recently said the Italian prison system was a national disgrace, and the jails an embarrassment to a civilised country. They are on the edge of what is acceptable to the European Convention on Human Rights. So think very carefully. The system works at a snail's pace over here. If they charge you, you could be waiting six, seven, eight months before you even get to trial. If you end up in the prison at Santa Maria Maggiore you might be the only English-speakers in a cell of six.' I was over-egging it now, but I just wanted a response that was something other than facetious.

Long Hair was hunched even lower over the table, and was crying, silently. Glasses stared at him with utter contempt, but I could tell he was shaken.

'Now then,' I said, 'shall we talk?'

Vanni was flicking through a report and smoking in cheerful contravention of Article 51. He looked up.

'What do you think, Nathan?'

'I think they're two stupid kids who should have stayed at home. As to whether they're dealing or not, I have no idea. They said somebody at the bar gave them the package to look after for a few minutes.'

'Well, we have one witness – the *barista* – who says he saw them selling the gear. Forensics will tell us about prints on the envelope. If there are any inside, we could probably make a case.'

'And will you?'

'Don't know. Maybe. Sometimes it's good to have a little clampdown. We get some nice publicity in *Il Gazzettino*. And it's a message to send out around the bars. "Be a good citizen", that sort of thing. How are they?'

'One crying when I left. Possibly both by now.'

'Goodness me. What did you say to them?'

'I described the Italian criminal justice system.'

He whistled. 'You're a hard man, Mr Sutherland.'

'They weren't even going to have a lawyer. I gave them a scare. Probably shouldn't have, but it's for their own good.'

'Okay. Well, we'll see what happens. Next time they'll think twice before they do some stupid bastard thing like taking unmarked envelopes from strangers.'

I gave him a watery smile, and went to give Long Hair and Glasses the details of their lawyer.

Chapter 5

It was past midday by the time I emerged from the *Questura*. Too early for lunch, not too early for a drink. I thought about it for a moment, but there were a limited number of bars around Piazzale Roma in which I thought it would be pleasant to drink a leisurely Spritz; and, besides, there were other things I needed to do. I patted my jacket pocket, just to remind myself that the package was still there. There was one person who might be able to give me some information about the book, and who I could trust to be reasonably discreet about it.

Vanni had said he would call me once they'd decided whether or not to charge Long Hair and Glasses. If they said no, my work would be finished and the two boys would be free to continue their Grand Cultural Tour elsewhere. If not, well, things might get busy. And messy.

I'd bottled the phone calls to their parents. Faced with two answering machines, I'd decided to ring off without leaving any messages. ' "Hi, you don't know me, but my name is Nathan Sutherland, honorary consul in Venice. I'm afraid to say that your son has been arrested for a serious crime for which, if convicted, he stands to pass a substantial amount of time in prison. Okay, if you can just give me a call when you receive this, that'd be great".' No. It would have to wait. In the meantime, it was a fine spring day and I had no surgery to worry about. I decided to take the *vaporetto* around to Santa Marta, one of the odder journeys to be taken in Venice.

The boat passed under the Ponte delle Libertà, and along the Canal de la Scomenzera. The boats moored at the side along here were barges for the transport of heavy goods, whilst the *fondamenta* was lined with industrial machinery alongside railway sidings. Through the window, I could see a giant fibre-glass hand resting upon an actual-size model of a tank, a relic of a previous Art Biennale that, it seemed, the artist had never bothered to come to pick up. To the right, a giant cruise ship lay moored in the terminal at Tronchetto. Only one, but the first of the year and a sign that the tourist season proper was on its way.

I alighted at Santa Marta, the only *vaporetto* stop in the city from where one actually needs to cross a road. The last traders from the market were packing up and loading the remains of their produce into vans, ready for the drive back to the main-land. To my right, the road led to the restricted areas of the port authority, whilst to my left it led back to the bridge across to *terra firma*. The area was a mixture of social housing, and nineteenth-century industrial buildings, now being used by the university. There was not a mask shop or a Not Murano Glass outlet to be seen. As I walked through the *calli*, canals started to appear and the architecture became older, remind-ing me that I was still, after all, in Venice.

I made my way to the Campo San Nicolò dei Mendicoli where the most undignified lion in Venice stood atop a plinth, looking over to the church of the same name. Shorn of mane, wings and self-esteem, he seemed embarrassed to be up there, like a man who suddenly realises he's arrived at work without his trousers.

The church glowed with old gold, and smelled of wood and incense. San Nicolò felt special, even in a city of over one hundred churches. There was something Byzantine about it, something ancient. The covered porch was a reminder that this had once been a place for the poor and needy to seek shelter from the elements. Directly inside, a sign on a table covered with tins of food and bags of dried pasta bore the legend *Per i poveri;* a reminder that we had not, perhaps, moved on as much as we should. *Oh Holy St Nicholas, pray unto God for us.*

In recent times, this had become one of my favourite places just to come and sit and think. But today, the meditative quality of the space was broken by a scaffolding rig. At its base, a couple of men in overalls and hard hats were checking instruments.

'Is Federica Ravagnan here?' I asked.

One of them nodded, without even looking at me. '*La Ravagnan, sì.*' He called up. 'Someone down here to see you, *dottoressa.*'

I craned my head upwards. Far, far above me, a figure appeared. Overalled, pony-tailed and dusted with dirt and white plaster.

'Nathan. *Ciao, caro.* Come on up.'

'Are you sure?'

'Of course. Come and see what we're doing.'

'Well I'd love to.' I looked up. It seemed a fearfully long way. 'Love to. Absolutely, yes. But I'm not insured or anything.'

'Don't be silly, that doesn't matter. Come on up.'

I was afraid of this. I should just have lurked outside until they broke for lunch. I made my way up along the systems of platforms and ladders. It wasn't that high, I kept telling myself, it really wasn't that high.

Federica greeted me with a big hug that I returned as best I could given that both my hands were firmly affixed to the railing. 'So what brings you here, *tesoro?*'

I kept my eyes half-closed, desperately trying to focus on anything beyond the fact that we were over fifty feet up. Modern-day scaffolding is rigid, sound and safe. I could not, repeat, could not possibly be feeling it move. Besides, hadn't Michelangelo spent years lying on a rickety wooden lash-up without complaint, whilst painting the roof of the Sistine Chapel?

'I know what you're thinking, Nathan. It's perfectly safe.'

'Can't help it. Just thinking of Donald Sutherland in *Don't Look Now.*'

'That was different, he'd been cursed or something. You haven't been cursed have you?'

'Sometimes I wonder.'

'Come on, try and open your eyes.'

I forced them open. Federica, wiping a cobweb from her hair, was smiling. There might have been a modest element of pity involved, but I thought she was pleased to see me.

'You're not wearing a hard hat,' I said, 'and the guys downstairs are.'

'*Beh*, if anything falls from here, they'll need one. If I fall from here, it isn't going to help. It's breaking the rules, but it's easier to work. Now take a look.'

I glanced up. A wooden mounting, flecked with gold, surrounded a bare circle of wood. I made the mistake of looking down. Immediately I clamped my eyes shut, and clutched at the rail with both hands.

'Francesco Montemezzano. Christ sits in Glory, as Nicholas is crowned Bishop. The Accademia are giving it a clean. We're just re-gilding the mounting, and doing a little bit of work on some of the *stucco*. It's not a big job, but it will look fantastic when it's done.'

'Lovely. Brilliant. Anyway, why I'm here . . . I've got something I'd like you to take a look at. A little problem of art history. I mean to say, I'd just like your opinion.'

'Of course, *caro*. Do you want to show me now?'

I tried to force my right hand to move from the rail to my jacket pocket. It, very sensibly, refused to move. I shook my head. 'No. No, not really.'

'No problem. I've brought a sandwich but you can buy me lunch instead. Thirty minutes, at the place around the corner?'

'Lovely. Delighted.'

There was a brief pause.

'See you there, then?'

I nodded, and inched my way towards the ladder. If I was very, very careful, I thought, I could get myself down to the ground without opening my eyes.

'You're doing very well, *caro*. Just don't think about Donald Sutherland.'

I was on my second Spritz by the time Federica arrived and ordered a Prosecco and some *tramezzini*. At least, I thought, I had stopped trembling. 'Your hands are still shaking,' she said, and took them in hers.

'I'm crap at heights. You know I'm crap at heights.'

'And I keep telling you there's no reason to be. You've been up the *campanile* at San Giorgio Maggiore with no problems.'

'That's different. It feels more stable. It's a big brick thing that feels like it's supposed to be standing up, not a huge wobbly metal skeleton.'

'Stop being a baby. Now tell me what this is about.'

I reached into my pocket, and withdrew the book. 'It's about this. It got, well, it got passed on to me yesterday. I don't know what it is. But there's something about it. Something that looks familiar.'

She plucked it from my hands, and flicked through it with, I thought, rather less reverence than it might have deserved. She raised her eyebrows. 'Of course you recognise this.'

'I do? Oh good.'

'Don't be silly. Of course you do. Tell me about it.'

'Well, it's the *Life of the Virgin*. Usual series of images. Birth, Presentation, Visitation, Marriage, *Pietà*, Dormition . . .'

'Very good. You ever thought about crossing over?'

'I'd love to. But my granny would kill me.'

'After she's gone then. Seriously. You'd be a great Catholic. Tell me more.'

I took a deep breath. 'Okay. I know I should recognise it but it's not quite clicking. There's something about the Virgin though.'

'Right.'

'Same model in every image?'

'Exactly. What else?'

'Very pretty. Beautiful even. That slightly rounded face . . .'

'Yes?'

'I've seen it somewhere before . . .?'

'Of course you have, Nathan, now tell me where?'

'I can't remember . . .'

'Yes you can. Come on now. Only one artist could paint Madonnas like this.'

'Titian?' I ventured.

She moved her empty plate to one side, and stared at me in wordless disappointment.

'Wait a moment. The Accademia. San Giobbe altarpiece . . .'

'Which means . . .?'

'Bellini?'

'Which one?'

'Giovanni, of course.'

'Of course. Well done. Your prize is you get to buy me another Prosecco.'

'Gladly. You know, maybe I'll have another Spritz.'

'You've had two, you can't have any more. Have a Prosecco instead. And at least have a *tramezzino*, you look like you need something solid.'

I waved at the waiter. 'How do you know I've had two Spritzes?'

'After the state you were in on top of the scaffolding? There hasn't been time for you to have had three. One wouldn't have been enough.'

We sat in silence for a while, until the waiter returned with our drinks and food.

'Okay, Nathan, now tell me where you got this.'

'It just got passed on to me. I assume it's stolen . . . I don't really know. I'm just curious.'

'Stolen, maybe. Probably a fake though.'

'Why so?'

She held the book up, and rubbed the cover between her fingers. 'I don't know. Not for sure. It's possible that somebody has passed on a genuine Bellini to you, but that doesn't seem likely. There's one guy that would know for sure. You go to the Banca Popolare in Campo Manin, and ask to see Giacomo Maturi. He's the archivist there. He'll be able to tell you all about it.'

'Because . . .?'

'Because they've got an almost identical book to this one, *caro*. Now I need to get back to work.' She leant over and kissed me. 'Call me, okay?'

I nodded. I still felt slightly shaky. Almost certainly, I told myself, due to the height.

Chapter 6

I put the phone down, and slumped back in the chair, rubbing my eyes in the hope of shaking off the weariness that had come over me. There had been two almost identical conversations. Two difficult conversations. Both of which had ended in the same way. *I'm sorry, there's nothing more I can do.* But at least I had done all I could. Something else was bothering me, had been bothering me from the moment I opened the package.

Only one person could help me now. I reached for the telephone again.

'Dario?'

'*Ciao, vecio!*'

'Listen, I really need a beer tonight. Are you free?'

He paused. 'I would be, but I promised Valentina I'd be home early for dinner.'

'Ah right. Okay, no worries.'

'Is it important?'

'Dunno. Just need some advice.'

'Anything I can do over the phone?'

'I don't think so. This needs a beer.'

There was another pause. 'Okay. I can't come into Venice

tonight though. Come over to Mestre, we'll have a few beers at Toni's and I can still be home in time.'

'You're a star. I'll see you there.'

I hung up and grabbed my coat. It was only fair. We nearly always met up in Venice. I worried at times that he thought I had the same attitude to Mestre as the tourists: dirty, unlovely, no reason to go there.

I walked down to Rialto, and caught the fast boat to Piazzale Roma. Within forty-five minutes, I was at Toni's bar on the Corso del Popolo. Dario was there before me, with two beers waiting.

'Drinks in Mestre. On a Tuesday evening. This has to be a big problem.'

'Not really a problem. I just don't know what to do.' I shivered. 'Why do we always sit outside here?'

He shrugged. 'Nicer outside.'

I looked around. Traffic whizzed past us on a busy street lined with tall grey buildings. 'If you say so,' I said.

'It's not so bad. Stay long enough and they sometimes bring you snacks. Anyway, it's ten minutes from the office and ten minutes from home. So what's going on?'

'That guy I told you about the other night. The one who wanted me to look after the package?'

'Yeah?'

'I've ended up with it. Long story, I'll tell you later. But it isn't drugs.'

'You opened it?'

'Yeah of course I opened it. I wanted to know if it, I dunno, was going to explode or something.'

'Nathan, usually the best way of getting something to explode is to open it.'

'Yeah all right, Mr Clever Army Man. I still opened it. It's not drugs. It's a prayer book, an artwork. I think it's stolen.'

'Mmm. You've been to the police then?'

'No.'

'No? You could get in trouble for this.'

'I know. It's just . . .' I took a long draught of my beer. 'There was something this guy, Montgomery, said that worried me. He mentioned the guy that had the consular job before me. Guy called Victor, don't know if you ever met him.' Dario shook his head. 'No reason why you should have. Anyway, Montgomery said, pretty clearly, that he'd left stuff with him in the past.' I paused.

'And?'

'That's the problem. If I go to the police I might end up getting him in trouble.'

'Yeah, but that's his problem, isn't it? Should have thought about that before accepting stolen property.'

'No, you don't understand. Victor's a good man. A decent man. I can't imagine him doing anything like this, unless there was a really good reason.'

'Mmm. Well, this other guy – Montgomery – he might just be lying. Makes sense.'

'I think so. I hope so.'

'Give this Victor a call then.'

'I know I should. I just keep dithering.'

'You're a consul, Nathan. You should be used to this sort of thing.'

'I know. It's just that it never gets any easier. I've got another problem on the go as well.' I ran through the sorry tale of Long Hair and Glasses. 'So, basically, I've got two scared kids locked up. I've got two sets of parents in bits back in the UK, demanding to know why I'm not doing anything.'

He reached for his beer. 'Seems to me you've done everything you can.'

'I have. That's the damnable thing. I can't do anything else.'

'Well then. There's no problem.'

'Not for me, I know. I just keep thinking I should . . . I don't know . . . maybe I should "have a word"?'

He burst out laughing, and reached across the table to grab my shoulder. 'Ah, welcome to Italy *Signor* Nathan. You're one of us now!'

'What do you mean?'

He finished his beer, then checked his watch. He paused for a moment, then held two fingers up at a passing waiter. 'How long have you been here, Nathan?'

'Nearly five years. Why?'

'This is how it all starts. What are you thinking of doing?'

'You know, just say to Vanni, "Look, these probably aren't bad kids. Is it really worth the trouble of prosecuting them? Won't it be easier for all of us if we just forget about it?"'

He laughed again. 'Yeah, that's how it all starts. One day it's, "Won't it be easier for us all if we do this?" Next day you're bribing a senator over a cheap land deal.'

'Ah come on, it's not the same at all.'

He waved his finger from side to side in admonishment. 'Look. Imagine you're back home. Would you say to a cop you've met three, four times just to "let something go"?'

'No, of course not.'

'So why would you do it here?'

I could see where this was going, but said nothing. He continued, 'Because you're thinking "this is Italy", right?'

I nodded. 'I'm sorry.'

He looked serious. I didn't think I'd ever seen him looking serious before. 'Yeah. This is Italy. You don't really know it yet. Don't do this.'

'Ah, you're right. It's just frustrating. It's the worst thing about this consul business. You want to help people and realise you can't.'

'Army was like that. There are times that you just can't. Let it go. You've done what you can. And at least nobody's going to get killed over it.'

'But would you do it?'

He seemed surprised. 'Yeah, of course I would. But you shouldn't.' He looked at his watch and drained his glass. 'Okay, I've really got to go.'

'Yeah. Thanks, Dario. By the way, what are you doing tomorrow night?'

'Probably at home. It's a bit difficult to get a night off at the moment.'

'Ah, no worries. It's just I've got a *thing* tomorrow. I suppose you'd call it an official reception. My first one.'

'Lucky you.'

'Anyway, I can bring a guest so I'd thought if you were free . . .'

'You thought of me?'

'Yes, of course.' I caught the expression on his face. 'Does that sound a bit tragic?'

'You thought of taking me? No, not tragic. Much worse than that.'

'Yeah, well you're my pal and . . .'

He buttoned up his coat. 'Forget about it.'

'I know, I know. Silly idea.'

'No. Stupid idea. Ask that friend of yours, the nice art-restorer lady.'

I said nothing.

He grinned. 'Ah, you've already thought about it!'

'No, no, not at all. Well, maybe.'

'Good. I'm blowing you off for tomorrow night, so now you have to ask her.' I opened my mouth to speak, but he waved his hand, 'And now I have to go.'

'Okay. Thanks again. Best to Valentina. How long is it now?'

'Just ten more days.'

'Wow. I've never asked you what you're hoping for.'

'I don't really care. Well, maybe a bit. A boy. Playing football together, all that stuff.'

I smiled. 'Any names?'

He hesitated, as if embarrassed. 'I think maybe Davide Riccardo Nicolo.'

'Okay. Would that be after David Gilmour, Rick Wright and Nick Mason?'

He said nothing.

'It is, isn't it? Does Valentina know you're going to name your firstborn after the members of Pink Floyd?'

His eyes widened in alarm. 'Not a word, okay? Not a word. She doesn't know yet. I'm hoping she won't notice. I'm still wondering if I can get away with Roger and Syd as well.'

'Dario, this is – as you've reminded me – Italy. Please, for the sake of our friendship, do not call your son Roger Sydney.'

'Too much?'

I nodded. 'Too much.'

He ran off to catch his tram, leaving me to pick up the tab. It seemed fair enough.

Chapter 7

The telephone rang in the middle of surgery. I wouldn't usually have taken it, but this time I recognised the number. It was Vanni. They'd decided not to proceed any further.

'What happened? Forensics?'

'No, we're not going to bother them. The *avvocato* made a persuasive argument.'

'Which was?'

'That it would be easier all round to let them go. Less trouble for everyone. To be honest we're all surprised here that you didn't suggest it.'

I spun around in my chair in a celebratory 360. 'That's fantastic. You've saved me some very awkward phone calls.'

'I'm glad. We're going to tell them to haul their arses out of Venice, and if they ever try anything like this again we'll put them away in the hardest bastard jail in the Veneto.'

'Do that. Thanks, Vanni. Until next time.'

I smiled back at the couple in front of me. 'So, you want to know where the nearest Internet café is then?'

I used to get annoyed if somebody turned up at the office wanting nothing more than directions, or recommendations of a good place to eat, or how to get tickets for La Fenice. I would politely but firmly send them on their way with directions to the nearest tourist information office. Then I started to think that, perhaps, it was one of the better aspects of the job. There was usually something concrete that I could do to help, and people would leave in a good mood. And given the small number of serious cases that I had to deal with, it was something to occupy my time.

Surgery had finished with nothing more serious than registering someone's iPad with VeniceConnected. Then I made two phone calls. Then I did a reasonable amount of basking in admiration. *No really, I did nothing at all. Really, I did nothing at all. Well, I'm glad it's worked out and I could help in whatever small way I did.* I managed to bite back *I'm just glad that justice has been done*, but it was a close-run thing.

Nearly the whole day ahead of me, and nothing to do except the day job. I took a pile of lawn-mower manuals from the drawer, placed them on the desk, and opened the first one. I read the first paragraph, then closed it, put it back on the pile with the others and locked them away again. They could wait. I'd spend a bit of time on my little mystery instead. Campo Manin was less than five minutes' walk away.

The Banca Popolare was an odd building. There'd been one in Manin since the nineteenth century. It was demolished at the end of the 1960s to be replaced with an elegant modern structure of glass, steel and reinforced concrete. The trouble was, it just didn't fit in. However many times you walked past it, it jarred in a 'Wait a minute what did I just see there?' kind of way. The most soul-destroying job in the world, I thought, must be that of being a modern architect in Venice. If you built anything new in the city you could guarantee that people would hate both it and you. If you built something as a Venetian-style pastiche, people would probably like it but you'd end up hating yourself.

I quite liked the Banca Popolare, but it was an opinion I kept to myself.

I hadn't imagined that there would be much work for an archivist at a bank, or that it would be particularly difficult to meet *Signor* Maturi. Nevertheless, he declared himself occupied with various archivey things and told me he could only grant me ten minutes. He didn't seem particularly pleased at the prospect of conducting a brief guided tour, but brightened up a little at the prospect of a chat about Giovanni Bellini.

The bank, he told me, could be considered one of the great undiscovered art galleries in the city. He led me up a glass and steel spiral staircase in the style of the great Venetian modernist Carlo Scarpa and along to the boardroom, a long, brightly lit space with engagingly old-fashioned 1970s furniture. One exterior wall was of glass, looking out upon the *campo*; whilst the other was illuminated at intervals by what – at the time – would have seemed a daringly modern set of Murano glass light fittings.

He must have been in his late sixties, but was spry for his age and I found myself struggling to keep up with him as he scuttled to the far end of the room.

'There. Take a look at that, eh?'

The painting he indicated showed a spiralling, swarming mass of people – saints, holy men, angels, cherubim and seraphim – illuminated by the light shining from the figure of Christ in the top left-hand corner.

'It's Tintoretto isn't it? A copy of the *Paradiso* from the Ducal Palace.'

He shook his head, and looked disapproving. 'Not a copy, no no. Much more interesting. A preparatory version, and not by Jacopo himself but by his son.'

He led me through into another meeting room, this one slightly less opulent and presumably for lower-level function-aries of the bank. A portrait of a Venetian nobleman hung on a wall. I'd seen this sort of thing any number of times – an elderly, bearded figure, clothed in velvet, silk and ermine stared out at us; his gaze projecting wisdom, serenity but, above all, power.

'Tintoretto?' I ventured.

'Very good.' His eyes narrowed. 'Which one?'

'Jacopo?' I managed to restrain myself from saying 'the famous one.'

His gaze hardened and he shook his head.

I could only think of one other but his son, I knew, had been noted as a portraitist. 'Domenico,' I nodded authoritatively.

He looked even more disappointed. 'Pfft.'

I wondered if every visitor was subjected to the same third degree. Moreover, if we were only supposed to have ten minutes, I wondered if we would ever get around to Bellini. Maturi was waiting for me to try again, but realised that I had run out of Tintorettos and took pity on me.

'It's attributed to Domenico, but I think not. For one thing, there is no signature – and every other example of his work is signed. Also, there are no *pentimenti* – no traces of correction and overpainting. These, again, are found throughout his paintings.'

'So who's it by?' I asked.

'I am confident that what we have here is nothing less than one of the few known pieces by Marietta Robusti. Tintoretto's daughter, *La Tintoretta*. She was supposed to have been one of the finest portraitists in the city, and yet hardly anything survives.'

'I didn't even know he had a daughter.'

He looked cross. I felt like I was letting him down. 'Go to the Uffizi. There is a self-portrait there.' He glanced at his watch. 'You want to talk about Giovanni Bellini?' he sighed.

'Yes. About his book, *The Life of the Virgin*.'

'Okay. Come with me.' He led me up to the top floor and a small room, smelling of old furniture. Each wall was lined with glass-doored bookcases.

'The bank archive. Maps, books, artworks. Everything that has come into our possession over the past five hundred years.' He moved to one of the bookcases, took out a set of keys, and unlocked it. Then he took a pair of white gloves from a drawer, put them on, and took down a small book – perhaps no more than four inches by three – which he laid with reverence upon the table. He opened it, and turned to the first page. There, enthroned in the company of saints, sat the Madonna. An image, to my eyes, identical to the one I was carrying in my pocket.

He noticed my expression. 'Beautiful, yes? Perhaps the most perfect, delicate work that *Giambellino* ever produced. Painted, they say, with a brush made from the hair of a new-born baby. Nothing would be softer, or allow for such precision work. And there is of course the symbolism, the purity of it. Have you read Vasari's *Lives of the Artists*?'

I half-nodded, half-shook my head. It was the kind of book that one thinks one ought to read, but I'd found it heavy going and gave up on it long before the author ever got as far as Venice. I didn't think this was the right moment to say so, however.

'No? If you had, you would know that Vasari gives little space to Bellini. He never had much time for the art of *La Serenissima*. He was Tuscan, so – of course – Tuscan art was best. Something of a blind spot. But he does, at least in some versions of his work, refer to this book. It was commissioned for Isabella of Mantova, of the Gonzaga family; and taken to one of their holdings in France. In the late nineteenth century it was bought by a Jewish collector in Berlin. After that, the trail goes cold. The book is lost. Stolen by the Nazis, almost certainly; then possibly looted by the Red Army. Destroyed or in the hands of an anonymous private collector.

'And then, in late 1989, the Soviet Bloc starts to fall apart. Hungary opens its borders with Austria. People start to stream from the East to the West. They have little money, and their currency is worthless here. What else can they use? Perhaps something that father brought back from the Great Patriotic War? Something lying in the attic for decades, in a chest under the bed. Or perhaps an old book, lost and forgotten in the middle of a shelf.

'There are rumours of the rediscovery of so many works. Some are true, some lead to nothing. Most of them are fakes. Then one day, I receive a phone call. A friend of a friend. An antiquarian in Vienna has acquired the book from a retired soldier from Budapest in search of hard cash. Acquired it for what today would be about five thousand euros. Would the bank be interested?'

I held my hand up. 'I'm sorry, but I don't understand. Why would he offer it to a bank?'

'He didn't offer it to the bank. He offered it to me. The art market is perhaps a perfect parallel to Italy itself. Everything works through friends.'

'But why didn't the Accademia or the Correr want it?'

'Oh they probably did. But the bank, of course, also has a responsibility to the city. If there is a chance for us to do something to protect our heritage, then of course we will do so. And if there is a chance to be seen doing such a thing, even better. It may seem hard to believe now, but in 1990 we had a lot of disposable money.

'The bank sent me to Vienna to acquire the book. For considerably more than five thousand euros. The unfortunate Hungarian soldier should have been a very rich man but the art market – and this is another parallel with Italy – is pitiless. Have you ever been to Vienna? No? You should. Like Venice, it is one of the great melancholy cities of the world. The difference is that Vienna feels, to me, sad only in the winter months. Venice, of course, is sad even in the brightest of sunshine. And Austria reminds me of how Italy would be if it were still run by the Austrians. Everything works so perfectly, and yet everything is also just a little dull.

'So I returned to Venice, on the train, with a work by Giovanni Bellini. Now you might suppose that I carried it in a briefcase chained to my wrist, accompanied by two gorillas in dark suits with guns; but no. I travelled alone, and tucked it inside my jacket pocket. I wanted to feel it there, next to my heart. Can you imagine how that felt?'

He let the question hang in the air. I suspected this was a story he had told many times. A little theatrical, perhaps, but it was a tale well told.

'I am seventy years old now. This, I suspect, is the closest I will ever come to having an adventure. When I travelled to Vienna to bring this lovely thing home.'

He gazed, rapt, at the frontispiece. I held my silence for what I hoped was a suitably respectful length of time. 'It is a lovely thing,' I said.

He harrumphed, and nodded absent-mindedly; almost as if he'd forgotten I was there.

It was time to get to the point. 'The book,' I asked, 'was there only ever one? Was Bellini ever commissioned to make a second?'

He looked surprised. 'Well, there is a story. That Cardinal Pietro Bembo, having spent some time in Mantova and having seen the book in the possession of the Gonzaga family, asked *Giambellino* – he was by this time a very old man – to make a work for him. But we know no more than that. There is only a reference in one of Isabella's letters. This work that he desired may have been an exact copy of her book; it may have been an entire altarpiece. We will never know.'

It was my turn, now, to be theatrical. I fixed him with a gaze and slowly withdrew the package from my jacket pocket. *Yes. Yes, I know how it feels.* I slid the book from the jiffy bag (a jiffy bag – why in God's name had I not seen fit to put it in something a little more suitable?), removed the layers of tissue paper and slid it across the table to him.

He picked it up, started to flick through it, then stopped. I'd expected a great cry of exultation, or perhaps a single tear rolling down a cheek; but there was none of that. He raised an eyebrow, put his head ever so slightly to one side and said, 'Interesting.'

I waited. At some point, I thought, there would be the moment of revelation, of exultation. Instead, nothing. He flicked through it a number of times, sniffed the pages, rubbed the cover together between his fingers.

'Interesting?'

'Oh yes. Would you mind telling me who gave this to you?'

'I can't give you a name. It's not just a matter of confidentiality. I really don't know who he is. But I think he's a client, of sorts.'

'Hmmm.'

It conveyed a world of disapproval. 'You think it's stolen?' I said.

He shrugged. 'Who can say?'

'So it is a work by Bellini, then?'

He placed the book down upon the desk, removed his glasses and stared at me. 'Of course not.'

I felt a little deflated. 'No? Are you sure?'

'Of course I'm sure. Look!' He grabbed my hand and directed it to the face of the Madonna. 'Look. Similar, yes? But crude in comparison. Now look at the robes.' With infinitely more reverence he drew my hand across the original, taking care to keep my finger a good centimetre above the surface. 'Look how Bellini makes them flow. This one – yes, the artist can draw a bit, he has some talent – but it looks like a statue. You see?'

I could see no difference at all, but thought that wouldn't be the right answer. I just nodded and smiled.

'The colours. Look at the original.'

I looked. He went to the shelves and took down another book, laid it on the desk, and flicked through it. A book of photographic reproductions this time. 'Look at the colours. Look at the golds, the blues, the reds. This book is supposed to be nearly five hundred years old yet the colours' – again my hand was drawn across my copy – 'these are too perfect. Those of *Giambellino* have faded with the centuries. These are too bright. We can go and buy inks like these in any tourist shop in San Marco. Now look at the cover.'

I picked the book up, and turned it in my hands as if handling a kitten. With a grunt of impatience he snatched it from me, rubbed it vigorously with his fingers, and shoved it under my nose for me to sniff.

'It feels new?' I said. 'It smells new?'

'Feels new, smells new. It is new. It's been treated to look old at a cursory glance, that's all.'

I'd never known much about conservation, but I thought I'd have a last try. 'Isn't it possible this version has been better looked after? Couldn't the colours of the original just have faded?'

'No. These are cheap inks. Whoever made this is not even trying to make a serious forgery. This is just a game, or a student exercise.'

From outside I could hear the Marangona bell. Midday. It had been interesting, certainly, but I'd wasted much of the morning here.

'I'm sorry. I've made a silly mistake. Thanks for your time.' I reached for the book, but he grabbed my hand.

'Are you stupid or something? We must talk about this! Come on, let's get a coffee.'

'I don't understand. It's a fake, you say?'

His face bore the expression of a long-suffering teacher in the face of an idiot pupil. 'Of course it's a fake. That's why it's interesting.' He replaced the original on the shelves, then bustled about checking that every cabinet was secure. 'Come on. No time to waste. Even I only get two hours for lunch. Now where are we going?'

Campo Manin was home to a couple of depressing-looking pizza and kebab shops. If we headed further into San Marco there'd be more of the same, only more expensive. I took him back to the Magical Brazilian. It was a mild day so I thought we'd sit outside. Within five minutes I realised this had been a mistake and drew my coat around me. We ordered a pair of *tramezzini* and a couple of glasses of wine.

'You been here before?'

'Yeah. Well, I live just upstairs. So I come here for breakfast. Maybe a drink late at night.'

He sniffed. 'I don't like it.' He looked across the road to Gabriele's bookshop. 'I know him, though. Good man. A scholar. You ever go there?'

'Erm, well I've looked in the window. Never bought anything though.'

He glared. 'Well you should. You'd learn something.' He picked at a *tramezzino*. 'These are terrible. Like eating cotton wool. Next time, I'll decide where we go. You look like you need some proper food.'

He finished his sandwich, looked at the empty plate and shook his head in disappointment. 'So this book. A fake of course.'

'So you say.'

'Of course it's a fake.' He sat back in his chair, and swirled his wine.

'So?'

'So?'

'So why are we here?'

He set his wine down. 'To have lunch of course. A very bad lunch, I have to say.'

Eduardo chose that precise moment to walk past. 'Is everything okay, *signori*?'

'Just fine thanks, Ed!'

'No. It's not okay. My friend says he has breakfast here everyday. How long has he been coming here?'

Eduardo looked at me, 'Maybe three years?'

'Three years! *Dio Santo!* No wonder he looks like this!'

They both stared at me for a little bit longer than I thought necessary.

'You are poisoning him with this terrible food. This is food for stupid tourists, not for Venetian gentlemen.'

I forced out a laugh. 'Eduardo, this is *Signor* Maturi from the bank in Campo Manin. As you can see, he has this wonderful sense of humour.' I clapped Maturi on the back. Seconds of terrible silence ensued.

He pushed his glass across the table. 'We will have two glasses of your best wine and I do not expect to pay. And when Mr . . .' He paused.

'Sutherland.'

'When Mr Sutherland returns tomorrow – if he does – you promise to make him a proper breakfast?'

Eduardo looked us both up and down. 'Of course, *signore.*'

'Good. I don't want to have this conversation again.' He waved Eduardo away. I tried to make conciliatory flapping motions with my hands.

'There something wrong with you?'

'No. Nonono. Nothing at all.'

'Good. And stop stuttering. Now then. The book.'

'The book. Oh yes, the book.' I'd almost forgotten about it.

'Very bad forgery.'

'So you keep saying. So why are we here? Unless you just want to force me to go somewhere else for breakfast in future.'

He shook his head. 'Very bad. To me. But I am an expert. You . . . you are just a *dilettante*. You saw this thing and thought "ah, a work by *Giambellino*, now I shall be famous and rich", no?'

'No. I just wanted to know what it was.'

'*Beh*. Whatever. To me it's an obvious fake. To you, no. To ninety-nine per cent of the people in this world, no. So why do it?'

I hovered over my sandwich. 'I don't know. Money?'

'Of course. But you can't sell a book like this on the open market. An expert would see it as a fake immediately. So the question is, why? Why do it? Find that out, and we find the solution to your little mystery. And now I'm going to have another one of these disgusting sandwiches.'

I flapped apologetically at Eduardo. For the second time in two days, I could see myself paying for lunch.

Chapter 8

Harry Gainsborough had a view from a hill. He was going to bring the very best of Britain to Venice, in the shape of a British-themed shop. Model red buses, piggy banks in the shape of telephone boxes, teddies with Union flag T-shirts. It sounded tacky. It sounded cheap. And I had to concede there was a good chance of it working. He was having a launch party and wanted me there to make a speech. It was going to be my first official opportunity for schmoozing and pressing the flesh.

I didn't really know Harry. He was well enough off to live here for three months of the year ('any longer and they'll clobber me for tax, Nathan') in which he went rowing every day with a local club, went to his usual stall at the Rialto Market to buy fish at a special discount price, and stood at the bar in an old *cicchetteria* to chat in *Veneziano* with the locals. He was, in many ways, more Venetian than the Venetians.

His reception was being held at the apartment of a friend of a mutual friend. Enrico, the honorary consul for Venezuela, knew someone with a top-floor flat overlooking the market. If you were going to have a launch party, a place with a panoramic view of the Grand Canal was the place to hold it.

I looked at the invitation again. I'd re-read it a dozen times but those damned words ' "plus one"' were causing me no end of unhappiness. I fussed and fretted over CDs, searching for something to put me in the right frame of mind. In the event I decided on Bach's *Goldberg Variations,* played by Glenn Gould. There was something about the Goldbergs, something about finding patterns within patterns within patterns that suited problem-solving.

And so I sat there, and listened to Bach, and tried to think what to do. My first opportunity to help build business relationships between Britain and Italy. My first attempt at being anything like a proper diplomat. All I needed to do was turn up, be charming, and make a good speech. Oh, and if I wanted to, I could have a plus one. And Dario had let me down.

I thought a drink would be good, but coffee would be even better. I went to the kitchen to look in the jar. I still had a couple of measures left before I'd need to go back to the *torrefazione.* There'd been a place in San Marco that I'd liked. I'd worked my way diligently through every coffee on the menu until I found my favourite. And then it closed. Nowadays I needed to make my way all the way up to Strada Nova in Cannaregio to get something that approximated to it. Every year useful shops closed down, to be replaced by useless ones.

I liked the daily ritual of making coffee in a Moka. Wash out yesterday's dregs. Fill the reservoir with water, and the filter with coffee. Put on stove. However, Gramsci assumed that food was imminent whenever I stood in the kitchen for more than thirty seconds, so I'd wander away and do something else until the pot boiled over. At which point, I'd go back, pour myself what little remained, and swab the remains from the surface of the cooker. It was an imperfect method, perhaps, but one I'd honed to a fine point over the years.

I sat back down to think. I didn't really need to bring anyone. Why should I? Just a very few quick words, a round of shaking hands and I could leave after thirty minutes or so. Still. Plus one. 'Call me'. What to do?

I looked up at Her Majesty. She looked down beatifically yet with a touch of severity, as if to say, 'Get on with it now and call her, you silly man.'

Gramsci hauled himself on to the arm of the sofa, and shook his head.

I put down my coffee and sprang to my feet. I was the honorary bloody consul in Venice, and no one – no one – could tell me what to do, whether it be Her Majesty the Queen or an unfriendly cat. I prodded Gramsci in the chest. 'She's right, you know. What do you know, anyway? You're just a cat. And not just any cat, you're a rubbish cat and she's the Queen!'

Then I slumped back down on to the sofa, and took a little more coffee. 'You know, if you two weren't here, I worry that I might actually go insane.'

I took out my mobile and punched in a number. I dithered, but only for a second, and then hit 'call'.

'*Pronto.*'

'*Ciao*, Federica. It's Nathan.'

'Nathan, *caro*. What can I do for you?'

I took a deep breath. 'Okay, well this is all really a lot of nonsense, but I'm supposed to be at a, well, I suppose you could call it a party tonight. Got to make a speech, that sort of thing. It's probably going to be terribly dull but, you see, I'm

allowed to take somebody else along and . . .' I paused. I realised I had nothing left to babble about.

'. . . and . . .'

'And, you know, as I said I can take someone along, this
"plus one" as they call it. Probably not going to be much fun,
and won't last long, but still I was wondering if . . .'

'. . . if . . .?'

'If you might like to come along?'

There was a pause.

'I'm sorry, Nathan, I don't think that's a good idea.'

I sank back into the chair, wanting it to swallow me up.
Gramsci looked at me in triumph. 'Oh fine, no worries. You're
quite right. All sorts of dull people droning on about business,
I mean, why would you want to . . .?'

She took pity on me and cut me off mid-babble. 'No, I
wouldn't want to.'

'Of course not!'

'Stand around at a boring party listening to boring men
making boring speeches? Why would I want to do that?'

'Exactly,' I dredged up a laugh. 'Waste of an evening. Wish
I wasn't going myself.'

'I bet. Still, I guess you have to.'

'I know, I know. Still, duty calls eh? The country expects,
and all that.'

'I mean, if you were to say you were going to a party and
you'd like me to come along so that we could spend a nice
evening together, that would be different. But if it's going to
be as bad as you say and you just need someone to keep you
company, then I think you need to find someone else. Have a
good evening, *tesoro.*'

'Hangonhangonhangon. You mean you'd come along?'

'Of course. But not if it's going to be as bad as you say.'

'Look, I've probably exaggerated. I've just got to make a speech. Won't take all that long. And the apartment is supposed to have this spectacular view. Drinks and snacks as well. I mean, I said it was going to be dull but it might not be so bad and . . . and . . .' *Screw your courage to the sticking place, Nathan.* 'And I thought it would be nice for us to spend the evening together.'

'Well that's different. In that case I'd love to come.'

'Really?'

She sounded puzzled. 'Yes, of course. Why not?'

'Fantastic. Great. Brilliant. Shall we meet at Stellina and grab a quick drink before? Maybe at eight?'

'I'll see you there. And Nathan . . .?'

'Yes?'

'You really are the most English person I've ever met.'

'Thank you. Really. See you at eight.'

I hung up. I patted Her Majesty's frame, and wiped some dust from the glass with my handkerchief. 'Well done, ma'am. We're a team, eh?' I put my hands on my hips and sneered down at Gramsci. 'How about that then?' I replaced Glenn Gould with Jethro Tull, and bopped around arrhythmically to 'Living in the Past'. Then I looked down at the third finger of my left hand and felt guilty.

Gramsci shook his head again and stalked from the room.

Stellina was not my kind of bar, but it was the only one in the vicinity that I really knew. The Rialto Market had always seemed a strange kind of place for the *movida* – the Venetian bar crawl – to pass through. Even at midnight, it never quite lost the smell of raw fish. It was also one of the first places in the city to be hit in the event of *acqua alta*. Still, there'd been no sirens that day so that was something not to worry about.

I scrubbed up as best I could. Federica looked as she always did. Slightly wonky teeth, hair tied back a little imperfectly, and even the odd dusty touch of plaster clinging here and there. And yet, as ever, she managed to carry it off. I ordered a pair of Spritzes and talked about Harry's plan.

A British-themed shop, catchily titled 'The British Shop'. It sounded like a stupid idea but – the more he told me about it – the more I was forced to concede that there might be something in it. Hordes of Americans passed that way every day, any number of whom might be attracted by the novelty of it all or by some ancient notion of 'heritage'. Britain, he told me, was a brand. Just look at the number of Italian teenagers who seemed to love anything with the Union flag on.

'So what sorts of things is he going to sell? Food? *British* food?' asked Federica with more than a touch of doubt in her voice.

'Just souvenirs, I think. Although he's got an idea for ice cream.'

'A Brit selling ice cream to the Italians? Isn't that going to be rather difficult?'

'Oh, not just any old ice cream. Irn-Bru flavoured ice cream.'

'Iron *what*?'

'Irn-Bru. Fizzy drink, Scottish, bright orange colour.'

Her expression cleared. 'Oh, like Aperol?'

'Erm, no. Nothing like Aperol. Apart from the bright orangeyness.'

'So what does it taste of?'

I racked my brains for a suitable comparison. 'Difficult to say really. Not really anything, and certainly not oranges. Just sweet, in a bit of a strange way. It's . . . well it's very Scottish. It's a great hangover cure, they say.'

She wrinkled her brow. 'Is there much of a market for that?'

'It seems so. He thinks he might even be able to get Grom interested.'

She crammed a few more crisps into her mouth and munched away. I think that was why I liked her so much. She had no qualms about not cutting *la bella figura* and even fewer about eating crap food.

'So tell me about Harry.'

I scratched my head. 'Well, I don't really know him. He's only here for a few months of the year. One of those people who doesn't have to work for a living.'

'You don't like him?'

'Oh, I didn't say that at all,' I said, protesting too much.

She raised an eyebrow.

'But no . . . not really. He's one of those people for whom everything just seems to fall into place. He turns up for a few months every year, hangs around with his glamorous pals, goes rowing every day and then heads back to Britain to tell everybody about his beloved city and how it's being destroyed by those *ghastly* tourists. He's got no idea about real life here.'

'Which is?'

'In my case, translating lawn-mower manuals for twenty euros an hour.'

'Don't put yourself down. You're the honorary consul. He's just a guy who's opening a shop. Remember that.' She drained her glass. 'Are we having another?'

I thought we ought to be heading off. But it was another reason as to why I liked her so much.

Harry lived in a modern condominium on Giudecca. Lovely as it was, it simply wasn't the right sort of place for this kind of party. Look in one direction, and you overlooked Palladio's church of the Redentore. Look in the other, and you stared at the brick wall of what had once been a bomb factory. No, for a proper launch, for the press coverage and magazine articles, he needed something altogether more Venice-like. He settled on the apartment of a friend of Enrico's called Thomas.

A ghostly, red-eyed skeleton of a man opened the door to us. I introduced ourselves, but he hardly seemed to hear me and just waved us in, running his other hand through his thinning blond hair. He looked like Klaus Kinski's unhealthy younger brother. This, I assumed, was Thomas. Either that, or Harry was now hiring his staff from amongst the undead.

Harry came to meet us. He looked tanned, muscular and healthy. The last time I'd seen him, he'd still been attempting a comb-over with the remains of his hair, but now he'd shaved it all off and looked ten years younger. He kissed me on both cheeks as if to underline just how Italian he was, and then turned to Federica. He kissed her hand.

'You're looking well, Nathan. Very well.' He grinned, and patted my tummy. 'Italian food and *la dolce vita* agreeing with you then?' He patted his own stomach as if to emphasise the difference. 'Better watch things myself.'

I wondered if it would be impolite to punch the host so early in the evening, and if it would cast a shadow over the rest of the proceedings. I forced a smile on to my face. 'You better had, Harry, I think you might have gained an ounce.'

He steered us towards the drinks and buffet. 'Anyway, I'm delighted you're here. Great pleasure to see you. We're very excited about the prospects of this little venture.' He spun through 360 degrees, holding his hands apart. 'Wonderful space, isn't it?'

It really was. The ceiling was frescoed in the style of the nineteenth century, with suitably *signorile* furniture to match. The windows led out to a balcony overlooking the Grand Canal, almost still now, and over to the great Gothic palace of Ca' d'Oro. I couldn't help noticing, however, that the noise from outside was oppressive. Inside the apartment, ever so tasteful light classical music was playing on an expensive but discreet hi-fi. Outside, a mixture of beery ranting and Young People's Loud Music was becoming louder and louder.

'Small cigar?'

'Do we have time?'

'Course we do!' He punched my arm, rather harder than I'd have liked. 'Come on, grab a glass, let's step outside.'

I drained my Prosecco and swiped another, as he steered me on to the terrace. The noise rose exponentially as we went through the door. Harry draped one arm around my shoulders and swept the other from left to right to indicate the expanse of the canal. 'Magnificent, eh?'

It was, of course. I thought of saying that I saw it from the Number One *vaporetto* every day, but he was trying to be nice. No need to be churlish. But magnificent as it undoubtedly was, it was also bloody loud.

Harry offered me a cigar. Not my usual poison of Café Crème, not even an Italian Toscana. 'Cuban,' he said, 'There's a small place in Edinburgh I use whenever I'm there. Little Havana.'

'I think I know it. Down at the foot of Leith Walk right?'

'That's the place. Seems a long way away from here, doesn't it?'

I nodded, and took a puff. I felt it light up my chest and head simultaneously. 'That's good. Very good. Smooth. So how do you know Thomas?'

'Pardon?'

'I said "how do you know Thomas?" Sorry, it's a bit loud out here isn't it?'

'Oh, he's a friend of Enrico's. Basically he's always happy to let out his flat for these sorts of things. It's an extra income.'

'I wouldn't have thought anybody who could afford to live here would need to worry about money.'

'You'd be surprised.'

'Sorry?'

'I said "you'd be surprised". The rent on this place is less than a thousand a month.'

'You're kidding!'

'Straight up.'

'Can't be. You can't possibly get a flat like this, overlooking the Grand Canal, for that sort of money.'

'Oh you can. Trouble is there's a catch.'

'I'm sorry, I missed that.'

'I said THERE'S A CATCH. We're listening to it now.' The noise was increasing all the time. 'It'll get louder and louder until about one in the morning. Then there'll be a lot of drunken shouting, maybe a fight or two, and then boats will leave, all blasting out music the whole time. For pretty much six nights a week, for ten months of the year. November and March, I understand, are slightly more bearable.'

'Good God, how does he stand it?'

'I'm not sure. Silly boy rented the place on a four-year contract. Now he's stuck here. It does explain why he looks the way he does.'

I looked back inside. Thomas was attempting to play the genial host to the great and the good, all of whom seemed bewildered and not a little disturbed, as if Kinski's Nosferatu was inviting them to cross the threshold into the land of shadows. Then I turned my attention back to Ca' d'Oro, limpidly beautiful in the moonlight above a wine-dark canal. You'd get used to it, I told myself.

A DJ in one of the bars said something unintelligible, but it was enough to get a great WHOOOAAAAH from the crowd.

And on the other hand, maybe you wouldn't.

'So when are you opening, Harry?' I asked.

'End of the month, hopefully. Just need to get a bit of work done on the shop. On Frezzaria. Used to be a coffee shop. Do you know where it is?'

'Yeah. I used to go there.' Within a few weeks, if Harry had his way, it would be selling Union Jack pencil cases.

'Oh right. Well, the owners got a good price. Too many coffee shops in Venice anyway. That's why it's so difficult for them. Whereas my little project is going to be unique.'

'Oh yes, Harry. I think we can safely say that.'

He checked his watch. 'Anyway, shall we get this show on the road. It's not going to get any quieter, so may as well do it now.'

I patted my pocket, to reassure myself that my speech was there. 'Of course. I'll just say a few words, and then I'll introduce you.'

'Great. Oh by the way Nathan. The girl you're with . . .?'

'Federica?'

'Lovely name. You're a lucky man. You've not let the grass grow under your feet then, I see?' He punched me on the arm. Again.

I blushed. 'Oh no, we're not together. She's just, you know, a pal. We met a couple of years back – I translated her abstract for some work she did at the Correr. So she's my plus one if you like.'

'Really? Well she seems nice. Very pretty.' And with that he gently, but firmly, steered me back indoors to where the impeccably tasteful classical music was in ever more danger of being overwhelmed.

'. . . and so it gives me great pleasure to welcome you all here and, most importantly, to welcome The British Shop to our lovely city of Venice. I'm sure you'll all agree it deserves to be a great success. So let's all raise our glasses to the man who's made tonight possible, and who's made this exciting venture a reality.' This stuff, I thought, really wrote itself. 'Harry Gainsborough!' Glasses were raised and chinked. Harry, I noticed, was conspicuous by his absence. The rhythmic BOFF! BOFF! BOFF! from outside sounded ever louder. As I looked around, I understood why. The door to the terrace was open again, where Harry was standing with Federica. His left hand was indicating the sweep of the canal and the buildings opposite, in an 'I am the lord of all I survey' kind of way. His right hand, every so often, would touch her shoulder, if only for a second or two.

Various people came up to shake my hand and make polite conversation. I remembered Enrico the Venezuelan consul, and vaguely recognised a couple of local restaurateurs. Thomas brought me another Prosecco and chatted away but, half-crazed through lack of sleep as he was, it was hard to keep pace with his train of thought as he skipped manically from one subject to another. I smiled and said 'yes' for as long as I could bear, before disentangling myself and striking out for the balcony.

I was waylaid by Enrico. An elegant, silver-haired man in his late fifties, I'd never been quite able to work him out. For one thing, I was never sure exactly what he did, given that on every occasion we met he seemed to have discovered yet another business opportunity. Last time it had been buying Russian ex-military helicopters to sell for civilian use in Caracas. This time he seemed particularly interested in the Irn-Bru ice cream.

'Really, Nathan, this is a brilliant opportunity. Venice needs entrepreneurs like Mr Harry right now. We just have to have support from the government.' My heart sank. I liked Enrico, but once he got started on the subject of the government there was no stopping him. I nodded away for five minutes, all the time trying to focus on what was happening outside. It was loud, but I felt there was no need for him to be moving quite so close to her as he appeared to be.

Enrico turned to see what I was staring at, then smiled at me. 'I don't think Mr Harry wants to be disturbed.'

'Possibly not,' I muttered, 'but he's going to be.'

'Sorry?'

'Oh he will be. Just a moment, Enrico.'

I made my way outside. Harry was in full flight. 'You don't have a boat? Call yourself a Venetian? Joking! Really, you must come out on mine. We'll make a day of it, I'll get a picnic made up and we'll go out to one of the islands. Poveglia, maybe. I know you're not supposed to go there any more but it's the most lovely place.' He stopped and looked at me. There was only the shadow of a change in his expression. 'Nathan, lovely speech, wonderful.'

'Thanks.'

There was silence, as if he was expecting to me to say something. I suddenly realised I had absolutely nothing to say. He looked at my glass. 'You need a refill. Go and collar Thomas, tell him not to neglect my guests.'

'To be honest Harry, I think I should be heading home. I've got a surgery tomorrow.'

'I love that. "Surgery".' He leant in again towards Federica. 'Makes you sound like a brain surgeon, Nathan!'

'Yeah, well. It's still my job and I'm still finding my feet. I need to be on good form.'

'Very sensible man. We should all be like you.' He moved away from her for a moment and grasped my hand. 'Thanks for being here. We must meet up next time I'm over. Grab a coffee at Quadri, maybe.'

'Depend on it, Harry.' I smiled at Fede. 'See you soon, Federica. Enjoy the rest of the evening.'

I turned and left before she could say anything; then made my farewells to Enrico and Thomas. I walked downstairs, the music increasing in volume the whole time, and emerged into the hell of the *movida*. Every bar full of people having a good time. The entire *campo* packed with youngsters drinking, singing, shouting as loud as they could in order to maintain the semblance of a conversation. I moved through the crowd like a ghost; unnoticed, unobserved. I no longer belonged in this world. If, indeed, I ever had. At the edge of the *campo*, I turned and looked back. The two silhouettes on the balcony seemed even closer together. I shook my head, and turned away. *One of those people for whom everything just seems to fall into place.*

Home then. I checked my watch. There'd be a *vaporetto* in five minutes, but a walk would suit me better. Enrico had once told me that, when he was a boy, the *traghetti* would run all night. How wonderful that would be, to be silently rowed across the Grand Canal, wrapped in one's own thoughts, the only sound being the plash of the oar and the receding noise of the revellers at the *mercato*. But those days were long past. I decided to walk over the Rialto Bridge. There would be no crowds at this time, and it was a rare pleasure to be able to cross it in peace and quiet. I paused at the halfway point, rested my elbows on the balustrade, and stared out across the water. Not a boat to be seen, the surface like oil.

'So what was all that about?'

Subconsciously I'd been aware of her heels tic-taccing purposefully up the steps of the bridge. It was still a surprise to find her next to me

'Oh, you know. Really, I do need to be up early in the morning.'

'So on your way home you decided to stop here and take a break to feel sorry for yourself?'

I sighed. 'Something like that, yes.'

'Tell me then. What's it all about?'

'*Beh*. Just feeling a bit . . . you know . . .'

'Jealous?'

'Jealous. Yeah, that's the word.'

'*Oddio.*' She lit up a cigarette, and smoked in silence for a few moments. 'You have a wife, Nathan, remember?'

'Yes.'

'And you love her?'

'Yes, of course I do.'

'You love your wife. Yet you're jealous if I talk to another guy at a party. This is not the best compliment I've ever received.'

'I'm sorry.' I took a deep breath. 'I mean, I think I do.'

'You think?'

'And sometimes . . . I'm just lonely. Sometimes.'

'That's not improving matters, Nathan.'

I took a few deep breaths, and tried to keep my voice steady. 'I miss her, you know. I miss the way things were. Before everything got broken. And when we're together – you and me – I know it's not anything. Not really. But everything seems nice and normal and fun again.' My voice was starting to break up. 'I'm an idiot, sorry.'

She stroked my arm. 'No, you're not an idiot. You're just lonely.'

Try as I might, I couldn't stop the tears, and my shoulders shook as I tried to hold back a sob. She chucked her cigarette over the side of the bridge, and hugged me. 'Hey now. It's all right.' And I softly cried on her shoulder for a few minutes. I breathed in the scent of her hair, mingling with smoke. I raised my hand and touched her cheek, almost imperceptibly. Then the moment was broken, and she gently but firmly pushed me away.

She reached for her packet of Marlboro again. 'Take one.' I was about to speak, but she silenced me with a wave of her hand. 'Don't tell me you've given up. Take one. It'll do you good.' She lit mine from hers, and we stood in silence and stared out at the canal.

'So what are you going to do, Nathan?'

'I don't know.'

'Is she coming back?'

'I don't know. It's only supposed to be for a year. But she was never happy here. She'd like to stay in Edinburgh.'

'Could you go back?'

'Oh I could. I could work there as easily as I can work here. But I don't really know anyone there. And I don't know if I could bear to leave' – I gestured out towards the Grand Canal – 'all this.'

She shrugged. 'Sure, it's beautiful. That's the trouble. So many people come here to visit. They look out at all this and think, "If I could always be here and always be able to look out on all this beauty, then I would always be happy". But does it make you happy? Is it enough?'

'Sometimes. Sometimes when I walk home through the *calli*. When it's late, when no one else is around. Everything feels so *ancient*. So magical. I feel so lucky, so happy. Then I get home, close the door, and I wonder when I'll next have a conversation with an actual person that doesn't involve lost passports.'

'*Che palle*. You don't have to feel alone. You've got me, you've got Dario, you've got an unfriendly cat. But you have to decide – is this enough? And if it isn't, then maybe you need to think about going home.' This time she laid her hand on my cheek. 'Look at you, Nathan. I don't like seeing you like this.'

I gave her a teary smile and blew my nose. 'I'm really not cutting much of a *bella figura* am I?'

She shook her head.

'So,' I said, trying and failing to keep my voice neutral, 'are you going to see him again?'

She gave me a withering look. 'I *don't* think so. I put up with my lack of personal space so as not to spoil your big night, but when he tried to grab my arse I figured it was time to leave. Also, it's a shit idea for a shop and this Iron-brew *gelato* sounds like the worst thing in the world. Oh yes, and his *Veneziano* is terrible.'

'I'm glad. You deserve someone better.'

'Someone like you?'

'Well now . . .'

'Someone like you, only someone who doesn't end up sobbing alone on the Rialto Bridge late at night like someone in a bad movie.'

I half-sniffled, half-laughed. 'Nobody's perfect.'

For the first time in our conversation she smiled. 'No.' She leant over and kissed me. 'Now go home. Go straight to bed. And tomorrow morning have a think about what I said. Okay?'

'Okay.'

'Good.' She stepped away from me, and turned to walk back down the bridge. 'And call me!'

I stubbed out my cigarette, and wished I had another. Then I smiled to myself, and set off down the other side of the bridge.

Chapter 9

12 Should the mower start to vibrate abnormally, stop the engine immediately. Disconnect the mower from the power supply. Check the blade for damage, and that the engine mounting bolts are secure.

13 In the event of striking a foreign object, stop the engine immediately. Disconnect the mower from the power supply. Check both blade and mower for damage.

I stopped typing and rubbed my eyes. I re-read my morning's work. Yeah, it looked okay. Anybody reading it would feel pretty confident in their ability to operate their new lawn mower.

Translation, as a job, could be even less interesting than consular work, which at least involved the need to talk to other people. It had the advantage of being able to be done almost anywhere, as long as there was access to a computer and an Internet connection. The disadvantage was that the amount of human contact required was minimal. In ninety per cent of cases, I would receive a document to translate from a third party, and send it back to them with little or no contact with the client themselves. And the material, it had to be said, tended to be soul-crushingly dull. Oh yes, I might hope for a novel or a film script. Sometimes I might get a thesis, or some website work which would at least involve a certain amount of creativity and contact with the original author. I steered clear of medical work, as the potential consequences of a mistake scared me. So, most of the time, I worked on instruction manuals for electrical goods.

The great exception was the period surrounding the Art Biennale, when work would flood in on translating artists' abstracts into English; even though I sometimes felt that I was merely changing an unintelligible Italian document into an unintelligible English one. It would at least get me the occasional invite to some opening parties. But in this non-biennale year, it seemed as if lawn-mower manuals were as good as it was going to get.

I read on. *Do not operate whilst under the influence of alcohol, drugs or other medication.* Then I closed my laptop, stood up and stretched. I'd done enough for the morning. The peoples of the world would just have to continue risking their lives whilst operating their lawn mowers after a beer. It was time for a coffee downstairs, and then maybe I'd go for a stroll. The city was at its best at this time of year, in that golden period before the weather became suffocatingly hot and the tourist-thronged streets baked in the heat.

I felt one of my phones vibrating. This time, however, it was my business line instead of the consular one. Possible work, then, and something that shouldn't be turned down. I sighed, and sat back down again.

'Nathan Sutherland, professional translation services.'

'Mr Sutherland? *Scusi il disturbo*. You are an Italian to English translator, I believe?'

'That's correct, can I help you?'

'I believe so. My name is Arcangelo Moro.' He paused, as if expecting me to say something. 'I am currently engaged in the sale of property, and my lawyer has need of some Italian legal documents to be translated into English. You have experience in this area?'

I had. Well, sort of. When one got away from the bland lists of dos and don'ts that comprised instruction manuals, translation was often the case of finding the right voice. And in the case of legal work, that voice needed to be a suitably pompous one. 'I've done some,' I replied.

'Good. Now the work, I'm afraid, does need to be done at short notice. That is to say, I need it completed today.'

'Right. Well I can make room for that. Can you just email me the documents? The address is on my card, if you have it. If not, it's . . .'

He cut me off. 'It would be easier if you came over. My lawyer will be with me shortly. He can pass you the copies requiring translation and then, when your work is finished, everything can be signed and completed. This way there is nothing left to chance.'

I supposed that was fine. He continued, 'My house is not so very far away. We are almost neighbours. At the end of Campo Santo Stefano, next to the Palazzo Cavalli-Franchetti. You know it?'

I tried to remember. The adjacent building, I thought, was part of the *conservatorio*. Still, it would seem to be impossible to miss. I told him I knew where it was. I glanced up at the clock on the wall. Nearly one. I got to my feet and walked into the kitchen. 'I'll be there directly after lunch,' I told him, as I opened the fridge door.

'Oh no, you must eat here. Please. Another way I can make up for the inconvenience.'

I was about to refuse, and then I looked inside the fridge to be confronted with a carton of milk, a jar of anchovies and an ancient piece of Parmesan that had been there so long it was in danger of growing ears. 'I'll be right over,' I said.

As I walked across the *campo*, I came across a tired-looking Gheorghe sitting at the feet of the statue of Tommaseo, munching upon a *panino* with limited enthusiasm. I could spare him a couple of minutes. I sat down next to him. 'How's things?' I said.

He brightened. 'Not too bad, Nathan. I think things are really starting to take off. Tiring, though.' He looked shattered. He was also, I couldn't help but notice, covered in dog hair and bearing not a few scratches on his arms. 'I think some people are being a bit exploitative. Do you think I should charge more for bigger dogs?'

'Seems only fair. A euro for sausage dogs, toy poodles, Pekinese. Two for anything bigger.'

'And Alsatians?'

'At least three. More if they're not muzzled.'

'Yeah. I think so too. Do you have time for a drink?'

'Love to, but sorry. A bit of work came up out of the blue, I'm just on my way over there now.' He looked disappointed. I reached into my pocket and drew out a few euros. 'Take a break, Gheorghe. Have an *ombra* at Da Fiore. And have one for me as well while you're at it.' He looked embarrassed, but took the money anyway.

I made my way over to the gated gardens of Cavalli-Franchetti at the end of the *campo*, turned left and there, sure enough, it was. A tiny shard of Venetian Gothic, dwarfed by the *palazzi* on each side. A narrow strip of garden, thrown into shadow by the tall buildings on each side, lay behind the entrance gate.

I pressed the doorbell marked, simply, 'Moro'. There was a short pause, and then the lock on the gate clanked open. The garden, in contrast to the immaculately kept grounds of the Cavalli-Franchetti, was overgrown and needed attention. Indeed, the dull red plaster was badly crumbling, revealing the brickwork beneath, the effect of years of *acqua alta*.

The front door opened before I could ring the bell and I found myself towering over Moro's *maggiordomo*. A tiny, wizened little man in a shabby blue suit stared up at me through thick black-rimmed spectacles. Somewhat taken aback, I started to stammer out an explanation before he nodded and ushered me inside.

I'd been expecting something grander. Instead of which, what I saw was little more impressive than the entrance to my own more modest dwelling on the Street of the Assassins. It needed, you would have to say, a lick of paint. The walls were of unpainted plaster, again crumbling, and the floor of bare stone. The entrance hall and space under the stairs were jammed full of sheets of timber, stacked up against the walls alongside tins of paint and bags of cement and plaster; in readiness for a much-needed restoration project.

The *maggiordomo* started up the stairs; first grabbing the banister and giving it a good shake, as if to indicate that I should put no great trust in it. He led me past a *porta blindata* on the first floor, and then up to the second. He paused for a moment outside an ornately carved wooden door, more than somewhat at odds with the spartan surroundings, and knocked. A voice came from inside, '*Avanti.*' He opened the door, just an inch, and then stepped aside to wave me through. The effect was startling.

The ceiling was frescoed, in the style of Tiepolo. A woman, crowned with a laurel wreath, accepting the tribute of Venetian nobles led by the Doge, and, more significantly, the Pope. *The Triumph of Venice,* signifying that the Republic – alone among the Italian city-states – did not bow down before Rome. The walls, lined with red velvet, served to display a number of paintings.

The floor-to-ceiling windows looked on to the Grand Canal and the underside of the Accademia Bridge, a view that few visitors or residents would ever see. Doors led on to a narrow balcony, but were blocked by a table supporting a chess board; to the left of which lay a battered leather armchair, and, to the right, an antique wooden wheelchair on which lay a mask connected to an oxygen tank.

I looked again at the art. An odd, inconsistent collection. Paintings were arranged in a seemingly haphazard way, with works from the Venetian Renaissance hanging next to those from the twentieth century, which in turn found themselves next to scenes of Venetian life from the eighteenth and nineteenth centuries. The overriding impression was of someone with impeccable taste but lacking either the time or the inclination to show it off to best effect.

'You like it?' I was startled and gave a little jump. The speaker was a slight figure, dressed in a red smoking dressing gown. A shock of untidy white hair surmounted a hawk-nosed, typically Venetian face.

'I do. Indeed I do. It's just . . .'

'Not what you were expecting?'

'No.'

He waved his hand. 'It surprises everyone. But then, if money is short, why waste it on those rooms of the *palazzo* that we do not use? One day, perhaps, we will have some proper restoration work done downstairs. In the meantime, *beh*, nothing except the bare essentials until those thieves from the *Comune* see fit to give us some money.'

'It's a lovely space.' I walked over to one of the paintings. An elongated, swan-necked female nude with a stylised, mask-like, yet beautiful face. 'This is Modigliani, isn't it? One of his portraits of Anna Akhmatova?'

He raised his eyebrows and, for a moment, looked displeased. 'Is that who it is?' His expression softened, 'I'm sorry, forgive my rudeness. I am Arcangelo Moro.' He extended his hand.

'Nathan Sutherland. Pleased to meet you, sir.'

'Likewise. My lawyer will be here soon with the necessary papers. In the meantime, perhaps, shall we take a coffee and something to eat?'

'That's very kind. I hope you haven't been to any trouble.'

He looked momentarily puzzled, as if the concept of 'trouble' was alien to him. He pulled on a bell rope and, shortly, the little retainer re-entered the room. 'Maurizio, some coffee, please, and something to eat. And remember those pastries from Tonolo.' He looked over at me. 'I always think Tonolo make the best cakes in town. Would you agree?'

I nodded. 'Indeed. I should go there more often. Trouble is, whenever I go there I always find the queue is practically out of the door.' Again, he seemed a little confused, and gave the thinnest of smiles. 'Well, you must let me know next time. I never have to queue.'

I looked around the room again. One of the works caught my eye. I strode over to it. It was not a large work, but there was no mistaking it. I turned to Moro. The ghost of a smile played about his thin lips, and he arched his eyebrows quizzically.

'This is Bellini, isn't it?'

He nodded.

'A copy, of course.' As soon as the words were out of my mouth I regretted them, and cursed myself for how rude I must have sounded.

'Of course. It would have to be,' he answered, in a controlled, monotone voice.

I walked over to investigate further. It was an actual copy, not a photographic reproduction. A sad-faced Madonna, dressed in black and red, holding a naked, curly-haired and (it had to be admitted) spectacularly unattractive Christ child. She was pretty, yet slightly coarse of feature with the hint of a double chin. Not yet the Queen of Heaven, but an earthier, working-class Mother of God. 'It's still beautiful,' I said.

'So I am told.'

Maurizio returned with coffee, a plate of cold meats and cheeses, and a tray of delicate, exquisite little cakes. He pulled out an occasional table, and set two chairs for us. We sat and ate in silence for a few moments. I looked out towards the window and my eye, again, fell on the wheelchair. He caught my gaze.

'My brother's. He is very frail now. We have spent our entire lives together, yet the day is very close now when I shall be alone.'

'I'm sorry.'

He shrugged. 'We will all be alone one day, Mr Sutherland. But it is important not to confuse being alone with loneliness.'

The doorbell rang. There were the sounds of footsteps upon the staircase, and then Maurizio entered.

'*Avvocato* Berti to see you sir.'

'Thank you. Please show him in. That will be all for now.'

Signor Berti was a big man in a suit ever so slightly too small, and he moved in a fussy, birdlike manner at odds with his size, which gave him a mildly comic aspect. After initial pleasantries, he took out the required documents. I gave them a quick look through. They looked standard enough. After you'd done a few of these you realised they could be knocked out fairly quickly. Moro and Berti settled down to talk over coffee and cakes, as I opened my laptop and set to work.

'You have a house in Cortina,' I said.

'We do. But not for much longer. We are selling it to an English gentleman, as you can see.'

'You never use it?'

'We used to. During the summer time. To escape from the heat of the city. But Domenico is too frail to travel now. I will feel happier knowing it is being used.'

'A shame,' I said as I continued to type. 'I hope the buyer will make good use of it.'

'I hope so, although I fear it will only be for a few months of the year. The English are buying up Italy, metre by metre, just to use for their holidays.'

Thirty minutes later it was done, and I passed the papers over to Berti for inspection. He gave them little more than a cursory glance prior to stuffing them away in his briefcase. We shook hands and he took his leave. I just needed to move the conversation on to the subject of my payment, and I could be away with much of the afternoon remaining to me. I discreetly checked my watch. Not discreetly enough.

'Oh, do you need to leave immediately, Mr Sutherland?' He looked disappointed. 'I had hoped we might take a glass of wine together.'

'That's very kind, thank you. No immediate hurry.' We sat down together at the occasional table. Maurizio entered bearing a silver salver with a half bottle of wine and two glasses.

'*Recioto,*' he smiled, and we clinked glasses. It was as golden as the sun, fruity and intensely sweet. I nodded appreciatively. Then he threw his hand to his mouth, as if a thought had only just struck him. 'I am so sorry, I had completely forgotten your payment. Please, one moment.'

He left the room. In his absence, I moved aside the curtain and looked out. The Grand Canal sparkled in the late afternoon sun. *Vaporetti* and water taxis passed back and forth, whilst gondoliers ferried excited tourists up and down. The loveliest of views.

'You are wondering, of course, why we did not sit outside.' I hadn't even heard him come back in. 'The reason is that the sight no longer thrills me as once it did.' He sat down next to me. 'Everything fades, Mr Sutherland, even in a city like this. When I was a child I would look out and think that I lived in a fairy land. Now I look outside and think that I live in Disneyland. The city no longer belongs to me and mine. The tourists have claimed it. Look at them.' He gestured towards the bridge. 'Swarming like ants. Threading their way past filthy *abusivi*. Stopping only to fix their stupid locks to our bridges or to buy stolen bags from *vu 'cumprà*. They come to Venice to look, but they don't look. They only gawk and stare. We Venetians now feel as if we are under glass, or behind bars, existing only to be stared at by crowds.'

I struggled to form a suitably diplomatic reply. Then, with a swift motion, he drew the curtains. 'I see you don't agree.'

I took a deep breath. 'Tourism brings its problems, of course. But I'm in no position to criticise. We first came to Venice as tourists.'

'And did you fix padlocks to our bridges and throw the keys into our ancient canals?'

'No. No, of course not.'

'That is the difference. Today, the wrong people are coming to our city. And the wrong people are living here. Not you, not you, of course. The foreigners, the Africans, the wretched beggars and thieves from the East.'

'It's a difficult situation.' I hated myself for the bland words. 'I know one Romanian. He's a decent man. Used to be a teacher he says. He's just trying to make a living. I guess not everybody who comes here can be a Ruskin.'

'A who?'

'Ruskin. John Ruskin.' He gave no sign of recognition. 'Author of *The Stones of Venice*. You must have heard of him?'

He was silent for a moment, and I thought I'd angered him; but then his gaze softened and he laughed, gently. 'I'm sorry. I've embarrassed you. One thing I love about the English is their wonderful sense of diplomacy.'

I wanted to get away before he could start on something else and so I checked my watch, more obviously this time.

'I was forgetting. You must forgive me, but it appears I have no cash in the house at this moment.'

I waved his apology away. 'No problem. You can just send me a cheque in your own time.'

'Thank you. Another thing I like about the English is their politeness. If you were Italian, you would have insisted that I immediately accompany you to the bank.'

'As I said, it's fine. Whenever you like.'

'Do you like the opera, Mr Sutherland?'

The question, out of nowhere, startled me a little. I nodded.

'Good. I have tickets for La Fenice tonight. Domenico, I regret, will not be attending. Would you do me the honour of accompanying me. Just as a small recompense for this slight inconvenience?'

I would normally have jumped like a shot at the opportunity of free tickets for the opera, but I was starting to find Arcangelo slightly hard work, as if I were stuck in a traffic jam with a taxi driver expounding his views on immigration. Nevertheless, there didn't seem to be any polite way to refuse. 'I'd be delighted,' I said.

'Excellent. It's Puccini. *Madama Butterfly.*'

I was unable to stifle a sigh.

'Oh, I'm sorry. You don't like Puccini?'

'I do. It's just that *Butterfly* was – is – my wife's favourite opera.'

'I see. A shame, but unfortunately I only have the one spare ticket.'

'No, it's not that. She wouldn't be able to come anyway. We're not . . . well, she's not living in Venice at the moment.'

His eyes widened. 'I must apologise. I must have seemed most indecorous.' He got to his feet. 'Well now, we will both need to prepare for the evening. We shall meet at – shall we say – seven thirty for a glass of Prosecco in the bar.' He reached to shake my hand, and I understood the conversation, and my work, was finished.

It was only when I arrived home that I realised I had not even told him what my regular payment was.

Chapter 10

The conversation stopped as soon as I entered the Magical Brazilian Café. Then, after a brief pause, Eduardo and his partner burst into applause. '*Che bella figura*, Nathan!'

'All right, all right. I'm going out tonight and thought I needed to look good. And then I decided it would be an even better idea to have a Spritz first. Steady my nerves.'

'Where are you going, a wedding?'

'His own, by the look of it,' cracked one of the regulars.

I straightened my bow tie ostentatiously. 'Tonight, I'll have you know, I have been invited to La Fenice.'

'Oooh.' Eduardo nodded to his regulars in exaggerated approval. 'The opera. But I've seen you go to the opera before, Nathan, and last time you didn't dress like' – he sniggered – 'this.'

'Yeah, but the guy who invited me seems a bit formal. It might be best to make a bit of an effort.'

'You're going with a man? Dressed up like that, I thought it must be *una vera bella signora*.'

'No such luck. Now, am I getting this Spritz or what?'

We chatted for a while as I worked my way through my drink, but what Eduardo said had worried me. It was rare for people – locals, at any rate – to wear anything more than a jacket and tie for the opera, and here I was in full evening dress – *uno smoking*, as they called it – and bow tie. Oh hell, if I looked ridiculous, I looked ridiculous. It was still a free night at the opera.

There was a brief flash of light. Eduardo grinned as he put his camera down. 'Photograph – for behind the bar!'

'Don't think you're getting a tip tonight, Eduardo!'

He laughed. 'See you after the show maybe?'

'Maybe. I have the feeling I'll be in need of a drink.'

La Fenice was only a five-minute walk away. I'd always wanted to live within walking distance of an opera house. The idea of it seemed so wonderfully civilised. And then, when it finally happened, I found myself unable to afford tickets. I still found it something of a thrill just to walk by there, on performance nights, to see the crowds gathering in Campo San Fantin and sometimes to listen to the sound of the singers warming up inside.

I walked up the steps, put my hand inside my jacket pocket, and then realised that, of course, I had no ticket. Neither did I have a mobile number for Arcangelo. I made my way as far as I could inside, looking this way and that, in the hope of spotting him.

One of the staff came up to me, a ticket reader in his hand. 'Are you looking for someone, sir?' He addressed me in English. I'd been in this city for nearly five years, and still people addressed me in English. By now I was resigned to the fact that I would never look remotely Italian.

'Yes, I've arranged to meet a friend but I can't see him. And he has my ticket. A *Signor* Arcangelo Moro.'

He smiled, and switched to Italian. '*Un attimo, signore.*' He exchanged a couple of words with the girl on the ticket desk, and returned bearing a ticket which he scanned with his barcode reader. '*Buon ascolto!*'

I walked up to the bar, and there he was. A tall thin man, clad in black evening dress and carrying a cane topped with a silver lion of St Mark. He hadn't gone as far as an opera cloak, but he could have carried it off. He smiled his thin smile, and came to greet me, kissing me on both cheeks. '*Mio caro.*' This, I thought, was going a little far considering our acquaintance stretched back little more than half a day. I returned his kiss and felt his skin against mine, papery and perfumed.

'Thank you again for inviting me *Signor* Moro.'

I was half expecting that he would insist that we should now be on first-name terms, but he gave no sign of that. He waved away my thanks. 'A pleasure. You are, I imagine, a regular visitor here.'

'*Magari!* If only. I'm afraid I find the cost of seats here too much for me.'

He sighed. 'Ah yes. Again, something the Venetians have lost. When I was a young man, the opera was for everyone in the city.' He suddenly switched to English. 'And now, who is it for? Fat Americans who think they have to come here for the "experience".' I caught a couple of irate glances from people standing nearby, and tried to flash a conciliatory smile. He switched back to Italian. 'Puccini, for example. We must have Puccini for the tourists.'

'You'd like something different?'

'Of course. This is a Venetian opera house. How often do we hear Venetian music?'

'Ah well, now that's an interesting subject. I'd love to see something by Luigi Nono here.'

'Nono?' He practically spat the name. 'Unlistenable rubbish and a communist pig. I meant we hardly ever hear a work by Monteverdi or Vivaldi any more.'

'Mmm. I suppose there are only three works by Monteverdi, and Vivaldi's operas seem to be out of favour at the moment. Perhaps that will change. Things are cyclical after all. It would be nice to see something by Stravinsky or Britten.'

'Stravinsky I know. Who is Britten?'

'Benjamin Britten. Twentieth-century English composer.' He gave no sign of recognition. 'Our greatest composer of opera,' I said, trying to keep the surprise out of my voice.

'I don't know him. Perhaps Britten is more famous in Britain?' He smiled, pleased at the little joke.

'He wrote a work called *The Turn of the Screw* specifically for La Fenice.'

'I don't know it. No matter. Now, my dear fellow, the lights are about to go down.'

He led me along the curving corridor to a box. 'My usual space.' Not directly facing the stage, but slightly side on. It nevertheless had a perfect view, in sharp contrast to my previous visits when I would spend the entire performance with my head craned painfully at ninety degrees to the rest of my body.

La Fenice is chocolate-box beautiful. So pretty, so ornate; the stereotype of what an Italian opera house should look like. The ceiling, adorned with paintings in sky blue and pink; the boxes ornate and gilded. It was easy to forget that this was nothing more than an elaborate fake, a painstaking reconstruction of the previous theatre after the great fire of 1996. I loved it, inauthentic as it was.

I used to think that the most tragic moment of *Butterfly* was her final suicide. Or perhaps the aria '*Un bel dì*'. I was wrong. The most terrible moment in the opera is at the end of Act One. The love duet that begins '*Vogliatemi bene*'. Terrible because we know this moment will not last. Pinkerton will return to the United States, and Butterfly will wait, and wait in vain. And when her dearest wish is granted, Puccini, with exquisite cruelty, will torture his little Butterfly and watch her writhe on the point of his pin.

We know the moment will not last. But Butterfly doesn't. And perhaps, at that moment, maybe even Pinkerton doesn't.

The applause died away and the audience rose from their seats to make their way outside. I thought we ought to leave straightaway if we were going to make it to the bar before the crush, but Arcangelo showed no signs of moving.

He touched my arm. 'This makes you sad, my friend, I can see.'

My voice was a little ragged. 'Yeah. Just a bit.'

'But of course it cannot work. How can it? She is a superstitious Japanese peasant. He is a man of the New World. It cannot work. That is the tragedy.'

I breathed deeply. 'No. There's more to it than that. We know that Pinkerton says that he will go back to America, to be properly wed with an American wife. But I like to think that at the end of the act, Pinkerton is in love with her, just a little bit. And he sails away but maybe – just maybe – he really thinks, at that moment, he'll return to his Butterfly.'

'You are a sentimentalist, Mr Sutherland. Would that make him any the less cruel?'

'Perhaps not. But I think it would make him more human.'

There was a knock at the door. *'Avanti,'* said Arcangelo, distractedly. A waiter entered with a bottle of Prosecco, and poured two glasses before nodding respectfully and retiring. We raised our glasses to each other. Arcangelo reached inside his jacket. 'Please,' he said, and passed me an envelope.

'Thank you.'

'Open it now, please. I want to be sure that everything is correct.'

This seemed like a bit of a performance for the sake of one hundred euros; nevertheless, I tore it open. I was expecting a pair of fifty euro notes and was a little disappointed to find that he'd written me a cheque; with all the associated hassle of queuing up to pay it into the bank. Then I read, and re-read, the figure he had written.

'There's some mistake here, *Signor* Moro. For two hours' work like this I would charge a hundred euros. Not' – I looked at the figure again – 'ten thousand euros.'

He said nothing, but reached over and grasped my hand. That dry, papery skin again. He drew it over to his chest whilst, with his other hand, he reached again into his pocket, extracted something, and closed my fingers gently around it. Then, equally gently, he released my hand.

I looked down. I was holding a photograph. A photograph of a bull-necked, well-dressed man with thinning hair swept back in a widow's peak.

I tried, and failed, to suppress a start. Arcangelo noticed, and smiled.

'You know this man?' he said. And at that point, the second act began.

Chapter 11

I recall very little of the second act of that particular production of *Madama Butterfly*. I do, however, remember sitting bolt upright for the entire length, every muscle in my body clenching. It was, I supposed, gratifying that total strangers seemed to be keen on pressing large amounts of money into my hands but there was also something more than a little odd, and probably highly illegal, about it all.

What the hell was I going to say to Arcangelo? I figured it was probably too late to consider lying. He'd seen my reaction to Montgomery's photograph. Then a wave of irritation rippled through me. He'd done this on purpose. He'd deliberately waited until the second act was about to kick off and then passed me the photograph, just to make me sweat for the next seventy minutes. Playing with me. Then I recalled the most famous words of the great Venetian philosopher Paolo Sarpi: *Le falsità non dico mai mai, ma la verità non a ognuno.* 'I never, ever lie. But the truth, not to everyone.' If Arcangelo wanted to play his little Venetian game with me, then I could call on some heavyweight support.

Eventually, Butterfly fell on her sword, and the opera came to its inevitable, tragic conclusion. I braced myself during the interminable applause and curtain calls for what was to come. As the applause died away, Arcangelo placed his hand on my arm once more. He gave me the thinnest of smiles.

'As I was saying . . .'

I made a great show of looking at the photograph. 'Yes, I know this man. Or, at least, I've met him.'

'You know his name?'

'Montgomery.'

'Perhaps that is what he calls himself now. What did he ask of you?'

'He wanted me to look after a package for him. Just for a couple of days.'

'Ah. A package.'

'I had to tell him, of course, that I couldn't possibly do so.'

'No?'

'No, it would be impossible. Firstly, the consulate is not a left-luggage facility. More seriously, I can't have an unidentified package just sitting in the safe. What if it were something illegal?'

'Or stolen property?'

'Exactly.'

'My property, to be precise.' His eyes were boring into me now. I said nothing, and let him continue. 'But you took nothing from him?'

'*The truth, not to everyone.*' I shook my head, 'As I said, it would be impossible and inappropriate. He hasn't returned since. I'm sorry. Obviously I had no idea that it belonged to you.' Good old Mr Sarpi.

Moro kept his eyes fixed on mine, but I held his gaze. 'A shame. A great shame. But of course, you weren't to know. No matter.'

I passed him the cheque. He seemed in two minds as to whether to take it or not, before folding it away. 'If he returns, or if' – and here he held my gaze again for an uncomfortably long time – 'you find yourself in possession of my property, you will of course let me know as soon as possible. And this amount could be considered payment for your services, should you be able to return it to me on the seventeenth of April.'

'Well, I'll certainly do that *Signor* Moro. But I have to give you the same advice that I give to all the people who come to me for help: if you've been robbed, you need to go to the police.'

He shook his head, slowly and sadly. 'I think not.' I made to pass him the photograph, but he shook his head. 'Keep it, please. A reminder.'

We made our way back through the dark streets together, but in silence. I noticed that he had no difficulty in walking. The cane, then, was just an affectation. When we reached Campo Santo Stefano he turned to me and said 'Do you play chess, Mr Sutherland?'

'I know the rules, that's all. I haven't played in years and was never much good.'

'I thought not. You are too much of a diplomat. Still, perhaps we will play, one day.' Then he turned to leave, said, 'Please think about what I said, Mr Sutherland,' and he was gone.

The Brazilians were still open, and my feet carried me automatically over the threshold. Eduardo smiled, then looked more serious as he saw the expression on my face.

'Negroni?'

'You had to ask?'

He reached for the gin. 'So. How was your date?'

'A bit strange. I think that sums it up.'

'So what's he like?'

'Kind of like a racist Count Dracula. He seems to be wealthy, he's got a *palazzo* full of original works of art. He can afford the best seats at the opera. But nothing seems to make him happy. He's one of those people that I can't imagine ever smiling. Not properly. He seems to suck the joy out of absolutely everything. He's also got a laundry list of things he hates. Gypsies, beggars, Africans, fat Americans – thin Americans for that matter – Russians, French, Germans. You name it, he's got a grudge against it.'

'How does he feel about Brazilians?'

'Don't know. We never got around to you.'

Eduardo looked at the level of my Negroni. 'Damn, Nathan, you've inhaled that one!' He pulled out the gin bottle again. 'Let me make you another. This time on the house, eh?'

'You're a star, Ed.'

One third campari. One third vermouth. One third gin. It felt like a friendly slap in the face.

'So. You going to see him again?'

I gave him a withering look.

'That's a no, then?'

'I don't know if it's up to me. I thought at first he was just this strange old guy who wanted to be my pal. Now I'm not so sure. There's something almost unclean about him. I think he uses people. I also think he might be a crook. How long have you been here, Eduardo?'

'Near ten years now.'

'You ever hear anything of the Moro brothers?'

He shook his head. 'It's a noble name though, isn't it? Wasn't there a Doge called that? Possibly more than one?'

'Probably. Kind of hard to keep track of them all, isn't it?'

'It's important though. The name. We had a guy working here a few years back. Just a bartender like me. But his surname was Bembo. When people found out, it was almost as if he should have a bit more respect.'

I finished my second glass. 'Ah, what's in a name eh, Ed? Right, three Negronis would be insane. I'm off to bed. I'll see you for breakfast.'

'Cheers, Nat. Good night.'

The downstairs door swung open at my touch. I appeared to have left it on the latch, although I had no memory of having done so. Stupid of me and asking for trouble, even in a city like Venice. I bent to pick up a few items of junk mail and a single letter that lay on the floor, which I tore open as I walked up the stairs. I unlocked my front door, although the key seemed stiffer in the lock than usual. I stepped back and took a look at it. Scratches around the keyhole. A few pieces of plaster chipped away around the frame. I didn't remember them. I closed the door behind me with my foot, as I extracted the letter.

Then I saw the handwriting, and I replaced it in the envelope. I went into the living room, and dropped it on the desk, as I went through to the kitchen to fetch a glass of grappa. Then I sat down, and held the letter in both hands, turning it over and over. I tugged at the folded sheets inside, and then changed my mind. I thought perhaps I should check my email, but decided against it. Deal with it in the morning, like the letter, Everything will be easier to deal with in the morning. As long as you don't open it, nothing is wrong.

I went to the rack of CDs and took down a recording of *Madama Butterfly.* I moved it on a few tracks, to the first meeting between Pinkerton and Sharpless, the consul. Pinkerton explains his entire plan, and, in Act 2, Sharpless has to do his best to pick up the pieces.

I listened to a bit more, but turned it off before the end of the first act. I was tired now, and feared that final duet would wake me up. Worse, it might push me into doing something stupid, such as reading the letter.

Poor old Sharpless, I thought. He wasn't the last consul to find himself in an impossible position.

Chapter 12

I slept uneasily that night, and was awoken by the sound of the bells of Santo Stefano. Only seven o'clock. The bells would start chiming in earnest at seven thirty, and even I would be unable to doze through that, but in the meantime . . . I turned over to go back to sleep.

I managed about five minutes until Gramsci came poddling around my head. He mewled. Feed me. I ignored him. He scrabbled at the duvet with his claws until I reached out and prodded him on to the floor. This was a game we had played over a thousand times.

He leapt back up. I tried to push him off, but his claws were sunk in this time and there was no moving him. I screwed my eyes shut and ducked my head under the sheets in the hope of muffling the sound of his cries.

He moved further up the bed until his head was next to mine, and jabbed again and again at my shoulder, meeowing all the while.

I gave up, got out of bed, and padded into the kitchen to fetch him some food. A game we had played over a thousand times. I was still waiting to win one.

I took a look in the cupboard. The magic coffee pixies had

yet to arrive to top up the jar, but there was just about enough to scrape a cup together. I checked the fridge to ensure it was still empty, then lit a cigarette and called it breakfast. It was becoming part of the morning ritual. I wondered if I should move in with the Brazilians.

I had no surgery that morning, so I shuffled from one room to another, from one radio station to the next, and generally pithered around without knowing quite what to do. I grouped all my papers into tidy little piles, organised my pens, and did the miniscule amount of administration that remained to me. And then I sat and stared at the opened, unread letter.

I should read it. I need to know. Whatever it is, I need to know. But, I told myself, nothing was wrong as long as it remained unread. At least for today. She wouldn't have expected me to have received it by now. It could wait another day.

I checked my email. There was a new message, as I'd expected, marked with a bright red exclamation mark. I closed my browser.

I stared at the safe, as if I could stare through it to the package within. A little riddle to solve. A problem to take my mind off things. Whatever it was, it seemed, somehow, more manageable than anything else. But where to start?

Montgomery had offered me a large sum of money to deposit a package. Moro had promised me a similarly large sum to give said package directly to him. Neither of them wanted to involve the police. *Ergo*, whatever was going on was almost certainly illegal.

So logic demanded that I should go down to the *Questura*, tell them everything and get the wretched thing off my hands.

Excuse me, officer, but strange men keep offering me money. For what? Oh, for a work of art which, according to an expert, is almost certainly a fake.

I tried to tell myself that going to the police would be a waste of time, but in my heart of hearts I knew it was the most sensible thing to do. I also knew that the whole problem was just a little bit exciting, and certainly a hell of a lot more interesting than lawn-mower manuals, lost passports and intractable domestic situations. I didn't have much else to do, and I remembered Maturi's story, about the closest he ever came to having an adventure. Well, maybe this was mine.

Okay, Nathan. Let's look at the problem logically. I took a clean sheet of paper, wrote 'Montgomery' at the top, and stared at it. I knew nothing about him. I didn't even know if it was his first name, his surname or if it was his real name at all. He was, probably, somewhere in Venice. I wrote down 'Somewhere in Venice. Probably.' I stared at the paper for another couple of minutes, then scrunched it up and threw it into the bin.

Perhaps Montgomery was not the best place to start. Maybe it would be easier to find something out about the Moro brothers?

I searched the Internet for Arcangelo and Domenico Moro, but there was precious little to be found. They didn't seem to be society people. I cursed the fact that so much of the Italian newspaper archive had yet to find its way online. I was on the verge of giving up when something caught my eye. An article from *Il Gazzettino,* from four years previously. A reporter had been released from prison after a three-year sentence. Paolo

Magri. An active member of the Communist Party. Something called 'the Moro case'.

I searched and searched again on *il processo Moro*, without success. Maybe I'd need to check newspaper archives directly. The offices of *Il Gazzettino* were over in Mestre, but I didn't know if you were allowed to just walk in there and start searching through back issues. There was an alternative, however. I could go to the Cini library on San Giorgio Maggiore and check the archives there.

It was a bit of a long shot. The Cini Foundation, I knew, held perhaps the world's greatest archive of information on Venetian history. I had no idea how far that extended into the present day. Similarly, there was no reason at all to assume it was the same Moro. Yet, after a further fruitless bout of searching, I had found nothing better to work on. The article referred to Magri living on Giudecca. There was, I knew, a Communist Party bar over there. It was a pleasant day. I could go over to San Giorgio Maggiore and do a bit of work at the library; then take the boat over to Giudecca and have a quick drink with the comrades.

I walked up to Zattere, flipping a euro to The Worst Busker in the World along the way, and took the next *vaporetto* across to San Giorgio Maggiore, a place I'd come to find invaluable, both as a space to work and as a retreat. In the summer, it became a little oasis of calm, in comparison with the tourist-choked city that it faced. There wasn't a great deal to do there, but on an unbearably hot day the temperature seemed just a blessed couple of degrees cooler. When San Marco became gridlocked under the sheer weight of people, and even the Street of the Assassins echoed to the sound of the crowd, I would come over to work in the silence of the library at Fondazione Cini. Then, if time allowed, I would go and sit in the calming white space of the *chiesa* and look at the two great works by Tintoretto; *The Fall of Manna* and his sepulchral *Last Supper*. On occasion, I'd even take the lift to the top of the *campanile*, to look across Venice and the lagoon from every direction. To remind myself why I was still here.

The library was cool and still, and I was the only person there. I walked to the end of the great hall, to look out through the windows and across the city. I was tempted just to pull a book from the shelves and read, and possibly doze off in a comfy chair; in the knowledge that the first thing I'd see upon waking would be the view over the lagoon to Piazza San Marco. But, tempting as that was, there were things that needed to be done; and I knew that if I spent a few hours in research I could at least kid myself that I'd done a proper day's work. I moved to the opposite end of the hall so as not to be distracted, took out my laptop and set to it.

As I had suspected, the recent archives on Venetian history were somewhat thinner than the historical ones. Indeed, one might have been forgiven for supposing that recorded history had come to an end in 1797, when Ludovico Manin, the last Doge, put his hat away for the final time. And of the brothers Moro, there appeared to be no record at all. The sheer lack of information was surprising in itself, as if they'd been erased from history in the same way as the traitorous Marino Faliero – the only Doge ever to be executed – was subjected to *Damnatio Memoriae* in an attempt to remove all trace of his existence.

There seemed little point in wasting any more time on it. I supposed it was possible that the Magri guy might be able to give me some more information, and so I decided the brothers Moro, like Montgomery, could be put aside. I leaned back in my chair, stretched and took a good long yawn. When I opened my eyes I was aware, if only for a second, of a shadow passing across the window at the far end of the hall.

I worried that I might have made too much noise. 'I'm sorry,' I said. '*Scusi il disturbo.*' There was no reply, and no words of admonishment. At least it hadn't been the librarian, then. I went back to my work. If there was nothing to be found on Arcangelo Moro, perhaps I could find out something about the book. I took the stairs up to the gantry, where the extensive art history section was to be found. There were multiple editions of Vasari's *Lives of the Artists* in various degrees of completeness. None of them contained more than a few pages on the Bellini family and they only served to confirm what Maturi had told me: there was little more information on the book beyond a few elliptical references to Cardinal Pietro Bembo, and his desire for a similar work.

It had been years since I'd attempted to read the *Lives*. I'd always found it a little dry. Yet it seemed to make more sense on a spring Venetian day than it ever had back in the UK. There was something about the city that, however one might try to resist, knocked the cynicism out of you. Vasari might never have quite understood the art of the Veneto, but he had at least tried to be nice about it. The language of art criticism had yet to be invented, and so he'd had to do it all himself. This led him to write an awful lot of sentences along the lines of 'and this, too, was very beautiful'. It seemed naïve, perhaps, in comparison with contemporary artists' abstracts and yet its honesty and innocence was endearing. How lucky he was, I thought, to have lived in a world where he felt himself surrounded by so many beautiful things. Perhaps I should make a proper effort and read the whole work. Then I looked along the shelf at the other twelve volumes in the series, and realised that I probably never would.

It seemed that Vasari was going to be unable to help me. Perhaps I needed something more visual. There were any number of catalogues of works, dating back centuries. I chose a recent-looking volume on Bellini, and sat down to leaf through it. As I did so, I heard footsteps from downstairs. I stood up, and leaned over the gantry and, again, thought I saw a figure move across the far window, blocking the sunlight for a moment.

There was no reason at all for someone else not to be there. Nevertheless, something was bothering me. 'Hello,' I called. Again, there was no answer; and so I moved slowly down the stairs to the main hall. I made my way along the great book-lined corridor to the far end. There was no one there, nor in any of the side rooms. Then, from behind me, I heard the clicking of heels on the wooden floor and I turned back to face the way I had come. There was nothing to be seen, but I could hear the sound of a door closing. I walked back, deliberately controlling my pace. 'Hello,' I called once more.

A sibilant '*Shhhh*' made me jump. I looked behind me to find a severe-looking young man in sombre dark suit and tie.

'I'm sorry,' I said, 'I thought I heard someone.'

'Of course, *signore*. The library is open to the public until eighteen-hundred. Anyone is welcome to visit.'

'I'm sorry. I don't know what I was thinking.'

He switched into English. 'This is a library, sir. People come here to work. It is important that everyone remains quiet.'

I bridled, just a little. 'I know. I'm working here too. I come here all the time,' I replied in Italian. 'Perhaps you can help me. I need an illustrated catalogue of works by Bellini.'

'Which Bellini, sir?' he asked, still in English, testing me now.

'Giovanni. I need the most recent one you can find.'

He made his way up to the gantry, and ran his hand along one of the shelves. With a faint air of annoyance, he regarded the dust on his fingertip for a moment; then brushed it away and pulled down a book. 'This, sir, is the most comprehensive and up to date.'

I thanked him. He reminded me again of the importance of silence, and we went grumpily along our separate ways. When I first arrived in Venice conversations of this type had been commonplace, each party obstinately sticking to the other's language and determined not to concede. They'd been rarer recently, which made them all the more annoying when they occurred. I pushed the irritation to the back of my mind, and settled down to read.

I didn't know much about the life of Giovanni Bellini. I don't know that much more to this day. Vasari doesn't devote many words to him, the adventurous life of his older brother Gentile proving more interesting to him than that of the stay-at-home Giovanni. But I like to think of him as being a good man. More than that, and banal as it may sound, I think of him as being a kind man. Whereas the art of his pupil, Titian, was gritty, masculine and kinetic, Bellini's was all about silence, and stillness. He was never one for action and movement, but that wasn't the point. Albrecht Durer visited him a full decade before his death and wrote, '*Giambellino* is very old now but is still the best painter in the city', at a time when his art had almost reached the point of anticipating photorealism by four hundred years. If I look upon one of his paintings, the thought that strikes me is that he must have been a gentle soul. I haven't tried to find out any more. I don't need to.

The book was of little help, lovely as it was. It was tempting to move down to the tables next to the window and leaf through it, illuminated by the light reflecting off the lagoon; but I was pretty sure I wasn't going to find anything more. I replaced it, and looked along the shelves again. There were dozens and dozens of books on Bellini, and I had no idea where to start. Then a spine caught my eye. It bore the simple legend 'Giovanni Bellini. Moro'. Almost certainly a coincidence, I thought but, nevertheless, I took it down. I looked at the author biography on the jacket. Domenico Moro. It could still be a coincidence, but it would be a great one.

His biography was concise, but described him as one of the great experts in his field. Born in Venice, with a doctorate in art history from Ca' Foscari, his other publications included works on Modigliani and De Nittis. He was evidently a man of eclectic tastes. There was a small black and white photograph on the inside rear fold of the jacket. A shock of dark curly hair, and hawk-visaged like Arcangelo. No doubt about it, this was his brother. The brother currently at death's door.

The book seemed to cover much the same ground as the other books on Bellini that I'd searched through that afternoon. I was on the edge of giving up, when I turned to the last chapter on 'Workshop and attributed works'. And there it was. An image of the first image in *La Vita della Vergine,* and identical – to my eyes at least – to the one currently lying in the safe. I turned to the back to look at the list of attributions. This one, it seemed, was the property of a private gallery in Florence. I turned back to the front pages to check the date of publication. 1989. A quarter of a century had passed. I had no idea if the gallery would still be there or not, but I scribbled the address down anyway.

I briefly scanned another couple of publications, but it seemed as if this was the best lead I was going to get. I said goodbye to the young librarian, who barely raised his head before giving me a sarcastic, 'Enjoy the rest of your holiday, sir', and made my way back to the *vaporetto* stop where I found the boat pulling away from the jetty. I checked the timetable. There wasn't much time to kill before the next one, but I didn't feel like waiting around on the pontoon or going back to the library and starting off another confrontation. I'd take a look around the church. More than that, I'd go up the *campanile*, look out over the whole city, and once more remind myself why I was here.

I paused for a moment in front of Tintoretto's *Ultima Cena,* searching in my pockets for a one euro coin to feed into the machine that would better illuminate it. I had a two euro piece, and a handful of small change. I remembered my first visit, years ago, when I blocked the machine by feeding in two fifty cent pieces, following which I had been forced to flee from the church pursued by an irate sacristan. I gave up and made my way to the ticket office by the entrance to the *campanile*. I took out my ID card to demonstrate I was eligible for a discount, and pushed a couple of euros across the counter. There was no one else around, and I had the lift to myself. I caught my breath, as I always did, when I emerged at the top. I pressed myself against the wall, closed my eyes, and counted to ten before opening them again.

The entire panorama of the city swam dizzyingly in front of me. I clamped my eyes shut again, and tried to control my breathing. It was always like this. Granted, I hadn't been up here in over a year, but I was no nearer to becoming used to it. I opened my eyes for a second time. Better now. I made my way to one of the viewing spaces, placed my hand on the metal security rail and gave it a good tug to ensure it was still sound. Then I stepped up to look out over the city.

It was almost enough to make me forget my fears. In one direction, I could see the Giudecca Canal, and over the city proper. A city that, from this perspective, appeared to be almost entirely devoid of canals. I moved to the right, and looked out over the Arsenale, and then turned my head towards the thin strip of the Lido. Another turn, and the view was towards the lagoon itself. Once more, and I looked out on Giudecca. The nearest part of the island was taken up by the Cipriani Hotel. In five years in Venice, I had been to eat there precisely once. It had been, I suppose, a memorable meal.

I've been offered a job in Edinburgh. Back at the University. I'm going to take it. It's only for a year, you could come too if you want to . . .

There was something terribly ambiguous about the way she'd phrased 'if you want to'. It would be fair to say it cast a bit of a shadow over the rest of lunch. I rested my elbows on the balustrade and stared out at the city. It was still beautiful. And it was, perhaps, still just enough.

I heard the hum of the lift doors opening behind me. Another visitor. I turned to look.

Montgomery smiled, and raised his hat.

Chapter 13

I opened my mouth to speak, but was interrupted by the bells chiming the hour. We looked at each other in embarrassment for a few seconds until they ceased, and our ears stopped ringing.

I reached behind me and patted with my hand to reassure myself that there was, indeed, a solid wall there; then leaned back and folded my arms. 'Mr Montgomery,' I said.

'Mr Sutherland. How are you today?'

'Not so good, if I'm being honest. And you?'

'I'm sorry to hear that. But I'm very well indeed, thank you. How's your lovely cat?'

'Resolutely unlovely,' I replied.

He was about to speak, but my mobile chose that moment in which to ring. I reached into my pocket. 'I'm sorry, just a moment . . .'

He waved a hand dismissively. 'Of course . . .'

I recognised the number, and immediately cancelled the call. 'Nothing important,' I said.

He nodded. There was another awkward silence.

'Mr Montgomery, are you following me?' My mobile rang again. I yanked it out, and stabbed at the keypad, holding down the off button with rather more force than necessary until it fell silent.

'If it's important, maybe you should answer it?'

I shook my head. 'It's not important. As I was saying . . .'

'. . . as you were saying. No, I'm not following you.'

'We do seem to keep running into each other. Or just missing each other.'

'Well, this is something of a holiday for me. I like to see as much of the city as possible whenever I'm here.'

'A holiday. Lovely. So where's home?'

'These days, usually Rome. Sometimes Florence. Naples. I move around a lot.'

'And the UK?'

'I haven't been back there in years.'

I decided it was time to get to the point. 'The book, then. Any reason I shouldn't take it straight to the police?'

'Now why on earth would you want to do that?'

'Because I believe it's stolen. From a small gallery in Florence.'

He chuckled. 'Well, Mr Sutherland, I can assure you it's not. I can show you the receipt if you like?'

I shook my head. 'You're telling me that you have sufficient money to buy a work by Giovanni Bellini, and that you'd then entrust it to a total stranger?'

'It's not by Bellini. Just his workshop. And that makes a considerable difference to the price. As for yourself, as I said, I need a secure place to keep it for a couple of days.'

'You tricked me into taking it.'

He looked pained. 'I'm sorry. But I really did need it to be with someone I could trust. And I am absolutely sincere about the payment we discussed.'

'I know. All of a sudden, people are queuing up to give me money.'

'I imagine that's not unpleasant?'

'Not unpleasant at all. I would like to know why, though. Incidentally, do you know why a man called Arcangelo Moro would want to give me ten thousand euros for the same package?'

If I had been expecting this to spark some kind of reaction, I was to be disappointed. 'I have no idea at all,' he said.

'You don't know why he would show me a photograph of you and offer me a large amount of money for what he says is his property?'

'None whatsoever, I'm afraid. As I said, I can show you proof – absolute proof – that the work is legally mine.'

'You also told me it was a picture of your mother.'

'Metaphorically speaking. Maybe I'm just a good Catholic boy?' He smiled. 'So the book is safely under lock and key, then?'

'As safe as it can be. It takes a lot of work to break into an upstairs flat with a *porta blindata*. Even more to break into a safe like that.'

'Good. Good.' He stepped up to one of the recesses to look out over the city. 'Wonderful, isn't it? You're a lucky man Mr Sutherland. How long have you been here?'

'A little less than five years.'

'As little as that? If you don't mind me saying, you're very young for an honorary consul.'

'They like people with a knowledge of the language. That's not true of all the expat community here. And they also like people who are prepared to make a long-term commitment. Gives a sense of stability, continuity.'

'I see.' He rested his arms on the parapet and pushed himself up, the better to lean over and stare down into the *campo* below; an action that sent a bolt of fear through me. I moved to the central area, and leaned my back against the lift, so that I could no longer look down.

He turned back to me. 'You don't like heights?'

'Not really. Fortunately they're quite easy to avoid in this city. If I see a *campanile*, I generally don't go up it.'

'But you came up here?'

'I like it over here. Gives me space to think.'

He nodded. 'There's something I'd like to show you.' He beckoned me over. 'Come on.' I moved over to him, taking my time, resting my hand on the wall the whole time. He shuffled over to make room for me next to him at the recess. 'Come on,' he repeated.

I stepped up, and gripped the rail with both hands. He suddenly leaned right over and the unexpected movement made my head swim. I clamped my eyes shut for a moment.

'Take a look out over there, Mr Sutherland.' He swept his hand across the panorama of the city. 'Tell me what you see.'

I kept my eyes fixed firmly on my hands, my knuckles white against the rail. 'Venice?'

He gave a little grunt, which I took to be one of disappointment. 'You know what I see?'

I shook my head. He patted me on the back then, almost without me noticing, he slipped his hand under my shoulder.

'You know what I see, Mr Sutherland? Sixty thousand Italians.' And slowly, but surely, he started to pull me upwards.

'Sixty thousand Italians. Sixty thousand people that I don't trust. Sixty thousand people who'd sell their precious *mamma* for the price of a good meal.'

He wasn't a big man, but he was powerfully built. I'd thought he was just running to fat but I was wrong. I felt my shoes scraping against the wall. Then he changed his grip, and started to push me forwards. My eyes were clamped shut, and my hands, sweaty now, started to slip on the railing. I found myself unable to speak, let alone scream.

'Open your eyes, Mr Sutherland.' He waited a few seconds, and then repeated himself. 'Come on, just open your eyes now. Take a proper look at what's out there.' His voice didn't change at all, but the pressure on my back increased. I forced my eyes open and the ground swam dizzyingly before me. 'That's better.' He moved his face closer until his cheek was touching mine. Stubble and expensive aftershave. 'As I was saying. Sixty thousand Italians that I can't trust. But I can trust you, Mr Sutherland, can't I?' He waited just a few seconds for my reply and, when none came, he pushed me forward perhaps a centimetre more. 'Can't I?' he repeated.

'Yes.' My voice was little more than a croak.

Then he gently released his grip and stepped back. I sank to my knees, clamped my eyes shut, and counted to ten. I became aware that he was kneeling next to me.

'Oh, Mr Sutherland, you really aren't very good at heights, are you? Now, as I said, I'll be along within a few days, just to be sure my property is being well looked after. It is, isn't it?'

I nodded. 'Yes.'

'Good. Then we're both happy aren't we? Aren't we?'

'Yes.'

He patted me on the cheek. 'And I'll make that payment as promised. And then I'll be on my way. Now, I'm heading back to San Marco. And you?'

I shook my head.

'A shame. We could have taken the same boat back together. Well, I'll be in touch.' He pressed the lift button, and then offered me his hand. I had no idea why, but I took it and he pulled me to my feet. Then the lift arrived and with another brief doff of his hat, he was gone.

Chapter 14

I gave it fifteen minutes. Fifteen minutes with my eyes closed, and my back pressed against the wall. Then I went down to the church, sat in a pew and gave it fifteen minutes more. Then I went outside and hovered around the pontoon until I was certain that Montgomery was no longer there.

I took the first boat back to San Marco and half-ran through the streets until I was home.

To hell with the communists.

I sat down behind my desk, took out my mobile and started to dial. Then I hung up. *Calm, Nathan. Don't do anything in a panic.* I took a beer from the fridge, and drank half of it as I thought back to twelve months previously . . .

A perfect early spring day. The city smelled of coffee and fresh brioche. Of cigarettes, and bright sun on ancient stone. I'd been halfway through my first glass of wine of the day when Victor arrived. We'd known each other since I'd arrived in the city. He was looking older these days, and moving more slowly. He'd started to use a walking stick in these past few months.

'Nathan. How are you this morning?'

'I'm fine. Very well indeed. Lovely day.'

'It is indeed. Spring never lasts as long as you want it to here, does it?'

I shook my head. 'Can I get you a drink?'

'Bit early for a Spritz. I'll just have a Prosecco. Jane always said that wasn't like proper drinking.' He pulled a seat across from the adjacent table, and sat down. 'So. Are you all ready?'

'Well, I think so. Ready as I'll ever be.'

'No need to worry. It's straightforward really. I did it for nearly thirty years, and I can't remember anything too serious. The simplest thing to remember is this: if there's a problem, just direct it to Rome or Milan. All the legalities are the responsibility of the Consulate General. You don't need to get involved with any of that. And it's vanishingly unlikely that you should ever need to be in contact with the ambassador himself. Unless there's some sort of party or reception here; they quite like to come up for that sort of thing. So just be there to hold hands and wipe away any tears.'

'I'm great at hand-holding. Tears, I'll muddle through with.'

'Good man. Remember, a large part of this is about giving the right impression – security, normality. A little home from home in the middle of a foreign city. If people come to you, it's because things have gone wrong. For most people, that means being robbed. In the worst case, that means they've got no passport. All you have to do is liaise with Milan to get them replaced.'

'And the police?'

'You won't have much contact with them. If you do, it will probably be returning stolen property. You just keep all that in the safe until such time as it can be collected. You might sometimes get called in if there's been any trouble. Drunk and disorderly, that sort of thing. It rarely happens. To be honest, nothing very much ever happens here.'

Our drinks arrived, and we toasted each other. '*Buona fortuna*, Nathan.'

'Thanks. So, what are you going to do now? Are you staying in Venice?'

'I don't think so.' There was a touch of sadness, of tiredness in his voice. 'This isn't a city to grow old in, Nathan. Every year becomes a little more difficult. All those bridges are just that bit more tiring to cross. Those freezing winters and damp autumns make the joints creak more and more. And I'm starting to find the summers unbearable.'

I pointed to an elderly lady making her way slowly across the *campo*. 'Oh, come on now. I see plenty of people older than you every day.'

He shook his head. 'It's not the same. They all have family here. They're all looked after. Since I've been on my own it's felt different.'

'But won't you miss it?'

He took a long look around the square, at the bustling bars and cafés and the crumbling buildings, and drew a deep breath. 'A bit. There was a time I thought I would never leave. But I think I'm falling out of love with it. Just a little. And that means it's time to go.'

'I don't think I'll ever grow tired of it,' I said.

'Maybe you won't. I hope not. I never thought I would.'

I nibbled at a couple of crisps and passed the dish towards him, but he shook his head. 'So what will you do? Back to the UK, or will you stay in Italy?'

'There was a time we thought we might move out of the city. Not to Mestre, but maybe one of the smaller towns along the Brenta Canal. But now I'm thinking of going home. I've still got family there, grandchildren. It'll be nice to spend more time with them.'

I finished my drink. 'Another?'

He checked his watch. 'No thanks. A bit early for me. I'll be heading back. You stay and enjoy the sun. The very best of luck to you, Nathan. And remember, you can always call me.'

'Thanks Victor. I'll miss you.'

He said nothing, but smiled and patted me on the shoulder. Then he left, to make his way slowly across the *campo* in the direction of the Accademia Bridge.

Gramsci mewled and tinked his claws against my empty glass, dragging me back to the present. I fetched another beer from the fridge, sat back down and dialled.

'Victor Rutherford.' He had such a lovely voice, I thought. And yet – like the last time we met – there was an element of tiredness to it.

'Victor. It's Nathan. Nathan Sutherland.'

'Nathan! Lovely to hear from you. How are things?'

'Fine. Absolutely fine,' I lied.

'Wonderful. I was just thinking about you the other day. When are you both going to be back in England? It'd be lovely to meet up again.'

'Erm, I don't know to be honest. Maybe this summer. Listen, Victor, you know you said I could always call. If there was a problem?'

'Of course, Nathan. Nothing serious I hope.'

Gramsci and I stared at each other. He tapped again at my glass. 'I think it's nonsense Victor, but it's just . . . Well, it's just that I got asked to look after something the other day. Something that I think might be stolen property.'

There was silence on the line. Only for a moment. Then he chuckled. 'My goodness!'

'You never had to deal with anything like that?'

'Dear me, no. It was never so exciting in my day.'

'Did you ever . . . did you ever meet a man called Montgomery?'

Another pause. Then, 'No. I don't recognise the name. Sorry.'

This time it was my turn to laugh. 'I thought not. Some people will try it on, eh? But I thought it best to check.' I paused. I took a draught of my beer. 'I'll just drop by the *Questura* tomorrow and tell them about it.'

'What?'

'Well, I think the guy's a crook. I ought to tell them about it.'

'Oh I wouldn't bother, Nathan. I wouldn't bother. I think you'd be wasting your time.' The words were tripping over each other now. 'And really, it's wasting police time as well. It's not the sort of thing a consul should be doing.'

'I know. I know. And if it were only me, I wouldn't bother. It's just that he mentioned your name.' I paused, again. 'I'm not having some cheap crook taking advantage of your name, Victor. I'll speak to Vanni first thing tomorrow.'

'No!'

'No?' Gramsci was staring fixedly at me. Strike now, Nathan. 'Why not?'

'It's a waste of time.' The words were tumbling over each other, and the velvet voice was cracking.

'Tell me why, Victor. Tell me why it's a waste of time.'

Silence.

'Tell me why, or I'll hang up right now and the next number I dial will be the *Questura*.'

'Nathan, for God's sake.' His voice had broken. 'For God's sake. Just listen. Please.' He was on the verge of tears. 'It was 2009. *La crisi*. The stock market crash. I'd lost money. A lot of money. And Jane was ill, you know that.'

I felt like a shit. 'I remember.'

'He offered me ten thousand euros. I needed the money, Nathan. I needed the money. Ten thousand euros. Just to look after something.'

'Look after what?'

'I don't know. It was well wrapped up. I think it might have been a painting. Or something like that.'

'Okay. Go on. What happened?'

'I said I'd look after it. And I did. And then, two days later, there was a break-in. Somebody took it.'

'Wow. And I suppose Mr Montgomery was very angry?'

'He was fine about it. Said these things can happen.'

'Let me guess.' I drained the last of the beer. 'He gave you the money anyway?'

'He did.'

I needed another beer, but I didn't want to break the moment. 'Oh, Victor, what were you thinking?'

'I needed the money, Nathan.'

'You broke the law. Accepting stolen property. In your position.'

'I needed the bloody money, Nathan. Jane was ill. She was so ill. And I bloody hope you never find yourself in a position like that.' His voice cracked, and I could hear him choking back sobs.

Well done, Nathan. You've been bullied today. And now you've taken it out on an old man. 'It's all right, Victor, don't worry. I'll sort it out. I promise.'

'Nathan. If you go to the police I'll be ruined. You understand. Ruined. Please . . .'

I sat there and listened to Victor Rutherford crying. A man who had been a good friend to me.

'I'll sort it out, Victor It's okay. Really.'

A moment of silence. 'Don't call me again, Nathan. Ever.'

Chapter 15

I had, it seemed, broken a friendship. I slept uneasily, and woke up late and in bad humour. I decided to skip breakfast and make my way directly over to Giudecca, where I took a coffee and brioche at the Bar Palanca. It was barely eleven o'clock, but the regulars were ordering Spritzes and *caffè corretti* with shots of grappa. It was tempting to join them, but I thought a clear head would be needed.

I never had much occasion to come over here, so when I did I liked to have a drink and just sit and stare. The weather was starting to turn but, for the moment, the sun shone down on one of the loveliest views in all Venice. To my right, I could see as far as the Basilica of San Marco and the Doge's Palace. Then, slowly turning to my left, the dome of the Salute rose behind the Punta della Dogana where, for centuries, those ships arriving from the far reaches of the Venetian empire would have paid their excise duties. Then the long stretch of the Zattere, merciless in both the blazing summer heat and the driving rain of winter, that led past the old salt warehouses that now served as galleries and artists' spaces. These gave way to bars and restaurants as the *fondamenta* stretched away to the port area at San Basilio, where real life started to intrude with the presence of actual road vehicles. Floating gin palaces lined the canal at this point. An elegant fifties-style yacht, the property of the widow of a long-dead Austrian businessman, was dwarfed by the passing of a giant cruise liner; a sad reminder of how the Most Serene Republic scratched out a living these days. Finally, my gaze landed on the distant Porto Marghera, dominated by the great Arch of Cracking, an almost classical-sounding name applied to an oil refinery. I didn't know what sort of cracking was involved, but one day, I told myself, I would find out. It seemed a whole world away. Incongruous as it was, I liked the fact that it was there. The view of Venice seemed to say, *Remember how lucky you are.* The one of Marghera replied, equally importantly: *This is not Disneyland.*

I walked along the *fondamenta* until I came to a bar where a window displayed a rumpled flag bearing a hammer and sickle and the legend *Partito della Rifondazione Comunista.* I steeled myself. I'd walked by a number of times in the past, and thought it looked like a fun place to have a drink, but had never quite managed to step over the threshold. Quite simply, I didn't know if you were supposed to be a member or not and I didn't want to be embarrassed when asked to demonstrate my revolutionary credentials. Still, I'd come all this way, so I stuck my *Manifesto* ostentatiously under my arm, and went in.

It was like walking into a cigar box. Wood panelling everywhere, save for the ceiling stained by years of defiant opposition to the smoking ban. A sepia photograph of Antonio Gramsci hung above the bar, whilst the opposite wall sported one of Enrico Berlinguer next to a Warhol-like image of Che Guevara. Some luridly coloured bottles of ready-mixed Bellinis behind the bar hinted at an attempt at gentrification. The layer of dust on them attested to its success.

Two old guys sat at a table, playing cards, whilst a bored-looking young man with a beard and topknot stood behind the bar. One of the older men briefly raised his eyes to look at me, before going back to his game.

What would be the most comradely drink to order? Spritz? Too effete. I scanned the bottles behind the bar. Would a beer be a safer option? I looked back at the guys playing cards. One of them looked back at me and held my gaze for a couple of seconds this time, before turning his attention back to his hand.

'*Un ombra per favore,*' I asked. The barman gave the ghost of a nod and a smile, and poured me a glass of red. I propped my *Manifesto* on the bar, and pretended to read. Five minutes passed, punctuated by the ticking of a clock and the occasional shuffling of cards. I kept my eyes obstinately on the paper, knowing that – should I raise them – I would find everybody else's staring at me.

I folded the paper away and attempted to give the barman a nonchalant smile. 'So, Paolo been in today then?'

He stared back at me, blankly.

'Paolo. Paolo Magri. Has he been in today?'

The blank expression became one of puzzlement. 'Magri? Why do you want to see Magri?'

'I just want to speak to him.'

He shook his head. 'He's a drunk.'

I was suddenly aware of someone standing at my elbow. One of the card players, old but powerfully built, glared at me from beneath bristling grey eyebrows. 'You want to see Magri?'

'Yes.'

'You a journalist or something?'

'No. No, I'm not. I just think he can help me.'

The barman threw back his head and laughed. 'He can help you? He's a drunk. A stupid drunk. If he comes in here and remembers his name and where he lives we think he's having a good day.'

The old guy's arm whipped out like a snake, grabbed him by the collar, and dragged him halfway across the bar. 'You shut your stupid face, *puttana di merda*.' Then he released him, pushed him back, and dragged me to the table.

He gestured at the kid behind the bar. 'He's an idiot. Only been working here a few months. He knows nothing. And nothing about Paolo Magri.'

'He comes in here then?'

'Every day, pretty much. Why do you want to know?'

I took a deep breath. 'Like I said, I think he can help me. It's about an old story he worked on. The Moro case.'

The other man at the table, a bespectacled professorial-looking type with a goatee beard, raised his eyebrows. 'What do you know about the Moro case?'

'Next to nothing. I don't know if it's at all relevant to me. I just wondered if it involved a man called Arcangelo Moro?' Neither of them said a word. 'It's just that *Signor* Moro contacted me the other day and asked me to help him. I wasn't happy and so I thought I should find out more about him. All I could find was this reference to Paolo Magri. I don't even know if he's the right Moro.'

For a moment I swore they were going to cross themselves. Then the bigger guy called over to the bar. 'Hey, *stupido*, bring us a bottle of red over here. Three glasses.' Then he turned back to me. 'So, Moro wants you to do him a favour?'

'He thinks I can help him get his property back.'

The Professor chuckled. 'Moro's definition of "his property" is a flexible one.'

His friend shushed him with a motion of his hand. 'Better to keep your distance from Moro. Okay?'

'I'm not sure I've got a choice. He seems to want me to be his friend.'

'He doesn't have friends. Just people he can use.'

I took a sip of my wine. 'Look, can you tell me a little bit about the case? I just want to know if Paolo can help me?'

'Paolo can barely help himself any more. But he was a good man once. A good man.' For a moment he looked terribly sad. Then he refilled his glass and continued. 'Paolo used to work for the *Gazzettino*. Back when it was a good newspaper. He was also researching a book. A book about art crime. Anyway, there was a story in the papers at the time. There'd been an attempted robbery at a *palazzo* in Bologna. The owner had been beaten to death by an *extra-comunitario*. Serbian. His story was that he was just looking for money.

'Only Paolo wasn't sure. It made no sense. The house was miles out of the centre of town, nowhere near the areas where the East Europeans live. And the old guy was a private collector of art. So Paolo went to speak to the Serb. He turned out to be a smart guy. The kind of guy who'd know exactly what it was he was stealing. And there he was, facing a life sentence, *un ergastolo*. He was ready to name names, do anything if there was a chance he could get his sentence reduced. So he said he'd been offered a stupid amount of money for the job, by a man called Arcangelo Moro.

'Now, if Paolo had been smarter, he'd have left it there. Or done some more work, got some more proof. But no, he publishes an article in the *Gazzettino* – "Rich Venetian's links to art crime". And next thing he knows, Moro sets his lawyers on him. Defamation of character. Six months later he's in prison and serving three years.'

'Wait a minute, he went to jail for libel? A journalist went to jail for *libel*?'

'Yeah, sure. What do you mean, it doesn't happen in your country?'

'No.' I paused to refill our glasses. 'Mind you, I can think of a few people who probably ought to.'

'The thing you have to know is this. This is Italy. Everyone thinks if you are rich, you can do what you like.' He shook his head, 'This is not true. Not quite. Everyone is equal under the law. Everyone is protected by the law. But the difference is, if you are rich you are protected more than the others. And Moro is rich. Very rich.'

'What are you saying? The police were involved? Judges?'

He smiled, sadly. 'As I said, this is Italy. Money talks. And it speaks to everyone in a language they can understand.'

'He has a noble name, I see. So presumably it was important to protect it.'

He snorted. 'Noble my arse. He's not even Venetian. Not properly. His father came here from Torino, after the war. Made a fortune in Marghera. Changed his name to Moro, just to sound important. Appearance is what matters to those people, sometimes all that matters.'

'What about the Serbian?'

'Withdrew his statement. Said he'd lied, said Paolo promised him he could get him off if he said the right thing. As I said, he was serving a life sentence. Except now he isn't. He was released and deported soon after.'

'And Paolo?'

The Professor removed his glasses in order to give them a quick wipe. 'Three years, and he served every single day. And prisons here are a disgrace. When he got out, well, he was not the man he was.'

'And now?'

'He still lives here. He drinks too much. And he can't work. He'll never get a journalist's card again.'

'Do you think he'd talk to me?'

'*Beh.* Possibly, if it's about Moro. Tell him that you've spoken to Sergio and Lorenzo. That may help. And take a bottle along as well. It'll help even more.'

I stopped at the Co-op to buy a cheap bottle of grappa. The skies were continuing to darken, and I was starting to think that the wine had been a bad idea. The address they'd given me was between the churches of the Redentore and the Zitelle. I'd missed the *vaporetto* and the next one wouldn't be for thirty minutes. I decided to walk, turning my collar up against the rain.

Giudecca is a lonely place on a miserable day. When the waters of the lagoon turn grey and the wind sweeps across the *fondamenta* it can feel desolate and empty. On a clear day, the Redentore shines like the sun. That day it looked cold and forbidding in the encroaching darkness. Too white, too cold. I checked the number of the next building. Still a long way to go.

I walked on along the *fondamenta* and towards the Zitelle, attributed to Palladio although nobody seemed to know for sure. There wasn't long now before I'd find myself at the end of Giudecca, and back facing across the water to San Giorgio Maggiore. And then, just as I was thinking I must have written down the wrong number, there it was. A gated entry to a *sottoportego* leading to a number of *condominia*. Rows of brass plates were attached to the wall outside, but I could see none with the name of Magri. I wondered what to do. Perhaps I could just ring a random bell and ask to be let in? I was about to do so, when an elderly lady appeared, dragging a shopping trolley behind her with some difficulty. I tailgated her through the doorway and into the *sottoportego* that lead through to a garden area surrounded by a number of modern red-stuccoed buildings. She turned to look at me with suspicion in her eyes.

'I'm trying to find Paolo Magri,' I explained. She grunted something which sounded like 'last one' and gestured straight ahead. She continued her slow progress along the corridor and into a courtyard.

'Can I help you with the trolley?' She looked across at me as if I were an idiot, and shook her head. I strode out across the yard. This was a side of Giudecca I'd never seen. The path led past a series of gardens, in various degrees of upkeep, lined on both sides by brick buildings best described as 'functional'. Presumably built for factory workers in the years just after the war.

I passed under a stone faux-Roman arch, incongruous in these surroundings, and almost immediately the buildings seemed shabbier, the gardens overgrown and unkempt; as if I'd passed into another Venice, a world away from Baroque and Byzantine palaces. A Venice Ruskin would never have recognised. I took a look back along the path. The other blocks, whilst they might not have been the loveliest buildings in the city, did at least look as if they'd been well-maintained. The building at the end of the path, by contrast, seemed to be falling to pieces before my eyes. Many of the windows, set in rotting frames, had been boarded up. The plaster on the ground level had crumbled away, exposing the brickwork, the effect of *acqua alta* that nobody had done anything to remedy. A few sad plants struggled to make themselves seen amongst the weeds that constituted the surrounding gardens.

A couple of steps, slippery with rain and moss, led up to the front door. The nameplates fixed to the wall were almost obscured by rust. I rang a couple, experimentally, but couldn't hear anything from within. It was raining harder now. The temptation was to give up and go home. Back to nice Venice, normal Venice. I gave the door a push, and it swung open. Oh well. At least I'd be out of the rain.

The entrance hall stank of damp, of stale cigarettes and desperation. There must have been a slow leak from a pipe as the floor was covered in a couple of inches of stagnant water, in which fragments of plaster floated around, slowly turning the pool into a filthy, cloudy soup. Bags of cement and household waste sat in the stairwell, where a half-deflated football bobbed, adding a mournful and slightly sinister touch.

Who in God's name would stay in a place like this? A pointless question, since I already knew the answer.

Abusivi, extracomunitari. The bag men, the street vendors. And the desperate and the penniless. I flicked the light switch, more in hope than expectation, but a bare light-bulb came on and illuminated the staircase. Was there any point in going on? It seemed I was going to have to check every flat in the block. But the rain was hammering against the few remaining windows now and I thought I might as well have a look around whilst waiting for it to pass. I grimaced, and strode through the foul-smelling pool to the staircase, trying not to think about what the water might be concealing.

The banister wobbled alarmingly under my hand as I made my way upstairs. And there, on the first floor, was a plain wooden door with 'Magri' on the name plate. I could hear music playing within.

I knocked. There was no answer. I knocked again. This time, the music increased in volume. Loud enough now for me to recognise it. Pink Floyd. *The Wall.* At first, I thought of Dario and it made me smile. Then I thought that this was one of the few pieces of music capable of making the place seem even more depressing than it already was. Still it showed he was awake, even if he didn't want visitors.

I made a third attempt. A stream of foul language came from inside.

'*Signor* Magri. I need to speak to you.'

'*Vaffa!*' was the only response.

'My name is Nathan Sutherland. I'm not a journalist. I've been speaking to Sergio and Lorenzo. They gave me your address.'

Silence. He'd turned the music off.

'Please. It's important. It concerns Arcangelo Moro.'

There was no sound. I was about to give up and go home, when I heard a bolt being slid back. The door, warped by the damp, juddered open with some effort.

Magri was younger than I'd imagined. He was probably only in his mid-fifties. Unshaven, puffy-faced, with thinning grey hair and red-veined eyes. Yet he didn't look as bad as I'd been led to believe.

'So, are you coming in or are we going to talk on the doorstep?' He stepped back to let me into a flat that smelled of damp and old books. Indeed, the place was lined with bookshelves. An ancient sofa and writing desk were strewn with papers. A cheap but functional CD player sat on the floor, in the midst of a pile of discs and cassettes. If not quite the desirable bachelor pad, it at least looked as if it was inhabited by someone who was trying to get on with his life.

He saw my expression, and grinned mirthlessly. 'You expected the crazy old drunk journalist, right?'

'Erm, well the guys at the bar told me . . .'

'. . . that I'm a drunk?'

'Well. Yes.'

'I only go to the bar to get drunk. The rest of the time, I have good days and bad days. Today is a good day.' He offered me a mug. 'Wine?'

I reached for my present. 'Or would you rather . . .?'

He looked at it and shook his head. 'You keep it. That shit'll kill you.' He cleared the papers from the sofa. 'Come on, sit down. Tell me about Moro.'

I related all I had to say of our first meeting, our strange night at the opera and an offer that it seemed I couldn't refuse.

At the end, he refilled our mugs and nodded, as if impressed. 'Well now. You're in a lot of shit, my friend.'

'But I haven't *done* anything!'

'You've got that package, right?'

'Well, yes.'

'Then you've lied to him. He won't like that.'

'So, what, you think he's going to kill me?'

Magri spread his hands, palms upwards. 'Who knows? He could have you beaten up, find some other way to hurt you. I guess he could have you killed.'

I put my head in my hands. 'You know, not so long ago the worst thing in my life was the translation of a lawn-mower manual. Now, I think it's safe to say the situation has gone into a bit of a decline.'

'I'm sorry.'

We sat in silence for a bit. I breathed deeply. 'Okay, Paolo. That's what I know. Now you tell me what you know about Moro. Tell me about the man who was killed in Bologna, and the Serbian guy.'

He nodded. 'Okay. First I fetch us some more wine. Do you smoke?'

'Every now and then. I'm trying to give up.'

'If you've pissed off Moro, I wouldn't bother.' He offered me a cheap packet of MS, or *Morte Sicura*, cigarettes. We lit up, as he refilled our glasses.

'Before we get on to Moro, Mr Sutherland, I need to ask you a question . . .'

Chapter 16

'Tell me something, Mr Sutherland. Be honest. Do you like this country?'

I hesitated. I felt I owed him a considered answer. 'I know there are big problems in Italy. There are things I don't like. The bureaucracy, perhaps, but you get that everywhere. Organised crime. The politics, of course. The corruption. I don't think I will ever understand how you put up with it. But yes, I do like it. In spite of everything, I love it.'

He stretched his arms over the back of the sofa. 'Then you are lucky. For us, it is not so easy. It is a difficult country to love now. Much more than even twenty-five years ago.'

'So what happened?'

'*Tangentopoli* happened. What do you know about that?'

This was something I thought I should know more about than I actually did. I tried my best to remember what I could. '*Tangentopoli*. In the UK we called it "Kickback City". I know there was a corruption scandal. The prime minister resigned. Bettino Craxi, wasn't it?'

'Craxi, yes. Those are the most basic facts. *Tangentopoli* began with the arrest of a man called Chiesa. He'd accepted a bribe to give a cleaning contract to a small business. Silly amount of money. Just seven million lire. Only then his ex-wife started to testify. Said he had several billion stashed away in Swiss bank accounts. So Chiesa found himself under arrest, and decided to start naming names. And everything snowballed from there. Half the *Camera* were investigated. There was hardly an area of life in this country that was not touched by it.

'So Craxi resigned. He might even have gone to jail but he fled to Tunisia. In the meantime, everything in our political system was being swept away. The Christian Democrats and the Socialists collapsed. The Communists never recovered from the fall of the Soviet Union. The very identity of the country changed. We became the Second Italian Republic.

'Everything changed, and yet nothing changed. You know *Il Gattopardo* by Lampedusa? "*Se vogliamo che tutto rimanga come è, bisogna che tutto cambi.*"'

I nodded. '"If we want things to stay as they are, things will have to change."'

'Exactly. And that is what happened after *Tangentopoli*. Everything changed. And so everything stayed the same. You know what happened next?'

'Berlusconi?'

'*Il Cavaliere, sì.*' It was as if he couldn't bring himself to speak his name. 'Everything stayed the same. Except perhaps it was worse.' He took a long drink.

'I'm sorry,' I said, 'I don't see what this has to do with Arcangelo Moro.'

'Moro and his brother were both investigated for bribing a senator. They'd wanted to acquire a large area of land outside of Verona. There'd been a factory on the land; they wanted the area certified as toxic so as to buy it cheap. Anyway, they were both charged.'

'What happened?'

He laughed. 'Domenico cried like a baby. He turned *pentito*, named names, and tried to shovel as much shit on his brother as he could.'

'And Arcangelo went to prison?'

'Oh no. People like Moro do not go to prison. Prison is for little people. But he was charged, and convicted and paid a fine. But if you are someone to whom appearance is everything, it is not good to have everyone know you are a crook.'

'So Domenico shopped his own brother. Must have made conversation over the breakfast table a little strained.'

'Exactly. Arcangelo could also have made a plea bargain, but he chose not to. So, to some people, he is the honourable one. Honour is important to these people. And because of that, he still has some friends.'

'This is more than twenty years ago. How could they carry on living together after that?'

'Arcangelo took his revenge. Domenico had had some success. He was a respected writer on art history.'

'I know. I've seen some of his books in the Cini library.'

'They must be old ones. Nobody takes him seriously any more. A story came out in the press that Domenico had accepted money for certifying fake works of art as genuine.'

'Including Bellini?'

Paolo, I could see, was becoming tired with my interruptions. He took another drink. 'Bellini, and others, yes. There was no doubt about it. It ruined his reputation overnight. No more invitations to speak, no more professorships, no more publishing deals. The two of them destroyed each other.'

'And so there they are, in the same *palazzo*. After all this?'

'Yes.'

I whistled.

There was silence for a moment. Paolo yawned, and refilled his glass. I'd noticed he was no longer refilling mine. 'So. Is that all you want to know?'

I sighed. 'I think there's a lot more. I think he might be involved in some sort of art crime. Theft, maybe.'

He laughed the same humourless laugh. 'Oh you think so? Might be involved? You've been inside his house. What do you think?'

'Well, he's got a lot of stuff. But he's a rich man. It could all be legal, or he might have inherited it.'

'Tell me, then.' His speech was starting to slur now, his voice warm and blurred by wine and cigarettes. 'Tell me, what did you see there?'

'I can't remember everything. But he's got a copy of a work by Bellini. And something that looks like a Modigliani. But there were a lot. Those are the only two I really remember.'

'Okay. You ever go to church, Mr Sutherland?'

'Erm, not really. Christmas, but that's about it.'

'Well you should. Good for your soul. Very important in case Arcangelo has you killed. Go to Madonna dell'Orto. Say a few prayers. Take a look around. And then come back tomorrow. I'll be at the club in the afternoon.' He got to his feet, slightly unsteadily, then stretched and yawned. 'If you don't mind, Mr Sutherland, I would like to get drunk now.'

I took a look at my watch. It was barely four o'clock.

'Okay, thank you very much *Signor* Magri. I'll see you t . . .'

I was outside the closed door almost without noticing it. The music started again. Paolo Magri, like David Gilmour and Roger Waters, was becoming 'Comfortably Numb'.

Chapter 17

Few things are as comforting as a dry pair of socks on a wet day. I lay on the sofa, my wet clothes steaming on the radiator, and listened to Glenn Gould. Gramsci perched on the back of the sofa, in the hope that he could leap on me in the event of my falling asleep.

Rain pattered against the shutters, and then the sound came. The great, tired wail of the *acqua alta* alarm. Then the first *pling*. Another, a tone higher. Then a third. And finally a fourth. Tonight was going to be the highest level. A hundred and forty or more centimetres above average, meaning over half the city would be affected. Poor Eduardo would need to be putting chairs on tables, and would be mopping up the water tomorrow morning. Yet, like the sound of the rain, there was something comforting about the sound of the *acqua alta* alarm when there was no need to go out. I looked at my watch. Six thirty now. That meant nothing would start to happen until eight thirty. I'd go and pick up a bottle of wine and a pizza and be back long before then. And then, perhaps, I'd have an early night. Just time for a snooze over the paper first.

The telephone rang.

'*Ciao, tesoro.*'

'*Ciao, Federica. Come stai?*'

'Not bad. Tired. I've spent a long day on top of scaffolding. Listen, are you doing anything tonight?'

'Well, Kate Moss is coming round in half an hour . . .'

'Ah, that's a shame. I need a – what do you say – a "plus one".'

'Right. Right. Well, I could put her off.'

'You sure?'

'Yeah, it's okay. To be honest she's slightly hard work. She's insisting we collaborate on a new translation of the *Inferno*, and my heart's not really in it.'

'Well I'm a lucky woman then. So let's meet at Maturi's apartment at eight. It's in San Giacomo dell'Orio.'

'*Maturi?*'

'Yes, we have dinner once a month. I worry about him being alone. He worries about me being alone. Anyway, we spoke earlier and he said he found you quite interesting. So I thought, what better than getting another lonely person along and we can all worry about each other?'

'Yes, that's a genuinely brilliant idea. I have to say I found him just a little bit scary.'

'Oh, he can seem like that at first. He's a sweetheart really.'

'Mm. Should I be jealous?'

'He's over seventy.'

'That needn't matter. My wife had a thing about Anthony Burgess and he's been dead for twenty years.'

There was a brief pause. 'Do you think perhaps you've got quite low self-esteem, Nathan?'

'Possibly so. Anyway, do you know how many drinks I had to buy off Eduardo until he forgave me?'

'More than you should, I'm sure. Now, it's *acqua alta* tonight so be sure to bring your boots. Bring something to drink as well. Nothing that comes in a Tetra-Pak, and definitely not a water bottle with some *vino sfuso* in it. Bring something nice. Something with a proper cork in it at least.'

Dai the Wine's shop was just a couple of steps along the *calle* from Da Fiore. It was called Dai Cancari in reality, but I had always liked to imagine it was run by a Welsh-Italian expat. So Dai the Wine he had stayed.

I entered the shop, and he instinctively reached for a plastic bottle to fill with *vino sfuso*. I shook my head. 'Not tonight, Dai. I'm going out. I need something good.'

He looked at me in disgust. 'It's all good, Sutherland. And stop calling me Dai.'

'Sorry. *Giovanni*. It's a special occasion and I think my host is a fussy drinker. I need something good from the Veneto.'

'Red or white?'

'Argh. Don't know. I should have asked what we were eating.'

'No problems. One of each then?'

I left the shop five minutes later, thirty euros lighter of pocket but with two bottles that contained, I hoped, 'something good'.

The rain had stopped, but a fine, damp mist was settling over the city. I made my way to the *vaporetto* stop at Sant'Angelo. It was quiet now, and chilly. Too cold, perhaps, to make it sensible to sit outside, but I did so anyway. It was a rare pleasure to get the outside seats to oneself.

The canal was almost clear at this hour. The commercial traffic had long since finished for the day. A few small private boats and taxis passed by. As we moved towards Rialto, the shape of a gondola emerged from the mist, ghostly in the blue half-light. There were no passengers – too cold, too late, too wet perhaps. A shame. I could think of no more lovely time to take a gondola ride. We passed under the bridge, and the figure of the gondolier was slowly lost in the mist.

We slid by the *mercato*, and the spell was broken for a moment, the sound of the never-ending *movida* echoing across the dark waters. Then past private *palazzi*, with frescoed ceilings and chandeliers of Murano glass. Houses, as Ruskin wrote, with Titians in. The Gothic palace of Ca' d'Oro passed on the right. And then we arrived at the *vaporetto* stop of San Stae, my favourite in the whole city. Somehow it never felt quite as chaotic and busy as many of the other stops along the Grand Canal during the daytime, whilst a sense of melancholy and loneliness hung over it after dark. There was something spectrally beautiful about it on a foggy night such as this, with the crumbling statues on the façade of the church being the only companions to the late-night traveller. Ruskin, of course, had hated it.

I stepped off the boat, and waited for it to leave. I was completely alone in the *campo*. The fog was so thick now, that all I could see of the opposite side of the canal was the diffused glow of the lights in the *palazzi*. Venice at its most serene and magisterial.

I made my way down the side of the church, and into the heart of Santa Croce. Through narrow *calli* and over bridges, into Campo San Giacomo dell'Orio. Bars and restaurants were open here, and the city felt alive again. I was starting to feel cold now, and stepped out towards the address Federica had given me.

Maturi's flat was on the top floor with a small terrace that would, on a clear day, have yielded a spectacular view across the city. Federica answered the door to me, kissed me, and took me through to the living room. Maturi emerged from the kitchen, incongruously dressed in an apron over a waistcoat and tie. We shook hands, and I passed over my wine. He examined both bottles in detail, and gave a half-nod in what I hoped was appreciation.

'Mr Sutherland. Make yourself comfortable and talk to lovely Federica. Please, have something to eat.' He offered me a plate of *cicchetti* – tiny portions of *sarde in saor* on discs of polenta – and a glass of Prosecco. 'Excuse me for a few minutes. I just have to finish in the kitchen.'

I raised my glass to Federica. 'These are great,' I said, between mouthfuls of sardine.

'Giacomo's an excellent cook. He's passionate about both food and art. And he gets very cross when they're less than perfect.'

'You're not kidding.'

'Anyway, he usually only cooks for close friends, so you're very lucky. You must have made a good impression.'

'Well I'm flattered. I thought he saw me as a harmless idiot at best. How do you know him, by the way?'

'I've known him since I was a child. He was a good friend of my father's. He was *zio Giacomo* when I was growing up.'

Maturi emerged from the kitchen. 'Mr Sutherland, some assistance please.' I followed him into a narrow galley kitchen where a pan of risotto was simmering away. 'Please just keep stirring that until I say so. If it starts to look a little dry, just add some more stock.'

I stirred away.

'Federica tells me you are a very good cook.'

'Well, I think she's just being nice. I don't cook as much as I used to.'

'You should do. Better than going to that horrible bar. And cheaper too.'

'You're right.' I could see him working with some small cuttlefish. 'I should make more effort.'

He grunted. With his left hand, he held the head of the cuttlefish; then pulled with his right, dragging out the innards along with the tentacles and body section. 'This bit is the most difficult. Well, not difficult, but get it wrong and you'll spend the rest of the evening cleaning up your kitchen.' He carefully removed the ink sac and set it aside; then repeated the operation with three more cuttlefish. Then he carefully rinsed the individual sections of head, body and tentacles before setting them aside. He looked over my shoulder and nodded approvingly.

'Thank you, Mr Sutherland. Now, just stand aside please.' He took an ink sac, dropped it in the risotto, and stirred it in until the rice turned a greyish-black colour. He reached behind him for a fork, and scooped out a couple of grains of rice. He nibbled away pensively, then shook his head. 'Not enough.' He threw in another sac, and stirred again, turning the risotto almost completely black.

'*Risotto al nero*?' I smiled.

He nodded. 'You like it?'

'Very much.'

'The trick is to be careful with the ink. You go to a restaurant, order a risotto for two, and they'll put in two *seppie* and two sacs. Too much. They do it so the rice goes as black as the night and it looks beautiful on a white plate. The first mouthful, you think it's maybe the best thing you've ever eaten. The second one is still nice, the third not so good. It's too rich. For me it's impossible to eat. One sac for two people, maybe two for three people is just about perfect.' He dropped the pieces of *seppie* in, and patted me on the back. 'Okay, your work is done. Go and be charming to Federica.'

Risotto al nero has the same problem as spinach, in that it makes you worry about smiling at people for the immediate future. It was, nonetheless, splendid. Maturi followed this up with *razza al burro nero*. Skate in black butter. Not perhaps very Venetian, he apologised, but it was a favourite of his.

He explained he'd never had the patience for desserts and so we finished with fresh fruit and cheese. 'Thank you *Signor* Maturi,' I said, '*una cena memorabile.*'

He waved away my thanks. 'No problem. I feel good seeing you eating properly at last. Next time you can cook.'

'Well, I'm out of practice.'

'No matter. We'll do it together. So, tell me, Mr Sutherland. How long have you been in Venice?'

I had my glass raised halfway to my mouth when the thought struck me that perhaps he was on the verge of asking me if my intentions were honourable and what my prospects were. 'Five years now.'

'So why did you come? Venice, I mean?'

'My wife had the chance of a job at the university – Ca' Foscari that is – for a year. In the English language depart-ment. I already did a bit of Italian-English translation, and it seemed I could do it as well here as anywhere. Her contract got extended and so we stayed.'

'You came because of your wife? Ah, I didn't know you were married.' He gave a little rumbling sigh, and went back to the kitchen. He came back with a bottle of grappa. Proper grappa, not Billa's own 'Clever' brand. He poured us all a glass.

'I also came to Venice because of my wife. We met in nineteen-sixty-eight. She was a teacher. History of Art, at Ca' Foscari. I was working at the Brera Gallery in Milan. It sounds impor-tant but I was very young, and it was a humble position. Then I found a job at the Correr. It was not much money, but it was a good opportunity. So I came to Venice to be with Maria Giulia, and I stayed.'

'That's lovely. How long were you married for?'

'Not long enough. Just ten years. She was very young when she died.'

'I'm sorry.'

'Well, these things will happen to all of us at one time or another. But they were ten good years. We were very happy. I don't remember us ever arguing, although I suppose we must have. And in all the years we were together, I only lied to her once.'

I hesitated. I didn't want the question to sound indelicate, but I had the feeling he wanted me to ask it. 'Which was . . .?'

'That I would marry again. I knew that I never would. But I also promised her that I would be happy and, for much of the time, I think I am.'

Federica patted his arm. 'Never so happy as when you have something to complain about though, eh *zio Giacomo*?'

He looked quite pleased. 'You should have brought your wife tonight, Mr Sutherland. Next time, I hope.'

'She's . . . well she's not here at the moment, *Signor* Maturi. There was an opportunity for her to spend a year working at the University of Edinburgh. That's where she is now.'

'Ah, I see. You must be missing her.'

'Yes. Yes I am.' Federica gave me a look. 'To be honest, I don't know if she'll be coming back. She was always happier back in the UK. I don't know what we're going to do.'

He nodded. There was a brief silence, then he got to his feet. 'I'll make us some coffee.'

Whilst he was gone, Federica took my hand. 'Sorry. Are you okay?'

'Yeah, fine. I need to talk about it. No point pretending the situation doesn't exist.'

Maturi returned, bearing coffee. 'Federica says you are also a diplomat.'

I laughed. 'I'm not sure I'd call it that. I'm an honorary consul. That means I don't do very much more than help tourists who've been robbed, or lost their passports or who just need a bit of help in general.'

'And you enjoy it?'

I sighed. 'Sometimes. I've got to say, I think I was expecting the job to be more exciting than it actually is. It's nice when people are pleased, of course.'

'Well I think you should enjoy it more. You have a job where you help people every day. That's good. Just in the city, or for the whole of the Veneto?'

'Just for the city. There's an HC in Padova as well, and also one in Mestre. There was a feeling that Venice needed a dedicated one, just because of the number of visitors.'

'Mestre, eh? Of course, many tourists end up there by accident. You ever go to Mestre?'

'Not often, I don't really need to. Sometimes I meet a friend for drinks there. Oh, and I covered for the consul there, just for a few weeks earlier this year.'

'You like Mestre?'

I rubbed my chin. 'Good question. I don't know. There isn't anything wrong with it and yet . . .'

'. . . there's nothing particularly exciting about it either,' said Federica.

'Yeah. Nothing particularly exciting. It's as if almost everywhere else in Italy is more interesting.'

'Maybe so,' Maturi said, 'There was a time, you know, that the area of Bissuola in Mestre was almost like one of the *sestiere* in Venice, as so many Venetians had moved there from the lagoon. You would hear *Veneziano* being spoken on the streets. But all that is changing now. Nevertheless, I like Mestre. It's important. It reminds us of real life.'

'But would you ever live there, *zio Giacomo?*'

He spluttered through his coffee. 'Good God, of course not!'

We all laughed. Time was getting on a bit now, and I thought I really should be going. It had been a good evening. I'd managed to avoid thinking about Montgomery and Moro and books that may or may not have been by famous artists the whole time. Federica was showing signs of being ready to leave, but something impelled me to ask, '*Signor* Maturi, you've been in Venice for over forty years, have you ever met a man called Arcangelo Moro?'

He raised his eyebrows. 'I've never met him. I know of him. Why do you ask?'

'He came to me with what I suppose I would describe as a business proposition wrapped up in a threat.'

'Hmmph. Sounds like him. You didn't accept, of course.'

'No. Although I don't think he's going to let the matter lie.'

'He won't. Very unpleasant man, Moro. Stay clear of him.'

'So people keep telling me. Trouble is, I don't think he's going to stay clear of me. What do you know about him?'

'He's like his brother. A waste of space. Never had to do a day's work in his life. Inherited money from his father, but never seems to have done anything with it. Certainly never put anything back into the city.'

'Is he actually, well, dangerous?'

'He could be. There have been rumours for years. That he's a thief. Or possibly worse. As I said, my advice is to stay clear of him.'

There seemed to be little more to be said, and so we said our goodnights. Federica and I pulled on our boots and splashed our way through the *campo*, and back along the *calle* to the *vaporetto* stop. The next boat was almost empty, and so we took our seats outside at the back. We were alone. As if being conscious of this, we left an empty seat between us.

'He's a nice man, your uncle. Underneath.'

'Oh he is. He just scares people a bit at first.'

'He scared me.' I paused. 'He seems very protective of you. I think he wants you married off.'

'Yeah. I think he does.'

'So. Fancy going to church tomorrow morning?'

'Why Nathan! And I thought you'd never ask.'

'Great. Madonna dell'Orto at ten o'clock. I need you to help me fight crime.'

Chapter 18

Venice is a city of over one hundred churches. There had been even more, before Napoleon had his way. Many of them are crumbling, and many will never open their doors again. Even after five years, I still had difficulty in identifying them from a distance. I tended to remember them by colour or style of the *campanile*: big ones (San Marco), green ones (San Giorgio Maggiore), falling-over-a-bit-more-than-they-really-should ones (Santo Stefano, San Giorgio dei Greci). Madonna dell'Orto, with its eastern-style onion-domed bell tower, was one of the easier ones to spot.

Federica, in leather jacket and jeans, was there before me. 'Right then, Mr Holmes. Where do we start?'

'I wish I knew, *dottoressa* Watson.'

'Oh. Do all our cases start like this?'

'I'm afraid so. I met a journalist yesterday. A guy called Paolo Magri. Have you heard of him?' She shook her head. 'He did two things. He put the fear of God into me by telling me the terrible things Arcangelo Moro might want to do. And then he told me to come here. I think maybe it's a test of some sort. To see if I'm being serious with him.'

'And that's it?'

'That's it.'

She gave me a disappointed look. 'Not much to go on is it? Well, let's go inside. Have you been here before?'

'Years ago. I don't remember much.'

'Then I'll give you the guided tour.'

A couple of tourists were fumbling for change at the entrance, but we just flashed our residency cards at the man on the desk and he waved us through.

She stood close to me, the better to whisper. 'This was initially dedicated to St Christopher, but that changed over eight hundred years ago. It was in a terrible state by the time the Austrians arrived, and they made a mess of trying to restore it. And then there was the great *acqua alta* of 1966. But today, it looks like this.' She turned through a full circle, her arms spread to emphasise the beauty of our surroundings. 'For me, this is one of the loveliest buildings in Venice.'

I had to agree. The ceiling was timbered and plain, but supported by striped marble columns. There were three chapels on each side. She led me along the right nave to show me a painting of a burly, bearded man carrying the Christ child upon his shoulder. 'They didn't completely forget about St Christopher. This is by Cima da Conegliano. Or at least it's a copy of a work by him. But this one' – she pointed to an altarpiece of someone who I took to be John the Baptist in the company of saints – 'this one is the real thing. But the best thing in the church is down here. Come on.'

She took my arm, and led me down to the end of the nave, where a huge canvas hung over the door that led to a separate chapel. It showed a flight of steps leading up to a temple, where a high priest stood in expectation as a young girl made her way up towards him. At the base of the stairs, illuminated by the light from a glowering sky, a mother – her hand on her daughter's shoulder – gestured up towards the temple, the better to draw our gaze. The effect was kinetic, almost cinematic.

'Tintoretto. *The Presentation of the Virgin in the Temple*,' she said.

'It's stunning. I'd almost forgotten about it. I'm never quite sure if I really like Tintoretto or not. But when he's at the top of his game – like this – there's almost no one to touch him. That use of light, that sense of movement.'

She punched my arm, which drew an 'Ow!' out of me, and a hostile look from the man at the ticket desk. 'Not sure if you like Tintoretto, eh? Well don't let him hear you!' She pulled me towards the chapel on the right of the apse, where a faded rose lay atop a memorial stone in the floor. Jacopo Robusti, *il Tintoretto*. Federica gave me a hard stare. 'This was his church you know? Show a bit of respect.'

I rubbed my arm. 'I was only being honest!'

She gave me a contemptuous 'Hmmph'.

I tried to change the subject. 'You know, I've always liked the way Italians commemorate the great and the good. Every time I go to the Frari, I see there's a rose on Monteverdi's tomb. I sometimes wonder if it's somebody's job.'

'Well it's important to remember them. People come to visit and still expect it to be the same country that produced Tintoretto and Titian. And it's not. For that matter, it's no longer the country of Fellini or Antonioni. It's not even the same country as twenty years ago. And so . . .'

'No more heroes?'

'Exactly.'

We moved on to the apse. To the left of the high altar lay Tintoretto's *Adoration of the Golden Calf*, in which, it was said, he portrayed himself, Titian, Veronese and poor, doomed Giorgione amongst the masses. On the opposite wall hung his monumental *Giudizio Universale*, the *Last Judgement*. Like the *Presentation*, the thing that struck you at first glance was the movement, a sense of being physically present at the instant of the damned being thrown down to hell. And there, just below dead centre, was the image that had always most disturbed me. A partly skeletonised figure. As if we were witness to the very moment of the flesh rotting from the bones. Small wonder that little Effie Ruskin had run screaming from the church upon seeing it.

'Fantastic, aren't they? But they don't quite get the top spot here. I've never understood why.' She gestured at the painting behind the high altar. 'Palma il Giovane,' she said.

'*The Annunciation*?'

'Of course.' She looked at me in expectation. 'Well? What do you think?'

'At the risk of being punched again, I've got to say I really don't much care for Palma il Giovane. They're just all so . . . brown. So dark. If somebody were to ask me to describe his work, all I'd be able to come up with would be "a preponderance of brown". But this one, I don't mind. There's just, well, slightly less brown.'

She smiled, and patted my cheek. 'Well done, Mr Holmes. We're making good progress.'

'Thank you, Watson. I have to say, I still have no idea what we're supposed to find here.'

She shrugged. 'No matter. Most of it's lovely to look at. The chapels on the left are less interesting. Most of them are by Tintoretto's son, Domenico. Still, they're all worth a look.'

We wandered slowly back down the left-hand side of the church, and we paused to take a look at a few works by Domenico. 'You're right, they're not as good. I mean, there's nothing wrong with them, they're all perfectly accomplished but they're not' – I threw my hand back in the direction of the *Presentation in the Temple* – 'they're not like that. Something that leaps out at you, and pulls you in at the same time.'

'Quite right. But it's important to remember that not everything from that period is a masterpiece. We only remember the exceptional works. For every Jacopo, there are dozens and dozens of dimly remembered Domenicos. All perfectly good painters. All of them with a talent greater than maybe ninety-nine per cent of the population. And their great tragedy is that they were merely "quite good". And now I think we've nearly finished. Shall we take another stroll round, or would a Spritz help inspiration to strike?'

It was definitely the Spritz hour by now, but I thought that – if this was the only useful information Magri was prepared to give me – I really ought to make a bit more of an effort. 'Let's cruise another lap. Maybe something will leap out. Oh, and we haven't done the last chapel on this side.'

She gave a wry smile. 'Nothing to see really. Which makes it the saddest place in the church. The Valier chapel.'

It was undecorated, although a small work was propped on top of the altar. I drew closer. At first glance, it looked like a panel painting but, as soon as I looked closer, it became immediately obvious that it was a photographic reproduction.

'I was still at school when it was taken. But I remember my father crying when he heard about it. He said it was one of the worst of crimes, to take something so beautiful out of the world. There are people, you know, who say that we waste too much money on preservation and acquisition. Why bother going to see *La Primevera* when you can look at it on a computer screen or in a coffee-table book. But it's not the same thing, not for a . . . What's the matter with you?'

My hands were gripping the edge of the altar in shock, as I read the sign underneath the painting. ' "Photographic reproduction, Giovanni Bellini *Madonna and Child* (1480). Stolen the night of March 1st 1993." ' The same sad-faced Madonna. The same unattractive Christ child.

'I think it's time for that Spritz,' I said.

Chapter 19

'You're telling me you saw a copy of the *Madonna and Child* two days ago?'

'Not a copy. The original. The exact same work.'

'How do you know? You saw it for, what, thirty seconds?'

'If that.'

'And this man, this Moro, said himself that it was a copy.'

'Yes he did.'

'Well then.'

'I know it sounds crazy, but there's something about him. Something *unclean*. He's got a room full of artworks, from pretty much every period. He's a wealthy man. Why would he just hang a print on the wall?'

'Maybe he just really likes Bellini. After all, there are still some things that money can't buy, even in Italy.'

'I'm not sure he really *likes* any of it. There was a portrait by Modigliani. He didn't even know who it was of. I think he just likes having them.'

Federica munched on the olive from her Spritz, then delicately dropped the stone back into her glass. 'So you're saying he's got a roomful of stolen artworks?'

'Maybe. I know that he was linked with an art theft five years ago.' I told her about the communists on Giudecca and my meeting with Paolo Magri.

'So that was just the word of one guy in prison, as part of a plea for a lighter sentence. And it never went anywhere. Come on, Nathan, do you seriously think that – in the heart of Venice – a man is sitting in his *palazzo* surrounded by stolen artworks, one of which just happens to be the most celebrated stolen painting in the city in the past half-century?'

'Yes. Yes, I think I am.'

She twirled her cocktail stick in her fingers, and tapped it on the table a couple of times. 'Nathan, what do you know about art crime?'

'Precious little. I have a feeling, however, that you're going to tell me all about it,' I added, with a touch of bitterness in my voice.

She jabbed the stick into my hand, drawing another 'Ow' from me. 'No need to be cross, Mr Holmes.'

'I'm sorry. Go on.'

'Everyone – the man in the street, that is – thinks that these things are stolen to order. That there's an oligarch in Moscow who drinks Martinis in a secret vault with a Caravaggio in it. It isn't like that. Ninety-nine per cent of the time, it's just collateral for organised crime. You steal a painting, cut it from its frame and you can carry it around in a poster tube. Easily transportable, and easy to use as security against drugs, arms, whatever you like.'

'And the other one per cent?'

'Okay, I'll concede there might – *might* – just be a few cases where works have been stolen to order and ended up in private collections. But the number of them is incredibly small. Think about it, you'd never be able to show them to anyone. And this isn't just one work you're talking about but a whole room.'

'It could happen.'

'No, it couldn't.'

'There was a case over ten years back. A French guy. He had dozens of stolen paintings at his mother's house.'

'Stephane Breitweiser. I remember. Okay, but that's an exceptional case. And he stole every work himself. You're not suggesting that Moro creeps out at night to loot churches, or flies off to exotic locations in order to locate his painting of the week?'

'What if he employs people to do it for him? Like the Serbian guy.'

'Firstly, we can't rely on the testimony of the Serbian guy. Secondly, every time he employed someone to steal for him, there would be the chance of getting caught. Multiply that risk for a roomful of paintings and the chances of him continually getting away with it are . . .'

'Are . . .?'

'Okay. Not zero. But small.'

'Look, let's just run with the possibility. We know Moro has a roomful of art . . .'

'As does almost every wealthy family in this city.'

'Just hear me out, eh? He has a roomful of artworks, some of which may be stolen. Magri has had suspicions about him for years. There was the initial statement of the Serbian guy where he came out and said that he had been directly employed by Moro.'

She looked underwhelmed. 'An alcoholic journalist, and the words of a convicted murderer. It's paper-thin, Nathan, paper-thin.'

I sighed. 'Okay. Maybe you're right. But something is going on here. We have a book that two people are interested in and prepared to pay for. And Magri says I'm in big trouble if Moro has taken an interest in me. Can we at least assume that there is something worth just a little bit of time and trouble to investigate?'

She drained her Spritz. 'Okay. I'll tell you what we're going to do. You go back and speak to Magri again. See if there's any more help he's willing to give you. Any sort of documentation that will give us something a little more concrete to work with.'

'It's a start. Thank you.'

'In the meantime, I'll go and speak to some of the archivists at the Museo Correr. I know a couple of people there. I'll ask them if there's any record in the past few months of a prayer book that might have been illustrated by Giovanni Bellini having been stolen. It's not much to go on, but it might help.'

'That sounds more interesting. Can't I do that?'

'No. Firstly, you don't know anyone there. It'll be easier for me. Secondly, I don't really want to have to go and meet a sad middle-aged man who drinks too much. I have you for that.'

'Thanks. I think.'

Her face broke into a broad smile. 'Come on. I agree that this is fun. We're fighting crime, aren't we?'

I smiled back. 'We certainly are. And it's been, well, it's been a nice morning.'

'Yeah. Yeah, it has.'

Chapter 20

I held a surgery that afternoon. Nothing serious. One travel document and a man with a query about his mobile phone. It was late afternoon, then, by the time I made my way over to Giudecca. The skies were clear, and turning pink in the sunset; an effect that even managed to make the distant refineries of Marghera seem beautiful.

Sergio and Lorenzo were sitting at the same table. They were dressed in the same clothes, and I wondered if they'd been home at all; although Lorenzo still managed to maintain a professorial air, as if gearing up for a late-night appearance on the Open University. Paolo was with them, looking much as he had the previous day, and the three of them were playing cards. I was about to speak, but I'd scarcely opened my mouth before Sergio interrupted me. 'Ah, it's you. Our investigator.' They all laughed but there was a warmth to it, and the Prof gave a little cheer.

I dragged a chair over to the table, opposite Paolo. The Prof clapped me on the back. 'Paolo says you and he are going to – what did you say, Paolo? – "nail this bastard to a wall"?'

Paolo shushed him, and turned to me. 'So. Did you go to church this morning?'

'He's a Protestant, Paolo, of course he didn't,' said the Prof.

'Quiet Lorenzo, this is serious. I'm trying to save his soul here. Not to mention his life.' They all laughed. Both the Prof and Sergio pounded me on the back again. Everyone, I realised, was cheerfully drunk.

'Church. Yes, I went to the church,' I said.

Paolo raised his hands for silence. 'Good. Well done. So what did you see?'

'A photograph of a stolen Madonna by Giovanni Bellini that looks like the one in Arcangelo's *palazzo*.'

Paolo nodded, and there was silence for a moment. Then he hammered both fists on the table in a little drum-roll of triumph, setting our glasses vibrating. 'I knew it. Didn't I tell you both? I knew it!'

The Prof reached across the table to steady the bottle. 'We can't know for sure, Paolo. It is most likely that it's just a copy.'

'Just a copy, my scrawny Venetian arse. He's had it for twenty years, keeping it under our noses all this time.' He leaned over and punched my shoulder. 'Well done. Well done. Now we need to think what to do next.'

I rubbed my arm. It was nice to be welcomed in such a comradely way, even if it was rather painful. Then I became aware that the three of them were staring at me, expecting me to tell them what the next step was. As if Trotsky had suddenly found himself in the middle of a bunch of co-conspirators all looking at him as if to say, 'Great idea Leon, but what is it we're actually going to *do*?'

I could only think of one thing. 'Does anyone know this man?' I asked and took Montgomery's photograph out of my pocket and passed it around. Sergio and Lorenzo both shook their heads. Paolo took a more detailed look before he passed it back to me.

'No. Never seen him before.' He drummed his fingers on the table whilst thinking, then reached inside a shopping bag under the table to withdraw a notebook and pen. He scribbled something down, tore the page out and passed it over to me. 'This is Sandro Adriatico. He's an officer in the *Guardia di Finanza*. In the art squad. He knows me a little bit. Give him a call, he might be able to help.'

'Anything else?'

He passed me the bag. 'I've got plenty of stuff on Moro. I was working on a book. Who knows, maybe I'll even complete it one day.'

I riffled through the contents. Newspaper clippings, photographs and a cassette tape. In one black and white photograph a young man with shaved hair, slightly Slavic in appearance, stared dead-eyed at the camera. Magri jabbed at it with his finger.

'That's the Serbian kid. The one who went to jail. Looks like a regular *naziskin*, right?' I had to agree, and nodded. 'That's what I thought at first. But I spoke to him twice, and then I wasn't so sure.'

The Prof gave a gentle cough. 'To be fair, Paolo, he did beat someone to death.'

Magri spread his hands wide. 'Sure, sure,' he said, as if this was the sort of unfortunate occurrence that could happen to anybody.

The Prof took my arm. 'You know what happened? No? You want me to tell him, Paolo?' Magri shrugged and let him continue. 'He was stealing a work by Medardo Rosso, you know Medardo Rosso?' He looked disappointed when I shook my head. 'Post-impressionist sculptor. Very good, you really must look at his work. Next time you go to Milan you should go to . . .'

'The point, Lorenzo . . .?' interrupted Sergio.

'Sorry. As I was saying, our young Serb was stealing a work by Rosso. The owner discovered him in the act. And before he could raise the alarm, he was beaten to death with the very same heavy bronze sculpture.'

There didn't seem to be much that I could add to that so I settled for what I hoped was a suitably grim nod of the head, and a 'Nasty.'

'I know. But as I said, I met him twice. And by the end I felt sorry for him,' said Magri.

'You're soft, Paolo. You went to prison because of him,' said Sergio.

'I went to prison because of Arcangelo Moro. Not because of some stupid kid.' Magri turned to me, and gave the bag a shake. 'Anyway, it's all in there. Take a look at it, see what you think.'

'Wait a minute, Paolo, aren't we working on this together?'

He looked surprised. 'Yeah, sure we are. But I've done all the legwork so you don't have to. It's over to you now.'

'Come on, Paolo, you know way more about this than I do. I'm not a private investigator or anything. You're the journalist.'

He shrugged. 'I'm an ex-journalist. An alcoholic ex-journalist. And I feel too old to be chasing around any more.'

'Look, it may be that Moro has another crime in progress. One that will finish on the seventeenth of April. I don't know why, but there seems to be something significant about that date.'

'Maybe.'

'But I need your help on this. Come on, we can nail this bastard together. You'll get your life back, your reputation back.'

'*Beh*, a journalist's reputation isn't worth so much. And it's too late to get my life back together now.'

I'd pushed him too far. He was visibly upset, his eyes even redder than usual. The Prof threw me a glance and ever so subtly shook his head. Magri reached for his coat. 'Have a look at what I've got. Come back if you've got any questions and I'll do what I can. But you be sure you come here, not to the apartment, okay?' He gave Sergio a light pat on the back, and left.

'I'm sorry,' I said.

'It's okay,' said Sergio. 'He gets upset easily.'

'I don't get it. I thought we were working together on this.'

'I think he'd like to. But he's scared of Moro. He won't admit it, but that's what it is. He frightens him.'

I couldn't think of anything else to say. 'I'm sorry,' I repeated.

Sergio waved at the barman. 'Come on. Let's have another bottle of wine.' He looked at me. 'You play *scopa*?'

'Not very well.'

They both cheered. 'Even better,' said the Prof, who started to deal.

I left a couple of hours later, light of head and emptier of pocket. I wondered if I should become a party member. And maybe, I thought, I had more than a few friends in this city after all. Yet, as I sat on the *vaporetto*, I remembered what Sergio had said. Magri was frightened of Arcangelo Moro. And, even though I had only met him for a couple of hours, I had to admit that he frightened me too.

Chapter 21

I crashed out on the sofa for perhaps fifteen minutes until Gramsci became bored with not being annoying, and jabbed at me until I agreed to give him some food. I wearily reached his box of kitty biscuits down from on top of the fridge, and measured out fifteen grammes into his bowl. He stared at me as if to say, 'Is that it?'

'That's it,' I said.

He continued to stare at me.

'Stare all you like. You know the rules. Fifteen g. now, and fifteen g. later if – and only if – you haven't destroyed anything in the meantime.'

We glared at each other like Lee van Cleef and Gian Maria Volonte at the end of *For a Few Dollars More*. Then I poured out some more food. He surveyed the contents of the bowl, gave a little yowl of triumph, and started to munch away.

I, evidently, was dismissed. I went back to the office and took a brief look through Paolo's files. There was work to be done, but I didn't feel up to it now. Whatever it was could wait until the morning. I'd call Federica and we could go through it together. In the meantime, I put the contents into a more robust canvas bag, opened the safe, and put in Montgomery's padded envelope as well. It made sense, I thought, to keep everything together.

The *acqua alta* alarm sounded again. Another four *plings*. Another very wet night in prospect. It seemed unlikely that I would receive another dinner invitation, so I wandered down to Rosa Rossa. A smile of recognition from the piratical-looking manager, who poured me my regular glass of house red as I waited for my takeaway. Then back home, where I ate it from the box, along with another couple of glasses of red, under the gaze of Gramsci, who evidently disapproved of my choice of toppings.

The telephone rang, and my heart gave a little leap. Federica, suggesting we do something? Dario, up for a beer? I looked at my mobile, and immediately felt sick with fear. An Edinburgh number. I considered not answering it, then I poured myself a large glass of courage with one hand, and pressed 'receive' with the other. It had been, what, two perhaps three days now? It had to be faced.

'Nat?'

'Hi.'

'How are you?'

'Fine.'

'You sound strange, are you all right?'

'Yeah, sorry. It's been a long day. My head's all over the place.'

'Important consular business?'

'That sort of thing. Yes.'

Silence for a minute, as unspoken questions hovered in the air.

'We haven't spoken for a long time. You haven't called for weeks now. You haven't even emailed.'

'Sorry, I should have. It's just things have been so busy here.'

'What things? What do you have to do? You can stay at home all day with the translating, and the consular work is, what, four hours a week?'

'It should be, yes. Look, there's something going on over here that I don't really understand. I had a guy come in the other day who gave me something to look after. I'm worried that it might be stolen property.'

'Well go to the police then. It's none of your business, is it?'

'I know it's not, but I seem to be getting dragged in.'

'Then don't. You're a consul. You fix up passports for people. You're not a, I don't know, private detective or anything.'

I rubbed my eyes and took a drink of wine. 'Okay, you're right. And yes, I should have called. I'm sorry.'

'Why do you hang up whenever I call?'

'It's never been the right time. I've always had people with me.' That, at least, was more or less the truth.

'I've emailed you as well. I even wrote to you.'

'Right. Ah well, I've had problems with the Internet. And, well, you remember what the post is like here.' A bare-faced lie this time.

I heard her taking a deep breath. 'Nat, there are things we need to talk about.'

I felt my heart start to race. My mouth was dry as I strove to keep my voice casual. 'Oh yes?'

'The university has offered me an extension on my contract. For another two years.' Again, a pause for breath. 'I think I should take it.'

I took another drink, but said nothing.

'So what are we going to do, Nat?'

'By "we", you mean "you", don't you?'

She sighed, as if trying to explain something to a particularly recalcitrant child. 'No, I mean what are we going to do? Us.'

There are those moments in a conversation in which each party realises that they are drifting inexorably towards a row, but feel unable to do anything to stop it. And sometimes the only thing to do is to accept it, embrace it. 'But you don't mean us. You've already decided. You're going to take your lovely university job. So what you mean is "What are you going to do, Nathan?"'

'Okay. If you prefer. What are you going to do?'

'What do you want me to do? Do you want me to come back to Edinburgh?'

'If that's what you want.'

'It doesn't matter what I want. Is it what you want?'

There was a short but significant pause. I pressed on. 'No answer?'

'No, Nathan.' She sounded tired now. 'No answer. I'm sorry.'

'Okay. Not what I wanted to hear, but at least it's an answer of sorts.'

'I'm sorry.'

'So you keep saying.' I could feel the bitterness, the bile, the sheer bloody misery rising in my voice.

'Nathan, if we can't sort this out we're going to have to talk about the flat. The one in Venice, I mean.'

'The one where I live, yes.'

'Look, I earn more money than you. A lot more, let's be honest. But I can't keep paying half the rent on that place indefinitely.'

'Ah, I see. Or at least I think I do. You don't want me to come back to Edinburgh, and, at the same time, you're going to make it damn near impossible for me to keep living in Venice. Have I got that right?'

'Nathan, are you drinking? Right now, I mean?' She was sounding on the verge of tears, but my sheer stubborn bloody pig-headedness, my urge to break something wouldn't let me pull back. Go on, Nathan, you're not the one at fault. You're not the one who walked out. You say what needs to be said.

'Yes. Modestly. But when I put this phone down I'm damn well going to start drinking immodestly.'

'Please don't do that. Please. Just go to bed. We can talk tomorrow. But it won't help if you get drunk.'

'Oh, I think it will.'

'Do what you have to do then. But the problem will still be there in the morning. And we will have to talk about it.' She paused. 'Do you still love me, Nathan?'

The question caught me unawares. I wanted to speak . . . *Of course I do, of course I do*. And then I realised that, this time, it was I who had no answer.

I don't know who was the first to hang up.

I breathed deeply, and forced myself to count to ten. I fought down the urge to punch the wall, or just to put my head in my hands and howl. I rubbed my face. What to do? Something self-destructive, sure, but perhaps not as self-destructive as all that. What did I have? Half a pizza remained. There was some beer in the fridge. A couple of bottles of wine. Some cheese and biscuits just in case I got hungry. A bachelor night in, with too much booze and comfort food. I'd need something to watch, as well. I went to the bookshelves. Maybe an old Bogart movie to start. *The Big Sleep*, perhaps? And then maybe *Casablanca* or something feelgood to take me through to the early hours. Or maybe it was an evening for something suitably nasty and Italian, and an old Dario Argento movie would suit my mood better.

It seemed I was now in the terminal stage of marriage. Within a few months I might even be homeless. But something would work itself out. It always did. Tonight, at least, I was in control. Except for one thing. There were no cigarettes in the house.

Proper smokers rarely run out of cigarettes. It is the curse of the occasional smoker that they often do. And one thing that the Italian smoker quickly learns is where and how to buy cigarettes out of hours. Only licensed *tabacchi* sell them which means that if you get the urge for 'just one' after seven p.m., you're out of luck. Unless, of course, you're in the Italian health system and have a *tessera sanitaria*, in which case you're in luck as long as you can find a vending machine.

I looked out of the window. It was raining gently, but the streets were flooded. I pulled on my wellies and a waterproof jacket, and went downstairs. I opened the door, stepped over the *paratia* (which was making a not entirely ineffective attempt at stopping the water ingress) and sloshed my way along the street. It was properly flooded in this section, well over a foot deep. I had learned to take my time when wading through *acqua alta*. Do it too quickly, and you risk creating waves which can cause an overspill into the tops of your boots, as well as really pissing other people off. I reached Calle della Mandola where *passerelle* had been set up, wooden platforms above the water level that allowed one to walk, for short stretches at least, in the dry.

Campo Manin was wet, but less flooded. I walked past the bank where I had met Maturi only a few days ago, and then into Campo San Luca, a seemingly impossible-to-avoid central point for any *passeggiata* through San Marco. There was a *tabacchi* with a vending machine, I knew, just off the *campo*.

I inserted my health card, and waited as the machine verified my age. I wondered if it was sending an automated email to my GP at the same time. Then I fed in five euros for a packet of twenty MS. *Morte Sicura* – 'certain death' – as they were nicknamed. They weren't great cigarettes, but I appreciated the joke.

I turned back through San Luca. A jazz band was playing in Bar Torino, and I thought about going in for a drink. I decided against it. I wasn't in the mood for the company of other people, and Bar Torino – its walls decorated with prints of fleshy Jack Vettriano nudes – had never really been my kind of place. I sloshed my way back through Manin, then on to the *passerelle*.

Then I turned into the Street of the Assassins, where four shadows waited for me.

Chapter 22

Four shadows?

I scarcely had time to register the anomaly before one of them moved. At first I thought he was holding one of those ridiculous selfie sticks that were sold on the bridges. Then a metal baton cracked across my knees and he was on me.

I didn't even have time to scream as pain shot through my legs. As I dropped to the ground he forced my head under the water, and pushed his knee into my groin. I lay sprawled in the alley, conscious only of the water seeping into my clothes and the pain in the lower part of my body; and desperate to draw in a breath.

Someone will come, I thought. Someone will be here soon. This sort of thing doesn't happen in Venice. He pushed my head further back under the water and held me there until I could hold my breath no longer. *I am going to drown. I am going to be found dead tomorrow, having drowned in the street.* He watched me draw in a lungful of filthy water, then dragged me upwards, spinning me round and allowing me to vomit it all up. Once again, he pushed me downwards, this time taking care to keep my mouth and nose just above the surface. He lowered his face closer and closer, until his nose was touching mine; and his knee worked its way ever more painfully into my crotch. He smiled, and then put his finger to his lips.

He dragged me to my feet, water sloshing out of my boots, and put his arm around my shoulders as if we were two old pals walking back from the pub. 'Easy now,' he said, and his voice had a light, pleasant German accent. He half-walked, half-dragged me to the door and I automatically fumbled in my sodden trouser pocket for the key. His grip tightened around me. 'Careful as we go.' My hands shook as the key turned in the lock, and the pain in my legs intensified as I barked my shin stumbling over the *paratia*. I reached for the light switch and, for the first time, saw the face of my assailant. Cropped blond hair, handsome, bright blue eyes. Something suitably Aryan about him to match the accent. He smiled.

'Best go upstairs, eh?'

Nobody lived downstairs. Nobody lived on the ground floor in Venice if they were in their right mind. The Brazilians were closed for the evening. I cursed the fact I hadn't been a better neighbour. Did I even have any neighbours? All I knew was that no one was coming. I unlocked the four bolts on the *porta blindata* as slowly as I could, trying to give myself time to think. Once that door was closed – a solid metal door sunk into stone – nobody, but nobody would be able to open it. If I could just gain myself a few seconds . . .

He had the same thought as me, and tightened his grip, painfully so this time. And then it struck me. I'd seen his face. I'd seen his face and he didn't care. He was going to kill me. I gave the key one last turn and the door opened. We paused for a second, and he applied the lightest of pressure to move me inside.

I read stories in the newspapers every day about another murder somewhere or other – in Italy, or the UK, it didn't matter. And sometimes I would wonder about the victim. Why hadn't they fought back? And of course, the answer was simple: they were frightened. *Perhaps if I don't fight back, perhaps if I can just talk to him, it'll be all right. If I try and fight, if I hurt him, he'll do something even more terrible. He can hurt me, properly hurt me. If I do nothing, just maybe he'll let me go.* And then the moment is gone. Too late for anything.

'The safe?' he said. I nodded. It was cemented into the wall and would have been nigh-on impossible to cart away. He released his grip, and made an encouraging 'hurry up' gesture. I dialled in the code, and opened the door. He waited for me to reach in.

'There's money in there. There is money. And passports. People will give you money for them. Just take them. But please leave me alone.'

He didn't move. Didn't even change expression. I reached inside. Picked up the canvas bag with the padded envelope and Magri's file. I handed it to him, unable to stop my hand from shaking. He took it from me, and nodded in acknowledgement. He turned it this way and that, as if weighing it up. Then he stopped, and nodded again, as if satisfied.

He reached inside his jacket pocket. *So this is it. He's going to kill me. He's really going to kill me.* You're supposed to see your entire life flashing before you, and all I could see were those moments when I could have done something. When I could have shouted, or tried to run or fight back. Perhaps every victim feels this way in their last moments, with the terrible realisation of how much power somebody who frightens you can hold.

He stepped back. Perhaps he didn't want to give me a chance at a desperate, last-minute lunge. Slowly, now. With almost infinite care. Slowing it down, just to prolong the moment, just to be cruel, just to scare me that much more. In the hope that I'd cry, or beg.

I was prepared for that. I didn't care about loss of dignity, I was ready to throw myself at his feet and beg him, beg him not to kill me. And then, from out of nowhere, came an unearthly, eldritch howl as if from the innermost circle of the Inferno. A scrabbling of claws, the tearing of fabric and a shriek of pain.

Gramsci. He'd stood on Gramsci. In the half-light I could see his sulphurous eyes blazing, as he sank his teeth and claws into the trouser leg of his tormentor, who kicked out furiously in the hope of shaking him off. As his body jerked, the bag flew from his hand and across the room.

There was, perhaps, just a second of opportunity. And a second of absolute clarity. *Do it now.* I grabbed the picture of Her Majesty, ripped it from the wall and brought it crashing down upon his head. There was another moment of fear. *My God, what if I've killed him?* I expected him to topple silently to the floor, but he appeared dazed only for a moment before beginning to struggle. The frame had settled around his shoulders and upper arms, and the more he moved, the more the wood splinters and broken glass cut into him. It must have hurt like hell.

Another second of clarity. I grabbed the bag. And, with only a moment of hesitation, I scooped up Gramsci, stuck him under my arm, and ran like hell. Down the stairs, into the street, along the *calle* under twelve inches of water. I had never imagined having to run for my life, and certainly not whilst wearing wellington boots and trying to control a spitting, clawing ball of fury. The flooding made it impossible to run, as in one of those dreams when you find yourself unable to move one foot in front of the other, and awake to find yourself kicking and thrashing against the weight of the bedsheets.

Think. Think clearly. It'll save your life. You're almost Venetian now, and maybe he isn't. Not down to Rialto, he'd be more likely to know the route. I checked my watch, and ran back the way, into Sant'Angelo and turned right into the Street of the Avvocati. The water would be deeper there, and slow him down as much as me. The water spilled over the tops of my boots adding to the weight and making it ever more difficult to run. I clutched Gramsci to my chest like a rugby ball. Then I was over the bridge and away to the pontoon for the *vaporetto*. All these years, living in the same *sestiere*, had left me with the departure times of each and every water bus from Sant'Angelo engraved upon my memory.

Please be there. Please be there. The boat was just pulling up to the pontoon, and I could have wept with joy. My lungs were aching and my hands stinging with pain from where Gramsci had clawed them. If I had had time to stop and think I might have noticed the agony in my legs. But I forced myself, chest bursting, for that last fifty metres and leapt aboard as the *marinaio* drew the gate shut.

Just a few more seconds of fear as my assailant pounded across the square, but the boat was too far away by now for him to attempt to jump, or for the captain to pull the boat back in sympathy for a late-night arrival. I could see him there, soaked and bloody under the street lights, as the boat pulled away. Gramsci was still struggling, but I felt confident enough now to tuck him under one arm and give a cheery wave. He stared back at me for a moment, then turned on his heels and ran back down the *campiello,* as fast as the high water would allow.

I squelched inside the cabin and slumped into a seat. I had perhaps three minutes' grace. The next stop was San Silvestro on the opposite side of the Grand Canal. He had, therefore, only two ways of catching up with me. Either run to Rialto and cut me off there – difficult, given the high water, but not impossible. Or go back to the Accademia Bridge and cross over there, but without any clear idea of where I was headed.

Three minutes. *Who to call, Nathan? Make this one count.* No choice of course. I took my mobile from my jacket pocket, thanked God it was still working, and jabbed at the 'favourites' list. It rang and rang and rang. *It's late now. They'll be asleep. It might even be switched off. Answer. Please answer.*

There was a crackle and a '*Pronto?*' at the other end of the line.

'Dario! Thank God!'

'I'm sorry, who is this?' The voice at the other end was thick with sleep.

'Dario, it's Nathan. I'm in trouble. Big trouble. I need help.'

'Sure pal, what's the problem? Just drop me an email or text me eh? It's a bit late now.'

'Dario, for the love of God, please don't hang up.'

He must have caught the desperation in my voice as he suddenly sounded more awake. 'Nathan. What's going on buddy?'

'I've been beaten up. I'm hurt. I don't know how badly.' True enough. As the adrenaline rush faded, the more the pain in my knees intensified. 'The guy who did it . . . I think he's following me. I need to get out of town, at least for tonight. Can you meet me at Piazzale Roma?'

'You're hurt? Do you need an ambulance? A doctor? Have you called the police?'

'Everything hurts but I don't think it's bad. And he'll be expecting me to go to the *Questura*. I'm on the Number two *vaporetto*. Can you meet me by the ticket office? I'll be there in maybe fifteen minutes.'

'Fifteen minutes? Christ, Nathan, I'll have to drive like a bastard.'

'Please do.' For the second time that night I could feel myself on the verge of tears. 'Whoever he is, I think he's going to follow me. I'm guessing he knows where I'm going. I think I'll have maybe ten minutes' grace before he arrives. And if you're not there in time, well, I think he'll kill me.'

I could hear movement at the other end of the line, 'I'll be there, Nathan.'

'Thank you. Thank you. Oh, and Dario?'

'Yes?'

'Could you bring a box for the cat please?'

I hung up, and slumped back in my chair. I held Gramsci out before me. 'We did it, old buddy! What a team we are, eh?'

He yowled and scrabbled his claws through the air, before I hugged him to me and bent my head over his, the better to hide my tears.

Chapter 23

'Did you have to bring him?' asked Dario, as Gramsci clawed and yowled from within a cardboard box on the back seat.

'I didn't know what else to do. I thought if they were left together they'd battle each other to the death, and I really didn't want that.'

We were halfway along the Ponte della Libertà to the mainland by now. I'd hopped off the boat at San Silvestro and ran as fast as I could up through San Polo and Santa Croce. I passed an agonising couple of minutes at Piazzale Roma, trying to get my breath back, to breathe normally, to ignore the pain in my legs and to stop the cat from struggling. Dario, of course, was there on time.

Mestre – grim, unloved Mestre – had never seemed so welcoming. Dario's partner, Valentina, had gone back to bed but had left a bottle of wine and some bread and cheese out for us. I took a shower to try and wash the stink of the lagoon off me. Dario gave me a change of clothes. I was aware they looked ridiculous on my frame, but no matter. It was good just to be warm again.

'Okay then. You going to tell me what this is all about?'

I took him through the whole story. He poured us a large glass of wine each.

'So why didn't you go to the police?'

'I thought he'd have guessed I'd do that. He'd be trying to cut me off.'

'Yeah, but why not just call them from the *vaporetto*?'

'Suppose I should have done. I just started thinking, what if I get in trouble here? Perhaps I've been handling stolen property – that sort of thing?'

'Yeah, but that's not your fault. You were just looking after a package for a client.'

'Dario, only a few days ago I spent a couple of hours in the *Questura* trying to get two daft kids off the hook for "looking after a package for a friend". And my fingerprints will be all over it by now.'

'Sure, but who cares? You're the honorary consul, not a silly kid.'

'I'd have to tell them about Victor. I can't do that to him. Give it a couple of days, maybe it'll blow over.'

'*Beh*. Maybe. Maybe not. Sleep on it, eh? And tomorrow go to the *Questura*.'

'Thanks. Really. I didn't know who else I could call.'

'It's no problem. Valentina's made you up a bed in the spare room. Sleep in tomorrow, you could do with it.'

I left the night light on in the spare room but awoke – how many hours later? – to find it was switched off. The only light came from under the door, a light that widened as the door opened, with the faintest of creaks. Perhaps that was what had woken me. A large silhouette filled the door frame. Dario, bless him, coming to check on me. I tried to speak his name, but my mouth felt thick and claggy, the taste of lagoon water still on my palate. I shifted, uneasily, sending shooting pains through my legs. Painkillers, aspirin even. That's what I needed. No wonder it was difficult to sleep. I tried to speak again, but the taste of foul water and vomit filled my mouth.

The figure came closer. Larger now. At his side hung a thin metal baton. I tried to raise my hands in protection, but the water pressure weighed them down as I felt myself sinking. A hand grabbed the sodden bedsheets around my neck and pushed me down, further down as the black water of the lagoon poured into my mouth. As I looked up, I could see the Rialto Bridge, this time from below and a face – Federica's – moving closer and closer to mine. She smiled, sadly. 'All this beauty. It was never enough. It never made you happy. Why didn't you go back home?' And I felt myself fall deeper and deeper, as the light faded above me. Into silence.

It was early, way too early, when I awoke to the sound of an argument. In my befuddled state I had difficulty in under-standing the machine-gun rattle of *Veneziano* but, Valentina, it seemed, was having the mother of all rows with Dario. I pushed myself upright, and swung my legs over the bed. Every part of my body hurt like toothache. My hands were badly scratched as expected. My knees had taken a bit of punish-ment. Badly bruised, but nothing seemed too serious. I took a tentative few steps. Yeah, it hurt but a few painkillers and it'd be bearable. It would be a while before I considered running the length of Venice in *acqua alta* again, though.

I struggled into Dario's clothes and made my way into the kitchen. The shouting stopped as soon as I entered. Valentina – tiny, spiky-haired and heavily pregnant – glared at me with-out saying a word, then pushed past me and left the room. Dario looked embarrassed.

I sat down at the kitchen table. 'Sorry. I guess this is my fault.'

He shook his head. 'No, it's not you. It's him.' He held up what might once have been a tablecloth, torn into ribbons.

'Gramsci? Oh Christ, I'm sorry. I'll replace it of course. As soon as Coin opens I'll go along and . . .'

'It's not so easy. This was a wedding present.'

'Ah.'

'From her grandmother. A christening gown. It was the most precious thing she ever gave Valentina.'

'Ah.'

'Her favourite grandmother.'

'Ah.'

'You know the Pink Floyd tablecloth? You imagine how I'd feel if your cat had destroyed my Pink Floyd tablecloth?'

I put my head in my hands.

'Well this is worse than that. A lot worse.'

I rubbed my face. 'Oh God.'

'Look Nathan. This isn't my idea, I don't want to do this. If it was up to me you could stay as long as you liked but . . .'

'But Valentina wants me to leave. Yeah, I understand.'

I put my head in my hands again. Gramsci padded over and prodded at my hair. 'That's sweet,' said Dario, 'he knows you're upset. He's trying to comfort you.'

'He's not, you know. He just wants feeding. If he doesn't get anything he'll jab harder and harder until he starts drawing blood. I don't suppose you've got any cat food?'

Dario shook his head.

I checked my watch. 'Okay. In that case I reckon I've got about forty-five minutes before he reaches critical mass. If I leave now I should just about be at home in time.'

'No time to waste then. We'd better go.'

'"*We?*"'

'Sure. You think I'm going to let you go home alone with all this shit going on? I'm coming to stay. I've got a bag packed and everything.'

I would have hugged him, but for the fear that he'd hug me back. 'Look. That's just . . . well that's just brilliant of you. But you can't do this, you've got Valentina and your job and you're going to be a dad within a couple of weeks . . .'

'I rang my boss this morning. Told him I had to take a few days off for family matters. He's not happy but he'll get over it. Valentina, well maybe it'll be good to be out of the house for a bit. Only a day or two. Let things blow over. It's going to be fine, really.'

'I don't know what to say. No, I do know what to say. Thank you.'

Gramsci jabbed at my cheek, more pointedly this time.

'We haven't got much time. We'd better leave.'

The front door was wide open, as was the *porta blindata* upstairs. This being Venice, nobody had paid a blind bit of notice to it. Dario walked into the apartment, and dropped his rucksack in the entrance. He whistled. 'Bastard did a good job on this place.' He walked over to the shattered picture frame. 'Even smashed up your picture of *sua Maestà*.'

'Yeah, that was me Dario, remember?'

'Lot of blood around.' He was right. The shards of glass and splintered wood were stained a rusty red-brown. 'Guy's going to be carrying some scars for a bit. If we want to find him, all we need to do is search Venice for someone with a face like a jigsaw.' He walked through to the kitchen. 'I'll make us some coffee.'

'Thanks. There's a Moka on the stove.'

I heard him unscrewing the lid, then, 'Christ, Nathan, when was this last cleaned?'

'Not sure. I don't think it was that long ago?'

'You've got things living in it! Jesus, this needs a good wash. And how many pizza boxes are here?'

'I don't know! What is this? "Guess Whose Crap Lifestyle"?'

'Rosa Rossa must be making a fortune from you.'

'Well, they do good pizzas. And they tell me they're thinking of giving me a loyalty card.'

He finished making the coffee and we sat in silence for a while.

'What's going on, *vecio*?' he said.

'Nothing. Nothing's going on. I could do without the scary Nazi assassin, but otherwise . . .'

'Come on. Be serious. Just for once. You used to cook all the time, now your kitchen is a disaster area. What's going on?'

I rubbed my eyes, which felt gritty and tired. 'Look. There was a time, when there were two of us. And it was fun to cook for two. She'd come home at the end of a long day, and I'd have spent hours working on dinner. Now there's just me. And it doesn't seem worth the effort any more.'

'Ah Nathan. What are we going to do, eh?' Then he jumped to his feet. 'I know what we're going to do. You're going to call that woman who definitely isn't your girlfriend and invite her over.' He checked his watch. 'I'm going to the Rialto Market to buy expensive fish. Then tonight, you're going to cook us all a feast. And then the three of us are going to solve the mystery!'

'Wait a minute, wait a minute. *I'm* going to cook us all a feast?'

'Sure. I'm a shit cook. I'll be back soon, okay? Best not to answer the door while I'm out.' And with that he was gone.

Chapter 24

'An eel. You got a bloody eel.'

'Typical Venetian dish. Great delicacy. It cost me a packet.'

The plastic bag in the sink shifted slightly. I gave Dario a hard stare. 'It's still alive, isn't it?'

He nodded. 'The guy said it would be best if it was absolutely fresh.'

'Right. You ever humanely killed an eel before?'

'No.'

'You know how it's done?'

'No.'

'Trust me, it's not easy. Okay, what else have you got?'

'A lot of shellfish. *Cozze, vongole, gamberi.*'

'Hmmm. We haven't got any stock. Not to worry, I can make some from the prawn shells; and the clams and mussels will generate enough juice on their own. Veg?'

He took out a bag. Onions, garlic, chilli, and a bunch of parsley. I took a look in the cupboard. There wasn't much there save a couple of tins of tomato, a bag of instant polenta and some risotto rice. It would do.

'Okay. I can do this. Bit out of practice maybe, but I can do this.'

'There's just one more thing,' said Dario. He passed me a small plastic bag. 'It's a present. I didn't have time to wrap it.'

I opened it up and took out a strip of black linen emblazoned with a skull and crossbones. 'Is this what I think it is?'

He nodded, happily. 'A bandana.'

'Why did you buy me a bandana, Dario?'

'You're the chef tonight. You've got to look the part. Like the guy in Rosa Rossa.'

'That's different, he's a friend of Johnny Depp's. Or he thinks he's Johnny Depp. Maybe he actually *is* Johnny Depp, I don't know. I'm not wearing that!'

'Oh yes you are.'

'I'm not.'

'We've got to change your mindset. Too many negative vibes. This is a start.'

I folded the bandana up and placed it back in the plastic bag. 'Dario, thanks. I appreciate the thought. But I'm not wearing it. And there is absolutely nothing you can do or say that will convince me otherwise.'

I checked my reflection in the bathroom mirror. I had to admit, it kind of suited me. I went back to the kitchen, took out a steel, and gave the knives a quick sharpen. Then I saw my reflection again in the polished surface of the refrigerator door. I stuck a knife in the wasteband of my apron at what I hoped was a suitably piratical angle, and put my hands on my hips. I nodded. A difficult look to carry off, perhaps, but I didn't look too bad at all.

'You've cheered up, eh? Nothing to do with your girlfriend coming round?'

'She's not my girlfriend Dario, and – technically at least – I still have a wife. I just happen to be in a good mood, that's all.'

'Christ knows why. Considering someone tried to kill you last night.'

'But I'm alive. I've got my friends on my side. And for the first time in my life I'm having an adventure.' I gave my biggest knife another quick shimmy against the steel. 'Let's go to work.'

I tipped the eel from the plastic bag and into the sink, where it slithered around half-heartedly. I brandished the knife.

Dario gave a nervous little cough. 'Tell you what, Nathan. I'm just in the way here. I'll let you get on with this, okay?' And he was gone, before I could ask him to lend a hand. I turned back to the eel. The eel, unfortunately, is not a creature blessed with plaintive, limpid blue eyes with which to stare at you. 'Sorry, old son,' I said, 'I'll make it quick . . .'

Half a kilo of prawns lay shelled. Tedious work, to be sure, but hopefully it would be worth it. The shells simmered away as I cleaned the mussels and clams, and chucked them into a pan along with a healthy slug of white wine. On another ring, chunks of eel were stewing in white wine and tomato sauce. I only had onions and garlic to play with for my *soffritto*, but it would be enough.

The doorbell rang. 'Shall I get it?' shouted Dario from the living room, where he found himself unable to choose between *Deep Purple In Rock* and the first Black Sabbath album.

'Aye. Just stick your head out the window first. If it's Fede, buzz her in. If it's the Nazi assassin, tell him I'm out.'

The door buzzed open a few seconds later. Federica put a bottle on the table, and gave me a hug.

'Are you okay?'

'Pretty much. A few bruises.'

'Okay. Now we're going to have a proper talk about this. After dinner. And certainly after you've removed' – she pointed to the bandana – '*that*.'

I did my best to sound pained. 'You don't like it?'

'Let's just say it takes a special kind of man of a certain age to carry off a look like that.'

'And I'm not special enough?'

She shook her head. 'Not in that way.'

I went back to the kitchen, and added the rice to the *soffritto*. I let the grains toast for a few minutes before adding a splash of Vermouth. In the meantime, I strained the prawn broth into a jug, discarded the shells, and poured the stock back into the same pan to start bubbling away. Then I turned to the other shellfish which were now cool enough to handle, and removed the shells. I added a few ladles of the cooking juices – any more than this and it risked becoming too salty – to the stock.

The Vermouth had now evaporated and I added a couple of ladles of stock. From now on, it would be straightforward. Just give it a good stir every now and then. I poured us all a glass of Prosecco and took them through to the living room. The doomy *diabolus in musica* of Black Sabbath echoed through the room. Federica did her best to smile. 'Do we really need this?'

I passed her her glass and bent to whisper in her ear. 'He's been a pal. Let him have this one. I'll stick some Bach on later.' I went back to the kitchen to give my risotto a good stir, and topped it up with more stock. Stir, drink Prosecco, talk with friends. Repeat until done. The best and easiest recipe in the world. I chopped some parsley and cubed some butter in readiness. I picked out some grains of rice with a fork and nibbled at them. A little too *al dente* still, but nearly there. I threw in the mussels, clams and prawns; added more stock, and gave everything a good stir. Then took a healthy glug of Prosecco.

I sampled a few more grains. Just about right. I turned off the heat, and beat in the cold butter. Then covered it and left it to stand. Not, perhaps, the healthiest way to finish the dish off, but the texture was never quite right if you didn't do it. And life was too short to eat virtuous *risotti*. After two minutes, I uncovered the dish, stirred in the parsley and dished up.

Dario pushed away his plate, and drained his glass. He smiled at Federica. 'See. I knew he could do it. We just needed to get him back in the game, that's all.'

Federica finished her last piece of eel, and nodded. 'He's right, Nathan, that really was very good. Mind you, I've never had *bisato in tecia* in April before.'

'Blame Dario, he did the shopping.'

'Worked though, didn't it?' said Dario. He shook me by the shoulder. 'Nathan's back!'

'More wine?' I proffered the bottle.

Dario nodded, but Federica placed her hand over her glass. 'In a minute. In the meantime we need to talk.'

I sighed. 'And we were having such a nice time.'

'I know. But it's got to be done. You were attacked last night. So what are you going to do?'

One thing about cooking is that it takes your mind off anything else. For ninety minutes or so, I'd managed to forget about it. 'Well now. It seems to me there are three choices. Number one, do nothing. Just wait in the hope that Montgomery will come back, pick up the package, and we'll never see him or it again. Two problems with that. Firstly, I don't know for sure that he's coming back. Secondly, just handing over the package might not be enough to stop the other interested party.

'Number two. Hand it all over to Moro. Problem being I don't trust him. More than that, I don't like him. I don't care if it's his property or not, I don't want him to have it. And he might also be indirectly responsible for murder, in which case we kind of have a moral duty to get him.

'Number three. We investigate. We find out what's going on.'

'Not much of a choice is it?' said Federica.

Dario nodded. 'Number three, then?'

I held up my hands. 'Well, actually there is a choice. You two don't have to get involved in this at all.'

Federica kicked me under the table, enough to get an 'Ow!' out of me, while Dario shook his head. 'I think we do, *vecio*.'

'*Beh*. I don't know what to say. But thanks.'

There was a slightly awkward silence. Federica broke it. 'Okay, let's talk about what I found today. I went along to see my friends at the Correr. I asked if there were any reports about missing works by Bellini. Specifically a small devotional book.'

'And . . .'

'Nothing. Nothing at all. Perhaps that's not surprising. If there had been a work by him stolen recently we'd have read about it in the papers. '

'Hmmm. Anything else?'

'Not much. There's a lot of doubt as to whether a second book even exists. There is a reference to a small private dealer in Florence who had one.'

'Had?'

'The owner's retired now, and his son took it over. It's not even a gallery any more, just "fine art supplies" and prints.'

'Now wait a minute. There was something I saw a couple of days ago. At the Cini library. There was a reference book, by a guy called Domenico Moro – Arcangelo's brother. It mentioned a private dealer in Florence who has – or had – a similar work.'

'Okay, well Moro's a fraud and a crook. But it doesn't mean he wasn't right about this one. So we should go and talk to the guy who runs the place now.'

'That's a start. Next thing is to look at Magri's file.' I took it out of the safe, and Dario and Federica stood behind me as I leafed through it. I fished the cassette tape out of the wallet. 'Dario, can you stick this on the stereo?'

He took it off me and bent to the hifi. 'Good thing you're an old man, Nathan. Not many people have tape players any more.' I gave him a withering look. He slipped the cassette in, clunked the window closed, and pressed play.

The first words were in Italian. 'My name is Paolo Magri and I am a journalist. The date is the twenty-sixth of May 2011 and I am in Barajevo in the city of Belgrado to talk with Adrijan Mihajlovic.' There was more. An introduction to the background of the case, and then Magri began to speak to the Serbian. At which point the language became incomprehensible.

Federica sighed. 'A shame. Perhaps Mr Mihajlovic had forgotten all the Italian he learned during his stay with us.'

'I don't even know what it is. What language do they speak there anyway? Serbo-Croat, isn't it?' I asked.

'So what can we do? Go to Serbia?'

'Oh yes. I can hardly think of a better idea than travelling to an unknown location in the middle of Belgrade in order to talk with a man who once beat someone to death with a sculpture.'

She shrugged. 'Okay. So find a translator.'

'Where do you find a translator for Serbo-Croat?'

'Oh I don't know, if only there was a nearby university with one of the finest language faculties in Europe.'

'Ca' Foscari?'

'Exactly.'

'Hmmm. It's a good idea. Trouble is we don't know what's on the tape. What if it's something we need to keep confidential?'

'It's just a risk you'll have to take. I can't think of a better solution. Well, there is. You go back and speak to Magri again. Presumably he understands what's on there. Or just try and convince him to get more involved.'

Dario coughed, gently. We turned to him, conscious that we'd not involved him in the conversation at all. 'You could ask me,' he said, with a slightly hurt expression on his face.

'You speak *Serbo-Croat?*' said an incredulous Federica.

'They just call it Serbian these days,' said Dario. 'You can guess why. There are other languages spoken there as well

– Romanian, Hungarian, Slovak. Also Albanian in Kosovo. But Serbian is what he's speaking.'

'Dario,' I said, 'how the hell do you know Serbian?'

'I was there for about three years. With the army, part of KFOR – the peacekeeping force, you know? Anyway, it was useful to learn a little. I've got some Albanian as well.'

'Wow. You're a man of hidden depths, Dario.'

The hurt expression returned to his face, but then he grinned. 'Well, it's not just progressive rock in *casa Dario* you know.'

'So what's he saying?' asked Federica.

'I'm not totally sure. He's speaking very fast. The quality isn't very good. He starts off talking about coming to Italy, looking for work, living as an *abusivo*. Give me a bit of time, let me listen to it once or twice, I can probably work it out. Either that or you go to Serbia.'

'Mmm. Do you think I ought to?' I asked.

He shook his head. 'I'll give it a good listen.' Then he checked his watch. 'Can I do it in the morning though?'

'Of course,' said Federica, 'it'll give you something to do while we're in Florence.'

'Oh, are we going to Florence?'

'Yes. It's only two hours away. The *Freccia Rossa* leaves from Santa Lucia at eight in the morning. That'll give us plenty of time there. To check out that gallery.'

'Why don't you just telephone?' asked Dario.

'*Beh*, where would the fun be in that?' She checked her watch. 'Early start then. So now I need to be heading home. I'll see you tomorrow, Nathan. Don't be late, okay?' She pulled her coat on, and kissed us both.

I closed the door behind her, making sure to lock every last bar of the *porta blindata*. Then I went back upstairs and poured us both another glass of wine. He regarded me over the brim of his glass, his eyes crinkling.

'What's that look for, Dario?'

'Nothing. I'm just happy that's all. My buddy's got a date.'

I thumped my glass down on the table with more force than was strictly necessary, the noise shocking Gramsci out of his sleep. He stretched, yawned and slunk from the room without giving us another look.

'It is not a date, okay? We're going to Florence to talk to some guy about a robbery. You're going to stay here and . . . and well, just keep things running. And when we get back, hopefully we'll have some sort of solution that will keep everybody happy and stop me being murdered in a horrible way. It is *not* a date. And even if it were, it would be the worst kind of date in the world. "Hey, let's go to Florence, it might stop me being killed".'

He waved his hands in mock surrender. Okay, okay. It's definitely not a date.' His voice changed and became more serious. 'But when this is over, *vecio*, what are you going to do?'

I poured myself another glass. 'I don't know Dario. I could go back to Edinburgh. I haven't lived there for five years, and I'm not sure if I have friends there any more or if they're just people I sort of know. But, yes, I could go back and try and make things work.'

'Is that what she wants?'

I shrugged. 'I honestly don't know.'

'Is that what you want?'

'I don't know that either.'

'You know what I think?'

'Tell me.'

'Stay here. Start over.'

'Mmm. But why?'

'Because if you go I'll have nobody to talk to about heavy metal.'

'You make a seductive argument.'

'I do, don't I? Okay, it's late. Let's just play a bit of *Wish You Were Here* and call it a night, eh?'

There was nothing to be said to that. I put the disc on, and turned the music up. Silence at first, and then David Gilmour's ethereal, bluesy tone emerged from the speakers; followed by that famous four-note arpeggio. I looked at the bottle. There was a glass left each. I topped us up, and we pushed our chairs back to listen.

'This song's about you, you know, Dario?'

His eyes were closed, and he opened them sleepily. 'You think?'

'Yeah. You're a crazy diamond all right.'

Chapter 25

I awoke, slowly and painfully, to the sound of Dario singing in the shower. It made a change, I supposed, from being clawed awake by the cat, although an off-key rendition of 'Child in Time' was not the way I would usually choose to start the day. I knocked on the door, just in time to stop him from attempting Ian Gillan's four minutes of screaming.

Mercifully, he stopped. 'Morning, Nathan.'

'Morning Dario. You going to be long in there?'

'Hope not. Shouldn't you be leaving now?'

'Now? What time is it?'

'It was seven when I got up.'

'Seven! Bloody hell, why didn't you wake me?'

'Ah, I thought you'd gone out already.'

I ran back to the bedroom to check my watch. 'It's seven fifteen! I've got to be on the bloody train at eight!'

'Oh. Sorry. Do you want to use the shower?'

'No time. Got to go.' I struggled into my trousers and searched for my least unpleasant shirt. I looked in the mirror. Hair askew, unshaven, I looked a state. Not the way I should look for a date. Which, of course, this was not.

I grabbed my jacket off the back of the door. Then I realised what day it was. Dario had started singing again. 'Dario, listen, this is important okay? I'm supposed to have a surgery from ten until twelve. So if anyone turns up, just say I can't be here today. If it's urgent, get their names and a phone number and tell them I'll call as soon as I can. If it's super-urgent give them my mobile number. Or call me yourself.'

'What counts as super-urgent?'

'Flight leaving tomorrow, no passport. Repatriation of body. Being under arrest. That's about it.'

'Okay. Anything else I'll deal with as best I can.'

'No! Don't do anything. Just leave it for me and work on the tape. Oh, and feed Gramsci.'

'When?'

'If he attacks you, he's hungry. Whatever you do, do not attempt to engage him in direct combat. See you later, right?'

'Have a good day.'

I slammed the door and ran for the *vaporetto* which I made with thirty seconds to spare. I ran my hands through my hair, trying to flatten it down, and rubbed my face. I looked around the cabin. The other passengers were reading newspapers, working away on tablets or talking on their cellphones. There were no rucksacks, wheelie bags or unfeasibly large suitcases to be seen. The morning commute. Most of them would be getting off at Ferrovia to head off to the bigger cities, or at Piazzale Roma to catch the bus over to Mestre. I stared out of the window at the Grand Canal. No gondolas as yet, and only a few taxis. An Alilaguna boat was ferrying a boatload of tourists to the airport. But most of the traffic comprised the large barges for delivery, or the refuse boats of Veritas.

At Rialto, two guys were unloading huge palettes of bottled water; the one in the boat throwing each one to his partner on the *fondamenta* who caught them unerringly, and seemingly without effort, as he stacked them at the side of the canal. This was the best time of day, I thought. Everyone going to work, and perhaps not even thinking how wonderful it was to start the journey by boat. Yeah. The best time of day. Then I caught my reflection in the window, and thought how much better it would be if I'd had a shave.

A Venetian friend had once described the area around the railway station as the casbah. On a busy summer's day, I could see what he meant, as illegal porters competed for business from the tourists emerging from the station, and crap merchants lined the *fondamenta* selling illegal or useless goods to the unwary. But at seven forty-five in the morning, most of the traffic consisted of people on their way to work. Federica stood at the top of the steps, searching me out in the crowd, and waved to me. Her expression changed as I drew closer, and she pushed me away as I tried to kiss her.

'What happened to you?'

'Sorry, I woke up late. Dario didn't wake me.'

'You look as if you slept in your clothes. Let me guess, you made a night of it after I left?'

'We finished the bottle and played some Pink Floyd, that was all,' I said, aggrieved.

'You might at least have had a shave. What's this guy going to think when I bring a homeless man along to speak to him?'

'All right, maybe I can scrub up a bit when we get to the station in Florence. Have we got tickets?'

'We have. You can pay me later. We need to step it out a bit, we've only got five minutes.'

Italians complain about the train service. I've never quite understood why. To me, they always seemed to run on time, they're relatively comfortable and not ridiculously priced. Yes, there was always the chance of a strike which might leave you high, dry and far from home, but on the whole I found them a delight to travel with. Italian friends found this impossible to understand. At least until they returned from holidays in the UK.

Federica settled into her seat, leant her face against the window, and closed her eyes. 'Goodnight, Nathan. Wake me up in Florence.'

'Wait a minute, don't we have lots of things to discuss?'

She opened one eye. 'What about?'

'About this guy we're going to meet. His Bellini. All that stuff.'

'Oh, all that stuff.' She yawned. 'I'm sure you've thought of everything. Goodnight.'

I hadn't brought anything to read. There hadn't been time to buy a newspaper. A sleep seemed as good a way as any to pass the time. I set my mobile phone to wake me up ten minutes before arrival; then closed my eyes, leant my head back and tried to think of something sensible that I could ask the man in Florence. It struck me that I didn't even know his name.

We arrived in Florence just after ten. Federica informed me that Gianluca Rossi had a small shop not far from the Piazza del Duomo and that I was going nowhere until I'd had a shave.

I bought a packet of disposable razors from a *farmacia* opposite the station, and scraped away as best I could in the station toilets.

'Better?'

She cocked her head to one side.

'Bearable.'

We set off. Florence was bright and sunny. There was still a chill in the air, but it felt good to be away from Venice and the all-encompassing feeling of damp.

'How's Dario this morning?'

'Oh he's fine. I've sort of left him in charge.'

'Really? Do you think the office will still be there when you get back?'

'Ah, don't underestimate him. He's a smart guy. He once rode a motorcycle along the Zattere, you know?'

'Just the person to leave in charge of a job requiring sensitivity and tact then.'

We walked in silence for a while. I had first come to Florence almost twenty years previously. I had never liked it as much as I thought I ought to. It was beautiful, yes. There was probably more great art per square metre than anywhere else on the planet. But, try as I might, I couldn't bring myself to love it. The streets felt crowded and choked with people. Everywhere there was the smell of petrol, the sound of *motorini* and the roar of traffic.

There were times, during *Carnevale* and the season for the great cruise ships, when Venice could feel swamped under the weight of visitors, but I'd become accustomed to that over the years. There were places where one just didn't go unless it was absolutely necessary. Piazza San Marco, during the daytime at least, was a no-go space for Venetians. Strada Nova, the great artery that funnelled the tourists from the station and down through Cannaregio, was also to be avoided if at all possible. The area around Rialto was nearly always hard work. Yet you got used to it. Stay away from those areas, and Venice was a pleasure to walk around. I had never found the same of Florence.

We stopped outside a small shop marked with a simple wooden sign that said 'Rossi'. The door was locked, but we could see someone moving inside. He stared at us for a moment, and then the intercom buzzed and the door clicked open.

The interior was dimly lit, the better to spare the paintings on the wall from the effect of direct sunlight. Dusty frames, in various states of repair, were propped all around and piled high on top of tables. On the wall facing the entrance, a selection of books lay open in a glass case; while a door led through into a back room.

I took a quick look around the art on the walls. Mainly reproductions of works in the Uffizi, together with some journeyman watercolours of the *duomo* and the other major sites. There were dozens of galleries like this in Venice, as there were, I presumed, in Florence. It didn't seem like the place in which one would discover a lost masterpiece of the Venetian Renaissance. The owner was a little bald-headed, bespectacled man, immaculate in cardigan, shirt and tie.

'*Signor* Rossi?' asked Federica.

'*Sì.*'

Federica made use of her title. 'I'm *dottoressa* Federica Ravagnan. I work in art restoration in Venice. This is my friend Mr Sutherland.' I nodded and smiled.

He looked a little wary as if wondering why a casual visitor should make a formal introduction. 'Gianluca Rossi. How can I help you?'

There was a brief pause, and then I became aware that Fede was staring at me in expectation. This, after all, was my adventure. 'If we're not mistaken, you have a work which may be by Giovanni Bellini. Could we talk to you about it?'

The wary look was replaced by one of suspicion. 'It's not for sale.'

'That's fine, we're not interested in buying it. I mean, we're not here to make you an offer.'

He shook his head. 'It wouldn't matter anyway.' Then he smiled, puffed up with happiness. 'I've sold it.'

I exchanged a glance with Federica. Sold it. That wasn't what we were expecting. Stolen, perhaps. Sold, no.

He looked at me, as if expecting more. 'Could you tell me about it?'

He shrugged. 'It was my father's. He bought it in the late 1940s. I forget the exact story. Some family, leaving for America, needing to raise cash. He never wanted to sell it. But now' – he waved his hands at the shop – 'well, some extra money was useful.'

'Of course. Is there anything else you can tell us? About its provenance?'

'*Beh*, my father always told me it was by the great Bellini. That's as much as I know. I'm no expert.'

I groped for the right words, trying to be diplomatic. 'But you do run a gallery?'

He laughed. 'It was my father's. He retired two years ago.'

I found it impossible not to look him up and down. However spry he may have been, Dad must have been of the age of Methuselah by the time he decided to call it a day. 'And so now the gallery is yours?' I continued.

'I wouldn't call it a gallery. Not any more. We just sell some art. Me, I used to work with wood. Most of these frames are mine. We probably make more money from framing than from selling paintings these days.'

I dragged him back to the original subject. 'So the book – you were saying you'd sold it?'

He nodded. 'Let me think. Perhaps two weeks ago, no more.'

'Could you tell me who you sold it to?'

He looked suspicious again. 'You're the second to ask me that.'

'The second?'

'The day I sold it. There was another man, just a few hours later. Are you from the police? I have copies of the invoice, the receipt, everything.'

'No, we're not police.' I rummaged in my backpack, took out Magri's file, and showed him the photograph of Montgomery. 'Can I just ask you if you've seen this man at any time over the last couple of weeks?'

He adjusted his spectacles, moving them to the end of his nose, and held the photo as far away as he possibly could. 'Sure I've seen him. He's the gentleman who bought it. The first time he came here was – let me think – maybe six months ago.'

'Six months?'

'About that. He was on holiday. One moment, I've got a card somewhere.' He opened a drawer and took out a stack of papers. Invoices mixed with receipts mixed with business cards. 'I must get this sorted, it's a *casino* at the moment.' He removed each individual invoice, and stacked them in a single pile. Then he repeated the process with receipts. He looked up at us. 'I'm sorry, I should maybe offer you a coffee?'

'A coffee? Yes, a coffee would be nice, thanks,' I said. Federica shook her head. I smiled at her. 'Not as if we're in a hurry, is it?'

'Come with me.' He led us through to a back room where a capsule-style coffee machine sat on top of a small refrigerator. 'This is the one George Clooney uses,' he said with a touch of pride. 'It's new. I spent some of the money from the book on it.'

'Splendid.'

'Now, I should have some coffee somewhere. Let me think. Ah yes.' He went back out into the main body of the shop, and returned with a cardboard box. He looked inside. 'Ah, just two left. We are lucky.' He clunked one into the top of the machine, and made to turn the handle before realising there were no cups. 'I had some plastic *bicchieri* here, I know.' He looked around, but every available surface seemed to be covered with prints. 'Hmmm.' He opened a cupboard supporting a perilous-looking stack of frames, and withdrew two large coffee mugs. He regarded the interiors with a touch of suspicion before deciding that they'd do. 'A bit large, perhaps, but no matter.'

He manoeuvred the first mug under the spout, and then paused as if struck by a thought. 'Sugar?'

'Sugar, yes please.'

His face fell. 'I don't think I have sugar. Maybe some *biscotti*?'

'That would be—Ow!' Federica discreetly trod on my foot, and smiled the sweetest of smiles at me. 'Actually, I think just black, no sugar will be fine. Really.'

He nodded, and turned the handle. Nothing happened. He looked puzzled, then rechecked the machine. 'Ah. Water. We need water.'

I returned Federica's smile. 'As I said. No hurry. All the time in the world.'

It wasn't a bad cup of coffee at all. It was always better in a Moka, I believed, but all in all George Clooney had chosen pretty well.

'*Allora*, what were we talking about?'

'The man who came to see the Bellini six months ago.'

He looked confused for a moment, then Federica waved Montgomery's photograph at him with slightly more emphasis than I thought necessary.

'Ah yes. Let me see.' He went through the pile of business cards, reading out the title on each one as if that would help to bring the image of each visitor to mind. 'And here we are!' He gave a little smile of triumph, and passed the card over to me.

'Sebastian Travers, Head of Valuations,' I read. Followed by the name of a prominent British auction house. I pointed again at the photograph. 'You're quite sure it was him?'

He nodded.

'And his name was Travers. Not Montgomery?'

'He said his name was Mr Travers. Like on the card. I don't understand, who is Mr Montgomery?'

I waved the question aside. 'What was he here for?'

'He said he was on holiday and that he was writing a book

about Bellini. He'd heard that we might have a work by him
– a little devotional book – and wondered if he could see it.
He came back every day for about a week to study it.'

'And what did he say?'

'He was certain it was the school of Bellini. Not his workshop, but his followers. I don't quite understand the difference, but I know it makes a great difference to its value.'

'Ah. That must have been a great disappointment.'

He nodded. 'A bit. My father always told me it was by the
great *Giambellino*. I think it would have broken his heart had
he known. Then Mr Travers returned just two weeks ago. He
was still interested in the book. It may not have been an original, he said, but it was still full of interest. He made a very
generous offer.' He rummaged around and brought out a
receipt which he showed me, his eyes twinkling with pleasure.

I looked at the figure scrawled on the receipt, and strove to
keep my expression neutral. I took the book from my pocket.
'*Signor* Rossi. Can you just tell me if this is the same book that
you sold to Mr Travers?'

He shrugged. 'Sure, it's the same' Then his expression
changed and he looked confused and upset for a moment. 'So
Mr Travers has now sold it to you?'

'No, no. Nothing like that. He just asked me to look after
it for him for a couple of days.'

His expression cleared. 'Ah, I see. Very good.' He smiled
again. 'The sad thing is, I think I could have sold it twice.
Later that same day I had another man also asking about it . . .
I don't remember his name . . . a handsome man, blond hair,
blue eyes . . . German or Austrian, he was.'

*   *   *

We walked aimlessly through the streets of Florence, heading away from the *duomo* in the hope of getting away from the crowds and giving us some space to think. I broke our silence. 'So let's think. What do we know? He thinks the book I've got is the same one as he sold. Can we take his word for that?'

Federica looked unconvinced. 'I'm not sure we can. He's no expert, as he said, and blind as a bat as well. They might all look the same to him.'

'Okay then. Now Maturi is certain that my copy is a fake. Not "school of", not "a copy of", but something made to resemble a work from centuries ago. Does that change anything?'

'It means *zio Giacomo* might be wrong. He only saw it for a couple of minutes after all.'

'Wow. Do you want to tell him that?'

'No. But I think he's wrong. I think that book is the real thing. Montgomery thinks it's genuine and I'm pretty sure Moro knows it too.'

We walked on in silence, again, and I found myself struggling to keep up with her as she started to step it out; her heels tic-taccing angrily across the cobblestones.

She suddenly stopped. 'Bastard,' she said, spitting the word out.

I couldn't help but agree. 'Bastard.'

'This guy – Montgomery or Travers or whatever the hell his name is – he knew what that book was. He knew what it was, and he screwed that little man for five thousand euros. He should be sitting on a fortune now, instead he's scraping away framing watercolours for tourists.'

She was properly angry now, and stepped out across the road without looking. I grabbed her arm to yank her back out of the way of a passing cyclist who tinkled his bell in admonishment. She shook my arm off and continued her way across the road.

'So what now?' she said.

'I don't know. What can we do? I don't even know if he's broken any laws.'

'Probably something about impersonation. Maybe fraud?'

'Maybe. But the evidence is pretty thin. Could we really make it stick?'

She shook her head. 'Probably not. So where are we?'

'Geographically?' I looked around. 'I have no idea, I haven't really been paying attention.'

'Not that. The problem.'

'We're not much further on. Montgomery has a book by Bellini, which he's conned an old man out of. So why was he so keen to foist it on to me?'

'He's looking to sell it on as quickly as possible and so he wants you to keep it safe for the time being. To keep it safe from other interested parties. Moro being one, the guy who attacked you being another.' She sounded tired. 'So what are we going to do now?'

'We could go back home. But what would be the point? Let's let Dario look after things back there and work on the tape. And in the meantime, I think we should go for an ice cream. There's a place one bridge down from the Ponte Vecchio that was good the last time I was here.'

I was half expecting her to say no, we had to return immediately, but she seemed happy enough. We went to a *gelateria* that I thought I remembered from years ago, and sat on the balustrade of the bridge across the river, breathing in petrol fumes and the warm spring air.

Federica licked away at a pale green ball of ice cream in a cone. 'What did you get?' I asked.

'Celery. When did you say you last came here?'

'1994.'

'Maybe it's changed hands.' She took another, thoughtful lick. 'You know it's not bad. I just can't get away from the fact that I'm eating a vegetable. How's yours? It looks like a ball of cement.'

She was right. A dark grey chilly mass sat atop my cone. 'Black sesame seeds. You know, it's actually pretty good if you can get over the colour.'

'Yeah. Grey food. Maybe this guy's just ahead of his time?'

We ate in silence for a while, then chucked our napkins into the nearest bin.

'Spritz?'

She shook her head. 'No. Once you get outside Venice everyone seems to consider it a cocktail. They cost a fortune down here.'

'*Beh*. Home then?'

She checked her watch. 'I suppose so. I don't know what we've really accomplished today.'

'We've proved Montgomery, or Travers, or whoever the hell he is, is a bastard. That's about it. We think he's probably a crook as well, but there's no evidence.'

'So maybe there's no mystery? Maybe it's all coincidence. He's bought something, perfectly legally, and he wants you to keep it safe for a few days'.

'No, that makes no sense. Doesn't explain me being beaten up. Doesn't explain Moro's interest. I think the three of them are competing for it, somehow. Remember, the gallery is mentioned in Domenico's book. It helps to explain how Arcangelo knew about it.'

I was thinking out loud now, but Federica took over. 'So they know there's a possible work by Bellini in a tiny, almost unknown gallery in Florence. They find out the original owner has died. It's not really a gallery any more. So Montgomery has the idea of posing as an authority from an auction house, spends a couple of weeks there before saying "Sorry, *Signor* Gianluca, but it's not an original work by the master. But as it's so pretty I'll give you five thousand euros for it anyway." No break-in, no robbery, nobody gets hurt.'

'And the German guy?'

'Working for himself, or more likely to be working for Moro. He doesn't strike me as the kind of man to get his hands dirty directly. *Mani pulite*, clean hands, you know? Only he's too late, the book has already gone. Which is good news for *Signor* Rossi, as he would probably have used more direct methods to get hold of it. Montgomery just needs you to keep it safe before selling it on, probably to someone in Venice.' She paused, and then a great smile illuminated her face. Then she grabbed me by the collar, pulled me towards her and kissed me full on the lips. 'I think we've solved it.'

I was stunned into silence, although I couldn't say if it was more from her theory than the kiss.

'You can speak if you like, Nathan.'

'Er, yes. It's a great theory.'

'No it's not, it's a brilliant theory.'

'Okay. So perhaps all I need to do is to take that package along to Moro, he'll be off my back, and everyone will be happy?'

'Apart from Montgomery. It is his property now, after all. And Moro might have you killed anyway.'

'Why would he do that?'

'He might be worried about how much you know. How much you've learned from Magri.'

'Oh.' My face fell.

'Try not to worry about it. In the meantime, I think we can spoil ourselves. Let's go and have an expensive Spritz.'

'Seven euros each, and you don't even get any crisps,' I grumbled.

'It's the view tax,' she replied. 'At least you get to look at the *duomo*. And besides, think how much we'd be paying in Piazza San Marco.'

'True.' I looked over towards Brunelleschi's masterwork and Giotto's elegant *campanile*. 'It's lovely. Yet I like it but I don't love it. I've always wondered why.'

'It's because you came here after Venice. It spoils you.'

'Yeah. It does. For all its faults, it spoils you. And that's why it would be hard to leave.'

'Do you think you might?'

'I don't know. I just don't know.'

A man with a bunch of sad-looking roses arrived, and stood by our table. We did our best to ignore him. He pushed one towards me. 'For the lady?'

'No thanks.'

He offered it to Federica. She shook her head. He placed it on the table, and stood there in anticipation, looking from one of us to the other. I turned back to Federica. 'As I said, I don't know.' I waited, expectantly.

'Do you want me to say "don't go", Nathan?'

I opened my mouth to speak, but the words would not come.

'Because I'm not going to say that. You have to decide. It has to be up to you.'

My mouth was dry, and I reached for my Spritz.

'I think you should stay,' said the man with the roses. I'd forgotten he was there.

'You don't understand. My wife is in the UK. We've been married for ten years. It's a lot to give up.'

'Could she come and live here?'

'We tried that. It didn't work. She never felt at home here.'

'But you do?'

I nodded.

'Would you be happy back in England?'

'Scotland.'

'Scotland, sorry. Would you be happy back there?'

'I don't know. Maybe. But I would miss being here.'

He shook his head, sadly. 'Then you have to stay here. If your wife comes here, she will not be happy. If you go to Scotland, there is a chance you will not be happy. In which case you will blame your wife. I think you must stay here.'

'But that's ten years of my life I'm giving up on!'

'No. You're not giving up. I think you have tried your best. But sometimes people grow apart, and you must decide if it is right for you to move on.'

'You're right, and I have thought of that and . . . excuse me, but why am I telling you all this?'

He shrugged. 'We have to talk about these things. It's important.' He made the lightest of gestures towards the rose. I sighed and passed him a euro, but he showed no signs of moving.

'I really only want one.'

He shook his head. 'One euro for the rose, and five euros for the advice.'

'Six euros!'

'It's a good deal. Look, I can make it five euros in total. That's the best I can do. Margins are very tight.'

I looked at Federica. 'I don't suppose you've got . . .'

'Don't even think about it!'

I took a five euro bill from my wallet and gave it to him.

'Thank you sir, madam. Have a lovely afternoon. And think about what I said.' He moved on to the next table.

I finished my Spritz. 'So. I've just been mugged by a man with a rose.'

Federica burst out laughing, and took out a handkerchief to wipe some tears away. Then she took another sip of her drink.

'Don't go,' she said.

The journey back was uneventful. Federica slept most of the way. Only Gramsci seemed able to compete with her unlimited capacity for sleep. I supposed that was the side effect of a job that required her to spend long hours on top of scaffolding. I bought a half bottle of Prosecco and a *tramezzino* from the bar, and made a phone call to the *Guardia di Finanza*. *Maresciallo* Adriatico seemed uninterested at first, but then I mentioned Paolo Magri and he agreed to meet me in Mestre the next day.

I took my drink back to my seat, and tried to think of something else in an attempt to clear my mind. Within a couple of days, one way or the other, this whole business would be finished and I would need to start thinking about the future again. I remembered my last, short, visit back to the UK. I'd lived for less than a year in Edinburgh, and it seemed grey in comparison to Italy. Still, there were people I sort of knew there, people who I might consider to be friends. And maybe, just maybe, if I went back the two of us would be able to make things work. But if we couldn't, would I suddenly find that my friends were not really mine at all, but hers, and find myself adrift in a city I hardly knew?

Yet what if I stayed? The people I knew best in Venice tended to be those who served me drinks. I had a paid job that I didn't like very much, and an unpaid one that I didn't like much more. Dario lived out in Mestre and was soon going to be a father. It wasn't going to be so easy to meet up for a casual beer on the off-chance any more. I looked across at Federica, gently snoring away, her face resting against the window. There was, of course, her. But I had no idea where we were going.

I must have fallen asleep, and woke up just outside Mestre. Only five minutes now until we arrived back at Santa Lucia. I gave Fede a gentle shake, and she opened one eye and stretched sleepily.

'Good sleep?' I asked.

'All sleeps are good.' She noticed my empty bottle. 'You might have woken me up if you were going to have a drink.'

'Didn't like to. You looked so peaceful.'

We alighted at the station and made our way towards the exit, through the throng of late-afternoon commuter traffic.

'Well now.'

'Well now. What are we doing?'

'I'd better go back to the Lido. I really need to do some work tomorrow. Are you walking?'

The weather was brighter now. It was going to be a clear evening, and no *acqua alta* had been predicted. 'It's a pleasant day. It might be nice to stroll down. But I'm tired. I think I'll take the *vaporetto*.'

'Okay. Let's both get the Number One then.'

We walked down the steps outside the station, along to the Ferrovia stop. Just as we got there I noticed a man descending the steps of the Scalzi Bridge, a small dog in his arms.

'Just a moment. There's someone I know. I'll just go and say hello.' She nodded, and I ran over to the foot of the bridge. I gave a cheery wave and opened my mouth to speak when I realised, to my surprise, that it wasn't Gheorghe.

He put the dog down, a miniature dachshund in a sparkly little coat, and exchanged a smile and some words with its owner, a burly, bald-headed man in a leather jacket. The predilection of tough-looking men for small, camp dogs was something I'd always found peculiarly Venetian. If nothing else, I admired their sense of security.

The dog handler waved to his client, and then turned to me with a quizzical expression. 'Can I help you?'

'I'm sorry. I thought you were someone else. Do you know Gheorghe? The Romanian guy, usually works around the Accademia Bridge?'

His eyes lit up with recognition. '*Sì. Signor Gheorghe*. My boss!'

'Your boss?'

'*Sì*. He's running a franchise now. There are four of us. Gheorghe does the Accademia route. The rest of us cover the Rialto, the Calatrava and the Scalzi.'

'So this is your regular one?'

'Yes. I was lucky. The Rialto is too busy. And nobody really wants the Calatrava Bridge. Too easy to miss your footing and hurt yourself. But this is a good route. I'm very pleased.' He looked me up and down, as if wondering if I might be concealing a dog about my person. 'You don't have one?'

'Sorry. I'm a cat person. Although I sometimes wonder why.'

'No matter. We're thinking of expanding into cats. It's a niche market, but Gheorghe thinks there might be opportunities there. Bring it along sometime.'

I shuddered at the thought. 'Trust me. I wouldn't do that to you.' He seemed puzzled by this, and looked around as if eager to get back to work. From the corner of my eye I could see the Number One *vaporetto* approaching. Time to be gone. I shook his hand and wished him well.

'So what are you doing tonight?' I asked Federica.

'Working, probably. There's a lot of documentation I need to produce for the San Nicolò project. Maybe I'll grab a pizza. How about you?'

'Don't know. I'll see what Dario wants to do, but I'll probably cook something. It'd be good to get back into the habit.'

'I hope Dario realises how lucky he is.'

'He is a lucky man. I think we make a handsome couple.'

'You do indeed. Well let me know if anything interesting's happened.'

We were pulling into Sant'Angelo by now, so I kissed her goodnight and made my way to the exit. It was dark now, and my eyes darted this way and that as I made my way through the narrow streets that led to the Calle dei Avvocati, in the fear of encountering a shadow where none should be. Then I was into the brightly lit Campo Sant'Angelo, and Calle della Mandola, mercifully busy at this time of night.

The Magical Brazilian was doing good business. A few tourists sat outside, braving the early spring chill. The inside looked welcoming and warm, and Eduardo gave me a wave as he saw me passing. Maybe I'd just throw some pasta on whilst Dario told me what he'd found, and then we could go down together for a couple of drinks.

My key turned in the lock, and Dario was there to greet me at the top of the stairs as I pushed the door open. He looked extremely pleased with himself. Gramsci padded up alongside him, and stared down at me, meowing in reproach.

'A good day, by the looks of things,' I said.

He grinned. 'Come and see.'

I walked upstairs into the living room. There was nothing unusual to be seen.

'Not here. In the office. *Viene!*'

He opened the door and waved me through, flamboyantly.

There, securely tied to a chair, was the bound and gagged figure of Montgomery.

Chapter 26

He stared at me in righteous, but inevitably silent, fury. I flashed him my most dazzling, diplomatic smile. 'Just one second please, Mr Montgomery,' and closed the door. An irate 'Mmph' came from inside.

I rested my head against the door, gathering my thoughts. Then I turned to Dario. He was still grinning away.

'So. What do you think?'

'Mmm. Let me see. In the office we have a man bound and tied to a chair . . .'

He nodded, puppy-like. 'And gagged.'

'And gagged, thank you, I'd forgotten that. A man bound, gagged and tied to a chair. A British citizen, who came to a British consulate for help, who you . . . It was you, wasn't it Dario?'

'It was.'

'Who you, Dario, have attacked, bound, gagged, and tied to a chair. Have I missed anything?'

He shook his head.

'So what was he doing here?'

'He just turned up. I think he was expecting to see you. I thought it would be good to stop him leaving. So we could talk to him.'

'Okay.' I ran my hands through my hair. 'So when I left this morning, I told you just to let people know that I wasn't here. And if there was anything important or an emergency, just to call me. Now this' – I pointed at the door – 'is kind of important, isn't it?'

'Sorry. I thought it would be difficult to explain on the phone.'

I closed my eyes and leaned back, resting my head against the door; finding its solidity comforting. 'You know, Dario, it's very, very hard to lose one's job as honorary consul. And yet, I think you might actually have found a way.'

I turned back to the door, and rested my hand on the handle. He grabbed my arm before I could open it. 'Wait a minute, we need to talk about what we're going to do.'

'What are we going to do?' I hissed, trying to keep my voice low. 'We're going to let him go and then plead with him not to go to the police.' I made to open the door again but, once more, his hand grabbed mine.

'No we're not. We're going to talk to him. We're going to talk about what he knows. And then he can go to the police, if he's got the balls.' He was serious now, not joking around in his usual Dario way.

I opened my mouth, ready to slap him down but something in his eyes stopped me. I took a deep breath, and nodded. 'Okay. Let's do it.'

We entered the office, and I closed the door behind us. I walked over to Montgomery, and squatted down, trying to project more confidence than I was actually feeling. 'Right then, Mr Montgomery. I'm going to remove the gag now. Then I'm going to untie you. And then we're going to have a little chat. Okay?'

He did nothing but stare at me. To be fair, there was little else he could do. I removed the gag, then went and sat down on the edge of the desk. I wasn't quite sure what to expect. Would he scream for help, or restrain himself to shouting, swearing and threatening me?

He broke the silence. 'Well now . . .'

'Well now. Do you want a glass of water? Maybe a coffee?'

'Coffee would be nice, thanks.'

Dario shook his head. 'Hot coffee. He could use it as a weapon.'

'He's not going to bloody use it as a weapon, Dario.'

'No? Look what I found in his pocket.' He reached into his jacket and tossed something on to the table. It landed with a clatter, and I took a closer look. A flick knife. I looked from Dario to Montgomery and then back again.

'Okay. He's probably not going to use it as a weapon. Just go and make us three cups, eh? One of us needs to stay here.' He looked hurt, but went off.

'Friend of yours?' asked Montgomery.

I nodded.

'Good. I was hoping he wasn't staff.'

'Are you hurt at all?'

'No, no. Please don't worry. He was very . . . *professional* . . . about the whole thing.'

'Good. Good.'

We sat in awkward silence for a while. 'You said something about untying me?'

I slapped my forehead. 'Completely forgot. Excuse me, it's been a long day. I'll do it now.'

I worried away without success at the knots. 'Sorry, we'll have to wait for Dario. He's more the professional at this sort of thing.'

'Evidently.'

I picked up the knife. 'Switchblade, Mr Montgomery?'

'Protection.'

'In Venice?'

He grinned. 'Not spent much time in Naples, have you?'

Dario returned with three cups of coffee on a tray. 'Could you perhaps untie Mr Montgomery Dario? If it's not too much trouble.'

He was less than impressed, I could tell, but he hunched down behind the chair and our guest was free in seconds. He stood up, slowly, whether from necessity or from the desire not to spook Dario into doing something stupid. He rubbed his wrists and flexed his fingers; and glanced at the coffee. 'May I?'

'Of course.' I passed him a bowl of sugar sachets, but he waved them away.

'No thanks. Gave up sugar years ago.'

'Well done you. I couldn't do it. At least, not with coffee.'

'Ah well, it's difficult at first, but – trust me – you soon feel the benefit.'

Dario looked from one of us to the other like a spectator at a tennis match. 'Is this the way they do things in Britain?'

I poured sugar into my coffee. 'It certainly is. We start with formalities, and then move on to "so what do we do now?"' I stirred my coffee. 'So, Mr Montgomery, what do we do now?'

He smiled, with his eyes as well this time. 'Well, I think this is the moment in which I finish my coffee and then go straight to the police.'

'Ah. In which case this is also the moment in which I remind you that you are a criminal and, as such, would not dare to go to the police.'

'Even if I were, even criminals have their rights.'

'True. But you won't go. You'd risk losing too much money.'

'What money would that be?'

'The money you're going to be paid for stealing a small prayer book by Giovanni Bellini.'

'I've stolen nothing. That book was honestly paid for. I have a receipt.'

'You paid a fraction of what it's worth, conning an elderly man out of his inheritance.'

He shrugged. 'Sharp business practice, maybe. Not a crime. Now, let's move on. You still have that package I gave you?'

'The one you tricked me into collecting, you mean?'

'If you prefer. You have it safe?'

'Against the odds, yes. Someone has tried to kill me for it, you know.'

'So I'd heard. I'm sorry about that.'

'Would you like it back?'

'Not just yet. I'm just here to check that it's safe. I'll be back to collect it tomorrow. Sometime after eleven p.m., if that's all right?'

'Then I'm going to have to disappoint you. I'm not going to give it back to you.'

'Well in that case I have no other option than to go to the police.'

I stirred my coffee, and placed my spoon down in the saucer. 'Of course. I understand.' I looked over at Dario. 'Could you pass me the phone? Mr Montgomery needs to make an important call.' He went through to the living room to pick up my mobile, and then set it down next to Montgomery. I could tell he knew what I was doing. I gestured towards the phone. 'Please. The least I can do is pay for the call.'

Montgomery's face remained impassive, yet there was a look in his eyes. Perhaps just the tiniest element of respect. He made no move.

'Go on,' I continued, 'call the police. Get your property back. Sell it to whoever the hell you like, collect your damn money and be out of here. And then my life can start getting back to normal. All you have to do is pick up the phone and call the police.'

He tensed in his seat and then sat back, composing himself. He looked me up and down, as if wondering exactly what he should tell me. Then he reached for his coffee, gathering his thoughts.

'He won't call.' The voice was Dario's. 'He won't call. Perhaps it breaks the rules of the game? Is that right, my friend?' He twirled the cassette tape around in his fingers.

'Dario? What are you on about?'

'The rules of the game, *vecio*. He knows what I mean. Let's have a listen, eh?'

Chapter 27

Dario brought through the cassette player from the living room. 'It's a bit long, so if anyone needs a drink, best to let me know now, okay?'

Montgomery rubbed his temples. 'You know, I think maybe a whisky would be good?'

Dario looked at me. I shook my head. 'Grappa's the best I can do.'

Montgomery looked disappointed.

'Trust me, you acquire a taste for it after a while.'

'Grappa it must be then,' he sighed.

Dario returned with three glasses, and placed the bottle on a coffee table between us. 'Everybody ready?' We nodded, a little surprised by our deference to this new Dario, and he clunked in the cassette.

'My name is Paolo Magri and I am a journalist. The date is the twenty-sixth of May 2011 and I am in Barajevo in the city of Belgrado to talk with Adrijan Mihajlovic. Can you confirm your name to me?'

The language switched to Serbian, following which Magri's voice cut in again.

'He says his name is Adrian Bratislav Mihaijlovic. He was born in Belgrade, in 1977.'

Dario continued translating, as the Serb started to speak.

'I came to Italy in 2005. People think that everyone from our country must be a refugee from the war. Not so. Everything was fine in Belgrade. I was just poor, that's all. I was a mechanic, a car mechanic. I thought there would be work in Italy. I had a wife back in Serbia. I thought I could send some money home.

'It didn't work. Life was difficult. It was hard to get work. In fact, there was no work. Try saying to an Italian, "I am a mechanic, I can fix your car. Oh, by the way, I am from Belgrade." It didn't happen. Imagine you are in Serbia. Someone says they are a mechanic, but they are from Finland and they don't speak your language. Same problem.

'I ended up in Bologna. There was some work. I washed plates. I cleaned apartments. I looked after old people. You Italians, you love your families so much. You love your old people so much you will pay for East Europeans and Asians to come and look after them.

'And one day, I finished work. I went to a bar, it was mainly Serbs, Ukrainians, Romanians who hung out there. It stayed open twenty-four hours a day, because they knew there would always be somebody needing a beer, no matter what time. Anyway, I was there, it was maybe eleven or so. And in came this guy. He was tall, blond haired. Blue eyed. Looked kind of Aryan. He had an accent, maybe German, Austrian, I'm not sure.'

'Whooah there,' I cried, 'stop the tape!'

Dario punched the button and the tape stopped with a satisfyingly old-fashioned kerchunk. He looked over at me.

'German accent, blond, blue eyed. It might be the guy who attacked me. The same guy who turned up at the gallery in Florence a few hours after Montgomery had left.'

Montgomery looked unimpressed. 'Germany isn't short of blond-haired, blue-eyed people. By the way, I don't suppose I could smoke?'

'Well supposed. Carry on, Dario.'

The tape continued. 'He said he could offer me work. One job at first, and then maybe more to follow.'

Magri's voice was heard again. 'And this job was a robbery?'

'Yes. You understand, it was a lot of money. More than I'd earn in a month of cleaning up old people.'

'So you agreed?'

'I agreed. He showed me a picture. All I had to do was steal this sculpture. He showed me a picture of the man who he said was the owner. He was rich, he said. He lived in a big house. I was to steal one sculpture, so what? He had many more, he would still be rich. It would be a crime with no victims.

'There was one strange thing. When I had the work, I was to wait to deliver it. I was to take it to an address in Venice on the seventeenth of April. Not before, not after. It had to be on the seventeenth or I would receive nothing.'

'Do you know why this was?' asked Magri.

'I don't know. I was just told it was "one of the rules of the game".'

I interjected, 'Dario, pause the tape please!'

He stopped the player. Montgomery had taken out a small silver case and was tapping a cigarette on it. I stared at him, challenging him. He acknowledged my gaze, then took out a Dunhill lighter and lit up.

'He said "the game". Dario, you mentioned that earlier. What does it mean?'

'Listen on, *vecio.*'

I looked back at Montgomery, nonchalantly puffing away. 'You know what this means of course?' He gave a half nod.

Dario restarted the tape. 'You understand this. I had never stolen. Not since I arrived in Italy. I had never stolen.'

'Then why do you think he chose you?'

'I think there were two reasons. At first, I thought it was because he wanted someone who was not stupid. He wanted someone who would recognise the sculpture, who would treat it with respect, who would not destroy things or cause trouble. Now, I think it is because he likes to play games. To use people.'

'Tell me about the events of that night.'

'The house was old, and on the outskirts of Bologna. I had no car, not even a *motorino* so if I was going to rob somewhere, it was going to have to be by bus. The day before, I went to check the place out. It didn't look difficult. I could get the bus there, take ten minutes for the job, and then get the next one back. Easy. And so, that night I took an old sports bag with my tools and travelled out there . . .

'If I close my eyes, I can see everything as if it were happening now. There is an iron gate leading to a gravel drive, but it isn't locked and it just swings open. I make my way across the garden. There are windows on the ground-floor level, but they are not fastened. I am able to push them up from the outside. Then I am inside. It is a living room, with nice furniture; it smells of stale cigar smoke. There are paintings hanging on the walls. I don't recognise them – never known much about art – but I recognise the piece I've been shown. Medardo Rosso, he told me the name was. I've never heard of him, but I can tell it is special. It's of a child, maybe a sick child. It's in a case, fastened to the wall, but I've got a screwdriver and I get to work.

'I unscrew the cover and lift it off silently. I remove the sculpture. I weigh it in my hands. It feels heavy, maybe it's made of bronze. I wrap it in cloth so that my tools will not scratch it, and place it in my bag.

'Then I hear steps approaching. I don't know if it's my fault. Maybe I've made a noise, maybe whoever it is is just doing an evening round of the house. I panic. I try and drive the screws back in, but I drop the screwdriver. There is no time to get out so I run and hide behind a curtain.

'The old man comes in. He looks around, everything seems fine. Then he sees the screwdriver. He picks it up. He looks at the case. He sees the screws have been extracted. He sees the case is empty. He stiffens, looks around. He walks backwards, looking in my direction all the time. There's a telephone on the table.

'If he makes that call I will be arrested. I will be deported. I will be sent back to Serbia with nothing. I have tools in the sports bag. Things I thought I might need. I reach inside, I'm reaching for a spanner or something. He picks up the receiver and starts to dial.

'I run at him. I have the heaviest thing in the bag in my hands, the sculpture. I strike him across the head. He screams, and falls to the ground. He's still moving, grabbing at me. I hit him again. He screams once more. I hit him again and again and again. I don't want to kill him. I just want him to stop screaming.

'And then he stops. He isn't moving any more. I stand up and wipe my hand across my face, and realise it is covered in blood. There are further sounds, from upstairs this time. I run, back through the window and across the garden. Through the gates. The street is dimly lit, there are only a few lights, and no traffic. I know I am covered in blood. I cannot get on a bus. So I run, along the road, back towards the centre of town.

'The police stop me, perhaps ten minutes later. They drive me to the *Questura*. I am crying. I am a murderer. And nothing now can ever be good or right again.'

There was silence on the tape at this point, save for the sound of gentle sobbing.

Dario stopped the machine, and glared at Montgomery. 'You bastard.'

He stubbed his cigarette out in his coffee cup. 'I'm sorry, but I'm failing to see what this has to do with me.'

'Yeah sure, you had nothing to do with it, right?'

'Nothing at all. Strangely enough, I've never, ever thought of beating someone to a bloody pulp with a sculpture.' He lit another cigarette and continued to smoke as he spoke, his voice gentle and controlled, his eyes fixed on Dario the whole time. 'Terrible story, though, isn't it? The good man who makes a mistake and ruins his life. Could almost be a Greek tragedy, couldn't it?'

I saw Dario starting to rise from his chair, and just about managed to drag him back down. Montgomery remained impassive throughout.

'Leave it, Dario, please. This won't help.'

'This bastard destroyed his life. He destroyed two lives.'

'Maybe he did. We don't know for sure. Please, just sit down. Let's hear the rest of the tape.'

He took a deep breath, and moved back to the tape machine. There was a pause of a couple of minutes, as Mihaijlovic pulled himself together. Magri then took up the story.

'When you were taken to the *Questura*, you were assigned a lawyer. Do you remember his name?' There was a pause. Magri continued, 'Did you tell him everything?'

'I did.'

'You told him that you had been employed to steal a work of art. You told him that you had to deliver it to Palazzo Moro on the seventeenth of April. Did you tell him these things?'

'I did.'

'Were these things mentioned during your trial?'

'No. The *avvocato* told me I would not be believed, that it would make more trouble. They would think I was lying. Better to make a plea bargain, and then I might avoid a life sentence.'

'And what happened?'

'I received a sentence of twenty years. Then, two years later, they told me I had a visitor. You understand, I had had no visitors in all this time. Not even my wife. The visitor was you, of course.'

'And what did we talk about?'

'You told me if I told you the complete truth, then maybe there would be the chance of a retrial, maybe of a lighter sentence. That there was a man you suspected of a series of art thefts throughout Europe, and that it might have been the same man. So I told you what I told the *avvocato*.'

'And what else?'

'I told you about the game. The two brothers. They play out some sort of game every year. They steal something. Not by themselves of course. They employ others. There seem to be rules, I don't understand what.'

'What happened after that?'

'A few weeks later – I forget exactly – I received another visitor. An old man, this time. This time we met in a private room, with no guards. I didn't think this was normal.'

'Can you describe him?'

'He was old, thin. He had grey, curly hair. Well-dressed. He carried a walking stick, but he looked fit and active. He told me he was sorry, so sorry for what had happened. There had been a terrible misunderstanding. Bad things were being written about him. I had to understand that he could not possibly bear any responsibility for the things that had happened. If I denied the things I had said to the reporter, if I went back on my statement, then he promised he could help me.'

'And if you didn't?'

'If I didn't, he said he could still hurt me. Even though I was in prison, he could still reach me. He took two photographs from his jacket pocket. One of them was of my wife. The other was of my daughter. I had not seen my daughter since she was a baby. I started to cry. He put his hand on my arm. Do not distress yourself, he said. He would leave me the photographs so I had something to remember. Something to think about.'

'What next?' Magri's voice was tight now.

'The next day I demanded to see an *avvocato*. I told him I had lied to the reporter, he had made me stupid promises and so I made up this ridiculous story.'

'How did you get this *avvocato*?'

'The old man told me he would pay for one. So, I told him I had lied. He smiled, and said it was the right thing to do. It would help me. Some months passed. Then one morning, I was told I was being released. I was taken from the cells, and driven to an airport where I was put on a flight to Belgrade. It had been five years since I left. My wife had long since moved away. I don't know where she is now. Or my daughter. So I live here, with my mother. She doesn't know what happened, only that I worked in Italy for five years. I have some work, fixing cars.'

There was a pause on the tape again. Magri's voice was heard, thick with emotion this time. 'I spent three years in prison, Adrian. I lost my job, my house, everything. Because you lied.'

'I'm sorry. But what could I do? He frightens you . . . you don't know how much he can frighten you.'

The tape came to an end, and the three of us sat in silence for a moment. I exhaled, slowly. 'You can make people do anything. If you can frighten them enough.'

Montgomery nodded. 'Very wise. Now, if it's all the same to you, I'll be on my way.'

'I don't think so,' said Dario.

I raised my hand, wearily. 'I think we have to let him go, Dario. He's a crook, I'm pretty sure about that. But I'm also pretty sure that he's got nothing to do with the murder, or with my being attacked the other night. It's not him.'

'It wasn't me. I think you know who it was. Now, I'm going to tell you one more time. I want my property back. At eleven p.m. tomorrow.'

I shook my head.

'And why not?'

'Because I'm going to find out what the rules of your game are. I think people have died because of it. And I'm going to make sure someone is punished for it.'

He nodded. 'As you wish.' He checked his watch. 'It's twenty-seven hours until midnight on the seventeenth. I won't be back. But someone will. I imagine he'll call soon. When he does, I think you should do what he says. Believe it or not, Mr Sutherland, I'm trying to save your life here. And not just yours.'

Chapter 28

Montgomery went upon his way. Dario broke the silence. 'More grappa? Or shall we go downstairs to Eduardo's?'

I shook my head. 'For once, Dario, I'm going to refuse. I think maybe clear heads would help.'

'So what now?'

'I don't know. If Montgomery's right, Arcangelo is going to call me in for a little chat. At which point, I guess I'll do what he says.'

'Nathan, he might be a murderer. Or at the very least an accomplice to murder.'

'I think you're right. But what can we do? There's no proof of anything. If I give him the wretched book, maybe he'll stay off my back.'

'Maybe so, maybe no. Look where he lives. You're practically *vicini*. Going to be a bit awkward when you keep running into each other at the shops.'

I opened my mouth to reply, but was interrupted by the sound of his telephone ringing. He made as if to hang up, then did a double-take when he looked at the number. He answered and stammered away in *Veneziano* for a few seconds before hanging up. He'd turned white.

'Oh God, that was it, wasn't it? That was The Call.'

'Nat, I'm sorry, man, but I've got to go.' He ran into the spare room to grab his coat and his bag. 'I'm really sorry.'

'It's fine, Dario, don't worry. You need to be back home right now.' He patted himself down. 'Have you got everything? You don't want to get to Piazzale Roma and find you've left your car keys here.'

'I've got them.' He exhaled, slowly. 'This is it then.'

'Bloody hell. You're going to be a dad!'

'Shit.' For a moment he looked terribly guilty. 'Are you going to be all right?'

'Sure,' I lied. 'If the worst comes to the worst, then I'll just have to give Moro what he asks for. And then at midnight tomorrow it'll be finished, and to hell with them all.'

'Call me if I can help, okay?'

'I will. Now run like hell, you've got five minutes before the next boat leaves.' Then, with a mercifully brief hug, he was gone. I made sure every lock on the *porta blindata* was secured, and then looked around the flat which suddenly seemed terribly empty.

It would be good, I thought, to talk to Magri but – I checked my watch again – he wouldn't be at his best by now. I'd meet *maresciallo* Adriatico from the *Guardia* tomorrow, and then head over to see him. And that would leave me, at best, eight or nine hours before Moro's deadline. At which point, I would have to decide whether or not to give him the damned book.

I was aware that I should probably eat something. I took a look out of the window. Only three shadows were there, but I didn't feel like going out on my own at this hour. Besides, it would be good to cook. There wasn't much left in the fridge, but I had a tin of tomatoes and some chilies. That was enough for a functional pasta sauce; and there was a bottle of red wine left over from the previous night. That would do.

Gramsci followed me into the kitchen, and I put some food down for him. 'Okay, Grams. Just you and me left now. This means you've got to be Watson. Do you think you're up to it?'

He meeowed, and prodded his now-empty bowl. I put more food down. 'All right then. You can be Holmes if you want to. So where do we start?'

He padded from the room. 'I understand. You want to work on the case alone. Let me know if I can do anything, eh?'

I made up some *penne all'arrabbiata* which I ate without much enthusiasm. Then I poured a glass of the remaining wine and walked through to the living room. I took the canvas bag from the safe and put Magri's file on the table. Gramsci immediately leapt on top of it and started scrabbling at the papers. I pushed him off. 'That's destroying evidence. We're the good guys, remember?'

I started leafing through the papers. Various photographs and clippings concerning the murder in Bologna. And more. Reports of a stolen work by Giuseppe de Nittis, in March 1995. One by de Chirico in April 1999. A sketch of Pulcinella by Giandomenico Tiepolo, in March 2001. Jacopo Bassano's *Adoration of the Magi*, taken from the abandoned church of Santo Spirito in February 2002. The bungled theft of the Medardo Rosso in 2006. And then nothing. He'd have been in jail, of course. I wished I could remember some more of the works in Moro's *palazzo* but all that came to mind was the Modigliani, and there was no reference to that.

There seemed nothing to connect the works by genre or by period, save for the time of the theft; always in the early months of the year. I collected the clippings into a single pile, in chronological order, and zipped them away out of the reach of Gramsci's claws. Then I lay back on the sofa to think the problem over.

I was no nearer to finding a solution when I awoke, stiff-necked and cold, a few hours later.

Chapter 29

Maresciallo Adriatico was an elegant grey-haired man in his late forties, who greeted me politely but with a touch of reserve and turned up his nose when I suggested a coffee at my usual Mestre bar. He took me to a smart, modern place over the road from the offices of the *Guardia*; one I had walked past several times but never visited. Too much glass and chrome, and drinks served in small measures in chic little glasses. I hadn't thought it looked like my kind of place.

'So how is Paolo Magri?' he said.

'He's . . . Well, I think he has good days and bad days. Do you know him well?'

'I haven't seen him for years. But I know him well enough to understand he was once a good man. Unfortunately, he wasn't always as smart as he needed to be.'

'I think maybe he was just unlucky.'

He snorted. '*Beh*. No question of luck. If you start bringing accusations against people – against powerful people – you make damn sure you have every last little bit of proof screwed down beforehand.'

'When did you first meet him?'

'Maybe seven years ago. Before things started to go wrong for him. He came to see us one day, said he had new information about some stolen artworks.'

'Which was?'

'He had a theory about a number of works that had gone missing over a period of nearly fifteen years, all stolen during the first quarter of the year. He thought they were being stolen to order by the same person . . . or by the same people.'

He paused. 'Who were . . .?' I prompted.

'If you've spoken to Magri, you'll know who I mean. But he thought it was more than theft. He seems to think it's some sort of game. That they actually compete with each other for stolen works.' He gave a little smile.

'You don't agree?'

'Magri is – was – a good journalist. But this is an obsession of his. And it's not one that makes any sense. He didn't have much evidence beyond that of the Serbian man who told him – off the record – that he'd been paid by Arcangelo Moro to steal a work for him.' He seemed embarrassed at having spoken so frankly, and added 'Of which, of course, there is no proof whatsoever.'

'Okay, yes. But you knew Moro had been involved in certifying fake works of art as genuine?'

'Of course. But Domenico, not Arcangelo. We were called in, over twenty years ago now – before my time – to investigate the claims. They were easy to prove in the end. This sort of thing happens a lot.'

'Really?'

'It's probably most of our work. In the art squad, that is. Let me give you an example. 2009 was a big year, the centenary of the Futurist movement. Overnight everyone, it seemed, had discovered a painting by Marinetti in the attic. We got calls from everywhere, from galleries being offered works that they thought were suspicious. Or calls from irate clients who'd bought fake works in good faith.'

'So if somebody called you and said that they knew of fake works by Giovanni Bellini being certified as genuine, you'd investigate?'

'Of course. As happened with Domenico. It's not a victimless crime, Mr Sutherland. We're talking about a criminal industry worth tens of millions of euros every year.'

'What about theft?'

He nodded. 'We deal with that too.'

'The Bellini that was stolen from Madonna dell'Orto in 1993. Did you work on that?'

He shook his head. 'Before my time.'

'Paolo mentions a painting being taken from Santo Spirito – what about that?'

'Not our responsibility. Theft from churches, from historic monuments – things that we might call national heritage sites – all that is the responsibility of the *carabinieri*.'

'You have two different squads dealing with art crime?' I said, trying to keep the surprise out of my voice.

He seemed amused by the question. 'Of course. In some ways it makes sense. We have more art crime in Italy than anywhere else in Europe. It might surprise you to know that we are also better at recovering it than any other country in Europe.'

'So if I want to know about the stolen Bellini or the work from Santo Spirito, I need to speak to the *carabinieri*?'

'You could try. The art team are based in Piazza San Marco. Not a bad place to work. We get Mestre, they get the Palazzo Ducale.'

'Is there anyone there I could talk to?'

He chuckled. 'I afraid I don't know anyone there. We don't talk to each other as much as perhaps we should.'

I rested my elbows on the table and ran my hands through my hair. This didn't seem to be going anywhere.

'How about Modigliani?' I tried. 'Did Magri ever mention a stolen work by Modigliani? An oil painting of Anna Akhmatova?'

He shook his head. 'There are always stolen or fake Modiglianis on the market, but he never mentioned one to me. It'll be the centenary of his death in 2020. We're expecting that to be a busy year. I'm sure all sorts of "undiscovered" works are going to surface.'

There was one thing left to try. I took out my photograph of Montgomery. 'I don't suppose there's any chance you know this man?'

He took it from me, gave it a brief glance, and shook his head.

'But could you check him out for me? Find out who he is? If he's involved in art crime, you might have a record of him somewhere.'

He turned the photograph over and over in his hands. 'I'm sorry, that's not possible.'

I sighed. 'I thought it probably wouldn't be. But is there no chance?'

'Officially, none at all. But I'll do it for Paolo. And absolutely off the record. Do you understand?'

'Perfectly. Thank you, *maresciallo*.'

He smiled again, then paused for a moment, and asked, 'Have you ever met Arcangelo Moro?'

'Only on two occasions.'

'And what did you think of him?'

'He has, shall we say, strong opinions on things.'

'You didn't like him?'

'No.'

'Anything else?'

'He seems like an intelligent man. A cultured man.'

He raised his eyebrows. 'Really? Why do you think that?'

'Well, he seems to know a lot about art. A lot about music.'

Adriatico said nothing. And then something clicked in my mind. 'Although, now I think about it, he's got a room full of paintings. Yet he doesn't seem to know very much about them. He's got a box at the opera, yet he seemed quite ignorant. And he professes to be an art lover, but one that's never heard of John Ruskin.'

He nodded. 'Exactly. Appearance is everything to *Signor* Moro.'

We shook hands, and I was staring to pack Magri's clippings away when he stretched out his arm and grabbed my hand. He took the pile from me, and quickly flicked through them with a quizzical expression on his face.

'Is everything okay?' I asked.

'Probably. I was just looking and suddenly wondered why he decided to give you the originals? Has he given up completely?'

The question threw me, and I couldn't think of an answer. We shook hands once more, and he made his way back to work as I waited for the next bus for Venice.

Chapter 30

I caught the first *vaporetto* to Giudecca from Piazzale Roma. I wished I had Magri's phone number. For that matter I wished I had a more intelligent phone so I could at least find out the number of the bar and give the boys a ring. I got off at Palanca, and half ran along the *fondamenta*. Paolo will be there, I thought, and everything will be all right.

He wasn't there. I checked my watch. It was a little early, but I understood he was usually there at this hour. Sergio and the Prof were sat at the same table, still dressed in the same clothes. I wondered if they actually had homes to go to or if they genuinely lived there. I was about to speak, but I'd scarcely opened my mouth before Sergio interrupted me. 'Ah, Investigator Nathan!' He held up three fingers to the young guy behind the bar, who went to fetch a bottle of red wine.

I dragged a chair over to their table. 'Has Magri been in today?'

They shook their heads. 'He's usually here by now, but he probably just had a late night,' said the Prof.

I rummaged in the bag and took out a handful of clippings.

'What's the matter, *compagno*?'

I spread the papers out on the table. 'It might be nothing. I don't know. But it's these. Look at the clippings.'

They stared blankly.

'They're original. They're not photocopies, they're the originals. Why would he give me these?'

Sergio's eyes widened in comprehension. 'He wanted you to have them . . . just in case.'

'In case anything happened to him. So that someone else would know exactly what he'd found.' I reached for my mobile. 'You have his number?'

Sergio shook his head, 'He doesn't have a telephone. We'd better go round there.'

I threw some coins on the bar, and we ran outside. And immediately there was a problem, as we saw a *vaporetto* pulling away from the pontoon. 'We'll have to run,' said Lorenzo. We looked at each other. The two of them probably had 150 years between them. Paolo's flat was over a kilometre away.

I thrust the bag into Sergio's hands. 'You take this. Then get the next boat and meet me there.' Then I turned and ran without even waiting for a reply. My lungs were burning by the time I reached the first bridge. When was the last time I'd run for anything more than a *vaporetto*? Over the bridge, along the *fondamenta*. Twelve months of no exercise. Twelve months of too much beer and not enough proper food. Over the next bridge and past the Redentore. Twelve months of late-night Negronis. The blood pounding in my head, and every muscle in my body crying for me to stop. Twelve months of too many bloody cigarettes.

Try as I might, I'd slowed to little more than a jog by the time I reached the entrance gate to the *condominia*. I pressed every doorbell in turn until somebody buzzed me in and it clanked open. Through the gardens, through the portico and into that other, darker Venice. The front door of Magri's building swung open, as it had last time, and I splashed my way through the pool of water in the entrance hall and up the stairs.

Music came from Paolo's flat. *The Wall*, again. 'Run like Hell'. Funny, I thought. I'll knock on the door, and Paolo will tell me to *vaffa*. I'll say who it is, we'll have a good laugh about it, and we'll crack a bottle when the boys finally arrive. A band of middle-aged and elderly men turned crimefighters. I knocked on the door, and it swung open.

Magri's flat had been in a state last time, but in a good way. There had been junk everywhere, but there had been a method to it, a kind of organised chaos. This was different. The place had been turned upside down and inside out. Papers were strewn everywhere. All his books had been swept off the shelves and the bookcases pulled from the walls.

He lay sprawled on the sofa. Nearby, on the floor, lay a broken bottle of wine. For a moment I hoped he'd got blind drunk and torn everything apart in a fit of rage. Then I realised that the red liquid pooling on the floor was more than just wine. He'll be okay, I told myself. He's drunk, he's fallen and hurt himself. You'll call a doctor, and everything will be fine. I reached to turn him over, to make him more comfortable.

His face was a bloodied mess, his hair caked in wet blood. And it was obvious he was never going to be fine again. I choked back vomit, stepped back from him and tried to think clearly. I dropped to my knees, and examined the bottle from a distance. Blood and wine merged into one on the jagged

edges. I got to my feet, breathing heavily. Music was still playing. How many times had Dario and I sat down together to
listen to *The Wall?* 'Run Like Hell' is somewhere near the end.
So it must have happened sometime in the last thirty minutes,
whilst I was still on my way to the bar. Which meant that
whoever had done this was not very far away.

Or still in the building. Or still in the apartment.

I stepped back. Quietly. Oh, so quietly. Pulled the door
open as gently as possible. I could see or hear no one. The stairwell was dark, but I forced myself to wait until my eyes adjusted
and I could see that I had a clear run to the door. Then I was
down the stairs, across the stagnant pool and through the front
door. I slipped on the steps and fell sprawling in the mud. My
feet scrabbled as I searched for purchase, and then I was away
along the path, through the arch that separated my Venice
from this unknown, dreadful one; and down the entrance
corridor. My hands banged and flapped at the side of the gate,
desperately searching for the opening mechanism. And then I
was through, and back on the *fondamenta* in the driving rain.
Soaked, muddy and breathless, I reached for my mobile phone
and stabbed out the emergency number.

Sergio and Lorenzo alighted from the *vaporetto*, and broke
into a run as soon as they saw me. I stammered out the address
to the police receptionist, and then sank to my knees, as four
words hissed again and again in my mind. *This is your fault.
This is your fault.*

Vanni offered me a cigarette and I took one, hands shaking.
We smoked quietly and illegally for a while, until he broke the
silence.

'Okay, Nathan. You want to tell me what this is all about?'

I rubbed my face. I felt unshaven, tired, dirty. 'I don't really know. It's difficult to explain.'

'I know. But you're going to try.'

What to do? Lie? Tell him the whole truth? What would Paolo Sarpi have done?

'I hardly knew the guy. Fact is, we met for the first time just a few days ago. I was interested in a story he was working on a couple of years back.'

'Which was?'

Vanni was a friend, of sorts. I needed to keep him on my side. 'The Moro story. The one he got sent to prison for.'

'I remember,' he replied in a noncommittal tone.

'I went to see him. He wasn't interested in sharing anything. I went back again today to see if I could change his mind. I was with the two guys from the communist bar. We decided to go down together and see him. And then, well, you know the rest.'

'Yes.' He sounded anything but convinced. 'Nathan,' he continued in a neutral tone, 'just why exactly are you interested in Moro?'

'He contacted me a couple of days ago. For some translation work. And then he offered me a considerable sum of money if I were to pass on to him a certain item, should it come into my possession.' *The truth, not to everybody.*

'Which was?'

'I don't know. He just gave me a description of the man who was likely to give it to me.'

Vanni looked at me quizzically. 'And . . .?'

I gave him as good a description of Montgomery as I could remember. He scribbled away furiously. A long silence followed.

'And . . .?'

'That's it.'

'That's it? You haven't been given anything which could be considered the property of *Signor* Moro?'

'No.'

He stared at me in silence, as I struggled to hold his gaze. He scribbled a few more lines, then clicked his pen closed and closed the papers away in a folder. 'Okay, Nathan, that's everything.'

'I can go?'

'Of course.'

'Thanks. Vanni. I think I need to go home and sleep for about a month.'

He gave a brisk nod of approval. Again, he held my gaze for a painfully long time. 'Aren't you going to ask me who was responsible?'

'I'm tired, Vanni. And I assumed you wouldn't tell me anyway. But, okay then, who do you think did it?'

'Probably one of the *abusivi* in the block. We've checked the records. There's a guy in Mestre who's letting out a whole set of apartments in that building to *extracomunitari*. Magri was the only Italian there. He didn't have much money, sure, but he'd have had a hell of a lot more than anyone else.'

I said nothing.

'What do you think?' Vanni asked.

I rested my elbows on the desk, and ran my hands through my hair. 'It makes sense. I suppose it makes sense.'

He nodded. 'It does.' Again, we sat in silence, and I stared at the back of my hands.

'Moro,' said Vanni.

I raised my head, but said nothing.

'If you do receive something that belongs to him – or even something that he thinks belongs to him – I should do as he says. He's not a man to cross, Nathan. You understand?'

I said yes, of course I did. Then got to my feet and walked from the room, feeling as tired as I ever had in my life.

Chapter 31

I had been back in the apartment for less than fifteen minutes when the doorbell rang. I buzzed my visitor up without even checking who it was via the speakerphone. I knew who it would be. I walked through to the bedroom to collect my jacket. When I returned, the tall blond man was standing in the living room, his face badly cut from the events of three nights previously.

I put my hands up, not so much in an act of surrender but more to indicate that I wasn't going to attempt anything stupid. Besides, Her Majesty's portrait was still propped against the wall, and broken. I couldn't depend on any help from *sua Maestà* this time, and Gramsci seemed to have disappeared altogether. But it was early evening, and the streets were still busy. This time, I hoped, he didn't have violence on his mind.

I broke the silence. 'I suppose we should be on first-name terms by now?'

'Karl.'

I nodded. Suitably Germanic. 'I'm Nathan,' I said, 'although you probably know that.'

He ran his hand across his face. 'I should hurt you for this.'

'Yeah.' I inclined my head towards the safe. 'So take the damn book.'

He shook his head. 'Not this time. *Signor* Moro wants to speak to you.'

'Okay.' I put my jacket on. 'He's got my number, though. Just ask him to give me a call next time. Save you the walk.' I paused, as a thought struck me. 'That is, if there is a next time?'

Karl just smiled.

We walked in silence past the Magical Brazilian café, and into Campo Sant'Angelo. It was a chilly evening but the rain had stopped, and tourists were gathering in their numbers at the cafés and bars along the way. We looked, I suppose, like any number of visitors or locals out for their evening *passeggiata*. Then into Campo Santo Stefano, and past the *conservatorio*. Someone was playing the piano. The *Goldberg Variations*. It seemed comforting. There was a beautiful logic and precision to it all. Karl rang the bell at Palazzo Moro, and we were admitted. The same decrepit retainer met us at the top of the stairs. He said nothing, but silently waved us in.

There were two of them this time, sitting at a chessboard. Both in brocade smoking dressing gowns. Arcangelo, wiry-haired and hawk-visaged. The other was little more than a skeleton. Wisps of hair clung to a cadaverous, sunken face. Yet enough remained for me to see that they were, indeed, brothers. Twins, of course. With faces of which my mother would have said, 'You don't get to look like that that by smiling too much.'

He sat, or rather slumped, in an antique wheelchair and occasionally drew a gargling breath of oxygen from the mask at his side. Arcangelo puffed away at a noxious cigar, the smell of which did little to dispel the stench of death in the room. Arcangelo waved his hand dismissively, and Karl and the retainer withdrew. I stood there in silence, watching them play. Should I say good evening? I tried clearing my throat, to no effect. Of course. This was all part of the game as well. I decided just to sit down, upon an elegant Rococo divan.

He turned, ever so slowly, to look at me; yet without any sign of recognition or greeting. Then he looked back to his opponent. 'He took the first move then, Domenico. Like you, he will find it is not always an advantage.'

Silence, again, for a few minutes. Domenico sat, reviewing the board, with his hands pressed together in an almost prayer-like attitude. Arcangelo spoke again. 'Tell me why you are here.' His gaze remained fixed on the game, yet the demand was evidently directed at me.

'I'm here because it seems I have something you want,' I said.

There was another achingly long pause. I looked from one player to another, and back again.

'Shall I just go?' I suggested.

I made my way to the door, and turned the handle. Outside stood the impassive figure of Karl. I closed the door and sat back down.

'Okay. Shall we talk? Or shall I just watch you play chess?'

There was another long pause. Arcangelo studiously avoided my eyes, and kept them fixed on his brother. 'You have something we want. Something I want,' he said.

I looked from one player to another, and back again, in the hope they would at least deign to look at me. Oh for Christ's sake. They knew damn well that I knew what they were talking about.

'A small padded envelope, maybe twelve or fourteen centimetres by ten or twelve. Right?'

Arcangelo nodded. 'You've opened it of course?'

I nodded.

'You know what it is?'

'I believe it's a book of worship illustrated by Giovanni Bellini.'

'Good. Well done. And where is it now?'

'You know damn well where it is'

He held up his hand as if my mild cursing had caused him physical pain. 'We do of course. In your office on the Street of the Assassins.'

'So why should I give it to you?'

'Because it's my property.'

'Bullshit.' I spat the word out with rather more confidence than I felt, and, again, he winced slightly. 'It's stolen property, obtained by fraud; it's got nothing to do with you.'

There was silence, again, for an unearthly long time. Then, 'You will bring it to me at midnight tonight. Not earlier. Not later. You understand?'

'No, I don't understand. I offered to give it to your gorilla just now. Why didn't he just take it?'

Moro folded his fingers together, and rested his chin on them. 'Because you lied to me. Because you were working with that drunk journalist to destroy me. And so I want you to bring it to me.'

'The rules, Arcangelo, the rules!' Domenico spoke, for the first time, in a high, paper-thin voice.

'To hell with the damn rules, Domenico. This will be our last game, and I am going to win it. You understand?' His brother slumped further back in his chair, his hand feebly flapping at his mask.

I leaned back in my chair. 'The rules of the game?'

'Strictly speaking, it should be one of our players to bring the piece. This year, I am prepared to make an exception.'

'The players being Karl and Montgomery?'

'Indeed.'

'So tell me, Arcangelo. Exactly what do you win?'

'The game. Yet another one to me. There was once a time that Domenico was an opponent to be reckoned with, but his mind is now nearly as feeble as his body. And he's chosen some wretched pieces as his pawns.'

'You win the game. Which means the book, of course.'

He smiled. 'Of course.'

'And why tonight?'

'Why tonight? I'm expecting my birthday present, of course.'

'Your birthday?' It was as banal as that then. 'Damn, you should have said. I'd have got you a card, or something.'

'No matter. It will be Domenico's last, but, sadly, there will be no gift for him this time. There haven't been any for some years now.'

'Well, you know how it is. Every year you drop off someone's list. One fewer card on the mantelpiece, eh? But Arcangelo, on the other hand, gets a splendid work by Giovanni Bellini to open up.'

Domenico merely hissed and rasped at his oxygen.

'I'm afraid my brother isn't one for conversation at the moment,' said Arcangelo.

'You must really love Bellini to go to all this trouble,' I said.

He smiled a thin and terrible smile. 'I don't give a damn about Bellini. I don't give a damn about his dismally pious virgins or his cutesy little cherubim or his sanctimonious suffering Christs.'

I sat bolt upright. He grinned back at me. He'd out-thought, out-played me again.

'That surprises you? I couldn't care less about the wretched book. I couldn't care less about that damned Madonna on the wall there. I don't care about Modigliani and that painting of – who did you say?'

'Akhmatova. Anna Akhmatova,' I replied, automatically.

'I don't care about them. But Domenico does.' He raised himself to his feet, leaned over the chessboard, and patted the motionless figure of his brother on the cheek. 'You care, don't you, Domenico? You care so much it hurts.'

'I don't understand.'

'Of course not. But Domenico does. Don't you, eh?' Again, he patted his brother on the cheek, as if playing with a small child. 'He understands that all these' – he waved at the wall behind him – 'are *mine*.'

'They're not yours, though, are they? They're stolen. All of them.'

'Every last one. And he has to look at them. Every day.'

'So why should that bother him? He still gets to look at them.'

Arcangelo looked genuinely surprised. 'But they're not *his*.'

'They're not yours either!'

'Of course they are. I won every one. And he has to look at them and know that they are mine and not his.' He walked over to the Bellini Madonna. 'I could stick my fist through this. Stick my hand into the canvas and drag it down and tear it slowly into pieces. I might still do that. Before he dies. Maybe one piece a day. Would you like that, Domenico?' His brother could only gaze at him, his watery grey eyes filled with confusion and terror.

I ran my hands through my hair, and breathed deeply. 'You're a piece of work, Arcangelo, and no mistake. You're an evil bastard, aren't you?'

If he was offended or angered he showed no sign. He reached over and took Domenico's hands in his. 'We are almost finished now, dear brother. The last game is nearly over, and the pieces must be cleared from the board.'

'And Paolo Magri was one of the "pieces"?'

He turned to me, but said nothing.

'You had him killed, didn't you? You had him killed because he interfered in your game, in this sick paper chase of yours?'

Moro did nothing but smile his thin, terrible smile. He looked at the ormolu clock on the mantelpiece. Barely half past eight. 'Plenty of time remaining, Mr Sutherland. Please stay and have a drink with us if you wish. But remember, I will be expecting my birthday present on the stroke of midnight.'

'What if I were to say I haven't got it any more?'

He cocked his head to one side, as if considering. 'Now, that is a possibility. It could be with your friend in Mestre. You might have left it with the pretty art restorer on the Lido. Perhaps you even sent it to your wife back in the United Kingdom?'

I said nothing, although I felt a cold chill in the pit of my stomach. He continued, 'In which case it will be necessary to be absolutely certain. I've promised Karl a few hours off this evening, but there are still a few friends I can call.' He reached into his gown for a mobile phone. His clear grey eyes remained fixed on mine, as his hand hovered above the keypad.

I breathed deeply. I summoned the pitiful vestiges of courage that remained to me, walked over to the table and dropped to my haunches in front of him. I moved my face as close to his as I dared, and hissed, 'Bullshit. You're full of crap, Arcangelo.'

He closed his eyes, and nodded respectfully. 'I understand. You are a man of great principle, Nathan.' He started to dial. Not slowly, as if he were calling my bluff on every digit, but as casually as if he were calling to book a table in a restaurant. He didn't even look into my eyes. His thumb poised for an instant above the call button.

My hand lashed out and closed around his wrist. He raised his eyes to mine, this time with mild interest. I released his hand. He replaced the phone on the table. I got to my feet, breathing heavily.

'I knew you would be no sort of chess player, Nathan. It transpires that you also have no talent for poker. Now, I think we'll just take a drink together for a few minutes. To give you a little time to think everything over.' He rang for the butler, who appeared carrying a tray with a bottle of wine and three glasses. Arcangelo pointedly poured one out for Domenico, who left it untouched. 'Not joining us, dear brother? A shame. *Salute*, Nathan.'

We clinked glasses. Then he turned away from me, to pore over the chessboard. For thirty minutes he assiduously ignored me. I drained my glass and poured another, but he paid me no mind. I took a look around the room again. That beautiful painting by Modigliani. The wonderful, perfect colours of the Bellini.

Arcangelo checked the clock again. He looked back at Domenico, wheezing pathetically in his chair, then down at the table. He moved his knight forward and captured a pawn. He rolled it over and over in his hand, then turned, almost absent-mindedly, towards me. 'Now then, Nathan. Be aware that Mr Montgomery is, of course, still in the game. He will want the package too, so take great care. But I know I can trust you. And now, I think you have work to do.'

I ran from the room. You can make people do anything, if you can frighten them enough.

Chapter 32

He's going to kill me, I thought. He's going to have me killed, and the best I can hope for is that he won't kill my friends as well. I sat on Tommaseo's steps, breathing heavily and trying to choke back tears. I put my head in my hands. *Come on, Nathan. Think. There must be a way out of this.*

I could, should go to the police. But Moro's arm was a long one. All he would need would be the time to make one phone call. No. I would have to sort this out myself.

From the *conservatorio* came more music, the *Goldberg Variations* still. I tried to concentrate on the lines in the hope it would help clear my head. The pianist had almost finished now and was playing the final aria, a repeat of the first. Dear old Bach, I thought. He'd have known what to do. Give him a simple theme and he'd twist it around and turn it inside out, without ever losing sight of his starting point. No matter how complex everything appeared to be, there was always that line to follow; beautiful in its precision and logic.

And then it hit me. The simplicity of the whole thing. If the complexities threaten to obscure everything, then ignore them and find your way back to that elementary theme. That was what I had missed. What we had all missed. The simplicity, the clarity of it all.

I ran, not in desperation now but in excitement. The bells of Santo Stefano tolled nine p.m. Three hours. Just about enough time. Gramsci mewled for food as I burst through the door of the flat, but for once I ignored him. I started up the PC, its ancient fan stuttering and wheezing, and I cursed the fact that I hadn't replaced it years ago.

I sat down, and tapped away. Modigliani. Anna Akhmatova. That beautiful painting of her. There were pages and pages of biography, but precious little in the way of concrete proof. It would have to be enough. I scribbled down the results and printed off the most useful stuff I could find. Then I re-read them. It was good. But it wasn't convincing, it wasn't enough on its own. I was going to have to give the performance of my life. And if I was going to do that, I needed a strong drink inside me. And more than anything else I needed a cigarette. I took the package from the safe and placed it inside my coat.

Gramsci scrabbled away at my heels, so I went to the kitchen to fetch him some more food. Before he could fall upon his bowl, I scooped him up in my arms and held him sufficiently far away from me for his flailing little limbs to inflict no damage. 'Okay, buddy. I'm off now. I might not be here for your next feed. But someone will come. And when they do, try not to hurt them. Do we have a deal?'

He yowled at me, which I chose to take as a 'yes' and I put him down. He didn't even raise his head as I slammed and bolted the door behind me. I strolled down to Campo San Luca, and bought a packet of twenty MS. Then back home again, and into the Magical Brazilian.

'*Ciao*, Nathan. Spritz or Negroni?' asked Eduardo.

I hesitated. A Spritz would leave me with a clearer head. On the other hand, a Negroni would help me to get into character. More than that, if I was going to die, I was going to die with a proper drink inside me.

'Negroni, Ed. It might be the last one.'

He looked shocked. 'Shit. You giving up?'

'No. It's just that I think someone's going to kill me tonight.'

He gave me a look as if to say, 'Jeez, he's started early tonight' and went off to fix my drink. I reached for my mobile. What to do? I could call Dario. He might be useful to have there. And on the other hand, he could get himself killed. It came as a moment of clarity to me. I was fine with being killed. I wasn't fine with anyone else being hurt. The thought made me feel very alone, and yet came as a great comfort.

Dario would be fine. But I needed to speak to Fede.

'*Ciao, caro.*'

'*Ciao, cara*. Listen, are you at home right now?'

'I am. I was thinking of going to bed though.'

'Okay. I need you to do something. I want you to lock every door in your house. Double check every window. Lock yourself in your bedroom. Have your mobile phone right next to you. Answer the door to no one at all. And if you hear so much as a mouse squeak, you call the police. You understand?'

There was a pause. 'Okay. I'll do that.' No *is this a joke?* No *have you been drinking?* 'Are you going to be all right? Is Dario with you?'

'Dario's gone back to Mestre. He's probably a dad by now. I need him to be there with Valentina. I need to know everyone is safe.'

'What are you going to do. Nathan?'

'I think . . . I think I can probably sort it out. And I think it'll probably be okay. It's just . . . Fede, when you were a little girl, did you ever get a birthday present that you didn't want. I mean, really didn't want?'

'When I was eight. I wanted a bicycle. I was so sure I was going to get a bicycle. And on the day, there was no big present, just a little box. It was a Barbie doll.'

'And what did you do?'

'I screamed and cried and ruined the whole day for everyone.'

'Yeah. That's what I'm afraid of. I'll call you tomorrow, okay?'

I thought perhaps she hung on the line longer than necessary, but maybe not. Eduardo pushed the Negroni across the counter at me. I passed the keys of my apartment over to him.

'Will you be open at one o'clock Ed?'

He looked confused, not to say a little troubled. 'I dunno, Nat. If you're going to be here I'll keep the place open.'

'Okay. If I'm not back to pick up the keys tonight, will you go and feed Gramsci in the morning?'

'Sure. You going away?'

'Maybe. If I am, can you look after him for the rest of his life?'

He'd decided now that I was just plain drunk, and played along with it. 'You ask a lot, Nathan.'

'It's a hell of thing to ask, I know. But I need to know he's going to be looked after.'

'I'll do it, Nat.'

'Good man.'

I checked my watch. Nearly midnight. Time to go. I patted myself down. Package, documents and, most importantly, cigarettes. *Coraggio*, Nathan, I thought to myself.

I reached the Palazzo Moro just as the Marangona bell of St Mark's chimed through the foggy night. Montgomery was there at the same time. I raised my eyebrows. 'I'm not sure that I expected to see you here.'

He gave a curt nod of acknowledgement. 'It's one of the rules of the game. I thought you knew that by now?'

'I see. So, shouldn't you be trying to get your property back? You know, threaten to kill me or something?'

'Not this time. Not in the hour before midnight. Too late in the game. Makes it too easy otherwise.'

'Well you're a remarkably gracious loser. I'm delighted to see you anyway.' I patted him on the back, and was pleased to see him flinch, however slightly, at the familiarity. The intercom buzzed, and the aged retainer was there once more to usher us in.

The game didn't seem to have progressed much in my absence. Both players sat hunched over the board in much the same attitude in which I had left them. Arcangelo made no sign of greeting, and Domenico appeared to be in no fit state to do so.

The last chime of the bell faded away, its sound muffled by the fog. I usually found the late-night bells of St Mark's comforting, like listening to the Shipping Forecast. Tonight it felt more as if it presaged an Event. As if Arcangelo had personally arranged it.

He got to his feet, and Karl entered the room. 'So, if everyone is here, I think we can begin. Mr Sutherland, if you please . . .?'

I took the package from my jacket and dropped it unceremoniously on the table.' He winced. 'Carefully, please. Domenico would hate to see it being damaged.'

We stood and looked at it in silence. 'Please open it, Mr Sutherland.'

I shrugged. 'It's your birthday present. I thought you'd be excited at the thought of unwrapping it.' I tore the seal open, withdrew the book and nonchalantly tossed it to him. He grabbed it out of the air, and glared at me with real anger this time. Karl made a step towards me and I couldn't restrain myself from flinching, but Arcangelo waved a hand and he stood back.

He flicked through it. '*The Life of the Virgin*. Giovanni Bellini. Thank you, Mr Sutherland. Mr Montgomery, it appears Domenico has wasted your time yet again.'

He placed the book next to his brother. 'Look at it, Domenico. So beautiful, so precious. And mine. The colours, so perfect after five hundred years.'

I nodded in agreement. 'They are lovely, aren't they. Just like this one.' I walked over to Bellini's painting of the Madonna. He flashed me an angry look, irritated by being interrupted whilst soliloquising. I lit up a cigarette, and dragged deeply until the tip grew red. Then carefully, ever so precisely, I drew it across the hair of the unattractive Christ child, tracing as carefully as I could along each delicate little follicle.

Fragments of paint flaked away and spiralled through the air like the tiniest fireflies. Arcangelo stared at me in disbelief. I took another drag on the cigarette, held the smoke down and exhaled slowly, trying to milk the moment for dramatic effect. Everything now depended on the performance.

'What are you doing?' he stammered out.

'What you've always wanted to do, Arcangelo. I'm wiping the stupid smile off her face.' And with that, I slowly pushed the cigarette right into the face of the Virgin. I withdrew it, equally slowly, and stood back to admire my handiwork as an acrid smell started to fill the room.

'There we go. What did you say to me? Something about sticking your fist through it and tearing it apart slowly piece by piece. Well, I've saved you the trouble.' Before anyone could move, I had moved on to the Modigliani.

The work was behind glass, so this was going to hurt. I was prepared for that. It needed to look good. I drew back my fist and smashed it as hard as I could into Akhmatova's face. The glass splintered as I clenched my teeth against the pain, dragging my knuckles over the surface of the canvas. I withdrew my hand, and wiped the blood on my jacket.

'Blood is a bastard of a thing to remove. You'll never get that off. It's ruined. Sorry. Now, is there anything else you'd like me to move on to?'

Karl and Arcangelo seemed too stunned to move, whilst Montgomery looked on with an air of wry amusement and curiosity. There was silence for a moment, broken only by the tinkling of a few more fragments of glass falling from the frame. Then, before anyone could speak, a gurgling, rasping sound came from Domenico. It must have taken all his strength, but somehow he had raised himself to his feet and was supporting himself on the table. His entire body shook, partly from the sheer effort of remaining upright but also from the great racking waves of laughter that were bending him double.

Arcangelo looked from him, to me, then back again. I dabbed at my bloodied knuckles with a handkerchief. 'Marvellous woman, Anna Akhmatova. Wonderful poet. Bore witness to Stalin's terror. Mentored Brodsky, inspired Prokofiev, admired by Shostakovich. A woman of great moral stature. And, of course, she was a great friend of Amadeo Modigliani.' I yanked the frame from the wall and let it crash to the floor. 'The only problem, of course, is that this is an oil painting. Whereas the orginal is in pencil.'

I moved back to the Bellini. 'Beautiful colours, aren't they? Could have been painted yesterday. And it pretty much was. Twenty years ago to be precise. Almost yesterday in the grand scheme of things.' Domenico continued to laugh his terrible, gurgling laugh.

'Now then. Anything else I should move on to, Arcangelo?' His face was frozen in disbelief and confusion. 'No? You still don't get it, do you? He's played you. He's been playing you from the day you started this game.

'You really thought you were so clever you could steal a work like the Bellini from a church two kilometres away and keep it secret? And in all those years, you never stopped to wonder why Domenico insisted on using Montgomery to do his dirty work, even though he kept losing? He must be the worst thief in the world. He left a trail a child could follow. He gave you every single opportunity to follow him to find out where he was leaving the goods before the end of the game. He gave Karl every chance to steal it off me. He's a terrible thief.' I paused. 'But he's a very, very good forger.

'Now, let me take a wild guess. It was always Domenico who selected the pieces to play for, wasn't it? And you let him.

How much more would it hurt him if it was something he wanted so badly, and he had to know it was you who had it? Oh yes, he won the occasional game. Even you might have become suspicious otherwise.'

Domenico slumped, gurgling, back into his chair and fumbled for his mask.

'And do you know why he did it, Arcangelo? Not for the money, although I think we'll find the originals were all discreetly sold off by Monty here. It's not even because he hates you. It's because you amuse him. You make him laugh. The great demonic Venetian philosopher-king, gloating over his collection of fake art.'

I looked over at Montgomery. 'Now, I think Mr Montgomery also has something you'll find interesting.' I pointed my bloodied hand at his briefcase. The adrenaline was starting to wear off now and the pain was growing. He hesitated. 'Come on, Monty, or Sebastian or whoever you are. Let's see the real thing. If you don't, Arcangelo will only ask Karl to shake you down.'

He shrugged as if it were all the same to him, and clicked open his briefcase. He took out a small object wrapped in tissue paper.

'May I have it?' I asked.

He passed it to me, with a quizzical look on his face, unsure as to where I was going with all this. I pulled the paper delicately away from its contents, a small book bound in black leather.

'Should I be wearing gloves, Monty?'

'Probably. I wouldn't want you to bleed on it. Unfortunately, I haven't brought any.'

'Of course not. This one wasn't intended to be handed over tonight, was it? Now, for my next trick . . .' I grabbed the first book from under the nose of Arcangelo, and dropped Montgomery's version next to it. I shuffled them around as fast as I could, as if I were playing a shell game; and then stood back.

'There you go. Here's your chance. Your last chance. Win the game at last, finally get one over on Domenico. No one's going to stop you. Just choose. Which is the real one?'

Arcangelo bent over the table, with one hand placed on each copy, his eyes darting from side to side as he strove to find something that could give him a clue. He picked one book up, and brought it close to his face; then repeated the same gesture with the other. He leafed through each page, one by one; poring over each matching set of illustrations. And then he stopped.

Domenico hauled himself from his wheelchair once more, clapped his hands and laughed hysterically. 'He doesn't know. Of course he doesn't know!'

Arcangelo sunk his head over the table, as if to re-gather his strength. He was silent for a few moments, then raised his eyes to mine. 'I could have you killed for this, you understand?'

The weariness in my voice was real, now. 'Yeah, you could. But what would be the point? I haven't done anything wrong. If anything, I've done you a favour. And the trouble is, Arcangelo, to threaten someone properly you really have to frighten them. And you don't frighten anyone any more. We're just laughing at you.'

Karl reached into his jacket and pulled out a small, snub-nosed revolver. I'd thought that he might. Nevertheless, I'd never had a gun actively pointed at me before. Everything hung on not being afraid. 'Come on, Karl. There's no point and you know it. You're never going to work for Arcangelo again. You'll just be making more trouble for yourself. And if you kill me, you'll probably need to kill Domenico and Monty as well to keep it quiet.'

Montgomery paused whilst lighting up a cigarette. 'Why Nathan, what a very clever thing to say.'

'True, though. You'll both be looking for a new job now. I suppose Arcangelo could continue the game on his own, but it won't be the same without a proper opponent. Although, if he did, I guess you could all compete for one of those prints of dogs playing snooker. I think that would be enough to keep him happy, given what we've learned about him today.'

Karl kept the gun trained on me, but I could see he was thinking now. I pressed on. 'Come on, Karl, kill us and you'll get a life sentence, and he'll get away free. And you know everything about him. Everything. How long will it be before he decides you're just another piece to be swept from the board?'

He stepped back, and for one terrible moment I thought I'd gone too far, remembering the moment in the flat when I was convinced he was about to kill me. But his movement was only to be better able to cover all four of us as he moved to the table, and picked up both copies of the book; stuffing them into the original package. He backed towards the door.

'One final payday?' I asked. He nodded.

'Bastards. All of you. Bastards.' Arcangelo, his voice constricted with fury and hate, could barely hiss the words out. It was enough to start Domenico laughing again, his gurgling rasp only interrupted by desperate draughts of oxygen from his mask. Then Karl, in an instant, had turned and run. Montgomery smoked quietly and intently, as if wondering what to do next.

I dabbed again at my knuckles. 'Well now. That seems to be that. It's late, and I should get this hand seen to. Nice to meet you at last, Domenico.' The dying man's eyes wrinkled and he nodded, as if in recognition of a joke well told and a game well played.

'I don't think so. I don't think so.' Arcangelo shook his head violently, as if trying to physically shake away the mixture of confusion, anger and hate that was blocking his thoughts. 'I'll take that damn book and I'll burn it in front of you tonight, Domenico.' He ran from the room, in pursuit of Karl, his turn of speed reminding me that the cane was, after all, just an affectation.

Montgomery gave me a thin smile. 'I got this one wrong, Nathan. I didn't think you'd get so involved. Still, chance for one final payday. One of us has to get it.' He dashed from the room as well and, after only a moment's hesitation, I followed.

Karl had a head start, but Arcangelo was spry for his age, and quickly made up ground. The two of them ran through Santo Stefano, and past the church of San Vidal. Karl reached the Accademia Bridge, and took the steps two at a time. I was in poor physical shape, but I had nearly twenty years' edge on Montgomery, and overtook him.

Karl was driven by little more than greed, whilst Arcangelo's wiry body was fuelled with twenty years of hatred. He drew level at the apex of the bridge, and hurled himself at Karl's legs, bringing him down. The package bounced and skittered across the ground. Karl rolled and raised a boot, stamping into Arcangelo's face. The blow should have been enough to stop him, but he appeared stunned for only a moment before emitting a scream of rage and frustration as he readied himself for another lunge at his adversary.

But Karl had spent a lifetime in crime, and the instinct for self-preservation took over. Before Moro could move, he had drawn his revolver and fired.

Arcangelo dropped to his knees. He muttered something. '*Impossibile,*' was all I heard. Then Karl fired a second time, and then a third, and he crumpled to the ground.

Montgomery and I threw ourselves upon Karl, as he reached for the package. Montgomery grabbed his arm, forcing the gun from his hand; whilst I punched him as hard as I could in the face. It was akin to hitting a brick wall, and the impact made my injured hand flare brightly with pain. The shock made me hesitate for a second, and that was enough. Karl caught Montgomery a blow across the face; whilst he threw me against the railing with his other hand. The impact knocked the breath from my lungs, and I had no time to react before he grabbed me by my shirt, hauling me up and over the balustrade. My feet bicycled and my hands scrabbled for purchase, as he forced me back, further and further. I grabbed at him, trying to pull him with me and use his own momentum to topple him. Then a shot rang out, and without a word, he fell from the bridge and into the dark water below.

I hauled myself back on to the bridge, sobbing with relief. Montgomery, gun in hand, was reaching for the package. Without even thinking, I threw myself at him. The two of us grappled for a moment, each of us searching for a proper grasp on the packet and then, with a tearing sound, it split into two and both books – copy and original – spun into the air.

I hurled myself at them, pushing myself up on to the railing just to give myself a couple more inches reach. One of them bounced off the tips of my fingers, and dropped, agonisingly, into the dark. The other one fell into the palm of my hand and I tightened my fingers around it. Too far. I'd pushed myself too far. I felt myself starting to fall.

Then a hand reached out, and dragged me back to the safety of the bridge. I lay there, my heart racing, the book safe in my hand. All I could hear was the sound of my own blood pounding in my ears mixing with the roar of an engine. I opened my eyes, and looked up.

Dario beamed down at me, and hauled me to my feet. I clung to him in thanks and relief. As I steadied myself and hugged him I became aware of the smell of petrol. I looked past him to the source of the noise, and burst out laughing. There, on its side, at the top of the Accademia Bridge, lay a Moto Guzzi Le Mans 850 motorcycle.

Chapter 33

We laid Paolo to rest a couple of days later. He didn't seem to have any family, so the mourners mainly consisted of some old journalist friends and comrades from the communist bar. Vanni had turned up to keep me company, and we sat at the back during the service. Then the funeral party set out by boat to the cemetery island of San Michele where Paolo Magri would be interred, at least for the next ten years; following which his remains, likely as not, would be removed to one of the communal ossuaries on the island.

It was a bright, sunny day but with the chill of early spring in the air. I pulled my coat tighter around me. Vanni offered me a small cigar, which I accepted. I had no idea if this was disrespectful or not but he, I assumed, had been to more funerals than I had.

We stood in silence for a while as the final rites were read. 'You know, Nathan,' he said, 'you lied to me.'

I could do nothing but bow my head. 'I did,' I said.

'According to the rules, I'm supposed to pursue that. Lying in a witness statement. People go to prison for such things.'

'They do,' I said.

He blew smoke through his nose. 'Trouble is, sometimes the wrong people end up in prison. And sometimes the right people don't.'

I nodded. 'It could all have been very different. If Arcangelo had gone to prison after *Tangentopoli*, we probably wouldn't be here now.'

Vanni smiled, sadly. 'People like Arcangelo Moro. They do not often go to prison, Nathan. You will learn that, the longer you spend in this country. It's one of the things that makes this job difficult.'

We smoked in silence for a few minutes. 'You lied to me,' he repeated.

'I'm sorry.'

'Don't do it again. Please.'

'I won't. But I have to ask. If I had come to you with the whole story, would anything have happened?'

He looked affronted. 'Of course. There would have been an investigation. A long investigation. By the end of which Domenico would have been long cold in his grave and so the investigation would have come to an end.'

I dropped my cigar and ground it out with my foot. 'Right. So justice, in any meaningful sense of the word, would not have been done.'

'Of course not. But at least we would have followed the right procedures.' He patted me on the back, and smiled.

'So what happens now? To Domenico, I mean.'

He shrugged. 'Like I said, we will open a case. And, I suspect, we will close it again within a few weeks. He seems to want to co-operate.'

'Of course he does. He's won the game, after all.'

'There's talk about some of the stolen works being returned. The few of them that were genuine. As to the others, well, the *Guardia* will investigate. Maybe they'll find a lead.'

'What about the Bellini? The *Madonna*, I mean.'

He shook his head. 'We'll never see that again. Well, probably not.'

Paolo was lowered in, and the gravediggers prepared to do their work. But not before Sergio stepped forward with a wreath in the shape of the Hammer and Sickle, and placed it at the graveside. '*Ciao, compagno,*' he said, and blew his nose.

Vanni patted me on the back again. 'I need to get back to the *Questura*, okay. I'll see you around.'

I walked over to Sergio, and we shook hands. 'I'm sorry,' I said.

He shrugged. 'Not your fault.'

'I worry that it was. If I hadn't got involved he'd probably still be alive. It's only because Arcangelo had me followed that he was killed.'

'Maybe, maybe not. But Paolo was going to do something with all that material. He might have written his book, for example. Arcangelo would have shut him up eventually.'

There seemed nothing to add. 'I'm sorry,' I repeated, tiredly.

He gripped my arm. 'Don't be. The two of you, you got the old bastard. He'd have been pleased about that. Now come on, let's go back to Giudecca and have a drink and play some cards for him, eh?'

Maturi asked me out for dinner. He didn't ask if I had a plus one, but I took the liberty of asking Federica anyway. Rather to my surprise, he suggested the Magical Brazilian, at least for an *aperitivo*. He grumbled his way through what, to me at least, appeared to be a perfectly acceptable Negroni before asking what he really wanted to know. 'So, Mr Sutherland. What happens now?'

'To be honest, I don't know. I doubt that Domenico will ever be able to stand trial. He'll be dead within months, weeks even. And there's little evidence against him, and no one to testify.' Karl's body had been fished out of the Grand Canal within a few hours. Montgomery had disappeared into thin air. He'd probably been on the first train out of Santa Lucia within fifteen minutes of Dario's arrival. 'Adriatico from the *Guardia* got back to me, you know. Interpol have files on Montgomery, or Travers or whichever name he happens to be using. He spent five years in prison in the 1980s for fraud. He's a man of many talents, it seems.'

'Evidently. Still, it was lucky for you that your friend knew exactly where to find you.'

'He didn't,' said Federica. 'Nathan was going to be wonderfully noble and sort it all out himself and keep us all safe. And I'm not saying I didn't trust him, but I thought I should call Dario. He was still at the hospital. He hadn't slept for about thirty-six hours.'

I smiled. 'So he left Valentina and baby in the hospital and hooned it back to Venice as quickly as he could. He was heading for Moro's *palazzo*. He knew he could get to the Zattere on his bike and from there, it was an easy ride down to the bridge.'

'How's he doing?' asked Federica.

'Oh, he's fine. He's probably going to lose his licence again for a bit, though. Not ideal with a new baby in the house. I'm not sure if Valentina is ever going to speak to me again.'

'More importantly,' said Maturi, 'what are you going to do now?'

I'd been wondering myself, but had kept pushing it to the back of my mind. 'I don't know. I really don't. I've got the rent paid on the flat for another six months and that's it. After that, I'll need to start finding the money myself. And I don't know if I can manage that.'

'But you're staying?'

I ignored his question. 'It would mean finding somewhere cheaper. Don't know where. Maybe out towards the railway station. Or further out in Castello, perhaps Arsenale or Sant'Elena.'

'Giudecca?' suggested Federica.

I shook my head. 'No, I thought about that. I liked the idea that I'd spend my days playing cards with the boys in the communist bar, but it's too far out for the consulate. If some-body's had their bag stolen they don't want to be told they have to get a boat to an island to sort it out. Besides, there's a big expat community on Giudecca, and I'm not sure I'm quite ready to be part of a community.'

'But you're staying?' repeated Maturi.

'I think so. It feels like admitting defeat, but I think so.'

'Good. I'm pleased. We both are, aren't we, Federica? Anyway, it seems to me you have a good job here.'

'Translating lawn-mower manuals?'

'No, not that. But if you say so, why not? If I buy a lawn mower, it is important for me to understand how it works. I mean, being a diplomat seems to be a good job.'

'As I said, I'm not really a diplomat.'

He waved his hand to shush me. 'And as I said to you before – you have a job where you help people. I think that must be a good job to have.'

I swirled the ice in the dregs of my Negroni. 'I'm not sure I helped Magri very much.'

'I think you did,' said Federica. 'I think he liked working with you. He had a project. He felt like a proper journalist again.'

'I got him killed.'

'Don't be melodramatic. Arcangelo would have come for him sooner or later. And now, well, he has his reputation back. That's nice for those who knew him. How do Sergio and his friends feel?'

'They're happy. I think they feel he did something honourable. That he was trying to put something right. But they'd have been happier if Arcangelo had been brought to justice. They think being shot was getting away lightly.'

Maturi shook his head. 'If they wanted to wait for justice, they'd have been waiting a long time. Nice to have ideals, of course. But this is why the communists never win elections.'

'More drinks?' suggested Federica. Maturi shook his head. 'Come on,' she said, 'it's still early.'

'I'll have a Prosecco,' he said. 'Another Negroni will kill me.'

'Look at Mr Sensible! So what happens to the book, Nathan?'

'I don't know. I'm not sure who it belongs to. Technically, I suppose, it's Montgomery's, but I doubt he's going to come and claim it any time soon. I suppose it'll become part of Domenico's estate.'

'Which means?'

'Which means,' said Maturi, 'that it passes to us.'

'Us?'

'The bank.' He looked exceedingly pleased with himself. 'I've already made a suggestion that we acquire it for the archives. It makes perfect sense. We will have both versions of *Giambellino*'s *Life of the Virgin*. It is only right that they should be together. And I'll make sure this man in Florence receives proper money for it this time.'

'I thought the banks had no money these days?' I said.

'We don't. But we don't have as little money as everyone else. That makes us rich.'

'But is it the real one?'

Maturi beamed. 'Do you really want to know?'

'I nearly got myself killed for the bloody thing. Yes I do.'

'Well it is not the fake. But that does not mean that it is certainly by Bellini. It probably, but not definitely, is. In the meantime, and until such time as we have it properly evaluated, the picture is like Schrodinger's Cat. It may or may not be by him. *Ergo*, it is both at the same time. My question is, does it matter?'

'Of course it bloody matters!'

Fede shushed me. 'But does it?'

Maturi took a couple of crisps, and nodded. 'Does it? It's still a beautiful thing. If it was painted by *Giambellino* himself, or by his students in his workshop, it is still a beautiful thing. And now it has its own history as well, perhaps even more interesting than the original. A shame, in fact, that the fake was destroyed. It would have been fascinating to display both together.'

I drained my glass. 'Maybe so. Okay, do we need some more drinks here? More sandwiches?'

'We need more to eat and more to drink. But not in this horrible place.' He patted my arm. 'My boy, I took the liberty of booking a table at Le Bistrot de Venise this evening.'

'You're joking! I've always wanted to go there.' Le Bistrot was one of the finest restaurants in the city. I'd walked past there on several occasions, window shopping for food and wondering if I would ever be able to afford to eat there.

'Good. This is my treat.' He waved to Eduardo for the bill. 'Le Bistrot can be yours.'

Federica linked her arm in mine, as we walked off. 'You're going to need to translate an awful lot of lawn-mower manuals.'

Epilogue

Dario faced the inevitable one-year ban with equanimity. His current boss, he said, was more understanding about this sort of thing and possibly even quite pleased with the publicity the case had brought. Valentina – well, Valentina would understand. Eventually. It might be as well if I didn't plan on coming round for dinner for the immediate future though.

I went downstairs to check the mail. There was only one item. A small jiffy bag. When I returned, Dario was standing in the kitchen, packed and ready to go, and finishing his coffee. I plopped it on to the kitchen table.

We looked at each other.

'Coincidence, right?'

'Almost certainly.'

'Where's it from?'

I turned it over. It was postmarked Venice.

'Should we open it?' said Dario.

Gramsci hauled himself on to the table, and prodded at it experimentally.

I sighed. 'He knows best. He always does.' Dario winced, but only slightly, as I tore the envelope open. I squeezed the sides, the better to take a look inside. Nothing seemed to be there. I turned it upside down and gave it a shake. Something dropped out and bounced on the table. I snatched it away as the cat swatted at it.

I opened my hand to reveal a small white chess piece. A pawn. We stared at it in silence for a moment. Then I rummaged in the bag and pulled out a stack of banknotes. Five-hundred euro bills. I had never seen a five-hundred euro note before. I wouldn't have known they existed.

'What do you think it means?' said Dario.

'*Beh*. Montgomery promised me ten thousand euros to look after the package. Arcangelo promised me the same amount to give the package directly to him. People have been falling over themselves to promise me large amounts of money. So perhaps this is Domenico saying thanks for a job well done.'

I riffled through the notes. There were twenty of them. Dario whistled.

'You're a lucky man, Nathan.'

'Well it was hard earned.'

'What are you going to do with it?'

'Pay the rent. This will cover me into next year. Well into next year if I'm careful. It buys me time.'

'And what about the chess piece?'

'Two theories. One is that it's saying thanks for the entertainment. That the pawn doesn't get sacrificed after all. I get to stay in the game.'

'The other?'

'Oh, the other is that it's a warning that I'm going to be killed in some particularly horrible way and that I should spend the money as quickly as possible. Best not to think about that.'

'You want me to stay a bit longer?'

I shook my head. 'No. I think it's okay. And if it isn't . . . Well, I think it would take more than two of us to deal with it. Anyway, if you don't go home tonight Valentina really will kill me.'

He grinned, the wrinkles around his eyes creasing. Then gave me a bone-crushing hug that I returned as best I could.

'See you again, eh? Might be a couple of months though.'

'Yep. And thanks again.'

The doorbell rang. I checked my watch.

'There's someone outside needing help, Dario. Perhaps they've been robbed. Perhaps they need a new passport. Or perhaps they just want to find a nice place to eat. Whatever it is, surgery is open!'

Acknowledgements

I am indebted to *Signor* Andrea Marcon of the Royal Thai Consulate of Venice for his invaluable help in explaining the works of the consular system; and to the *Guardia di Finanza*, Mestre for their help in explaining the work of their art crime department, and that of the *carabinieri*.

I am extremely grateful to Penguin Random House, for permission to quote from Giuseppe Tomasi di Lampedusa's *The Leopard*, in the translation by Archibald Colquhoun.

Finally, this book would not have been possible without the hard work and encouragement of my brilliant agent and great friend John Beaton; and the love and support of my dear wife Caroline, the first person ever to read Nathan's adventures.